MAGGIE and the MOUNTAIN OF LIGHT

A Wayfinder Girls Novel

D1637404

Light the path, lead the way.

MARK SNOAD

To Mikayla and Hannah, the two stars which help light my way.

THE HISTORY OF THE WAYFINDER GIRLS

The Wayfinder Girls is a worldwide organization founded in England in 1910 by Lady Solana Mapleston. Its mission is to strengthen and develop girls' ability to lead, both in their personal lives and in service to the community. The organization grew rapidly and spread to other countries, with *The Wayfinder Girls of America* founded in 1912. Today, Wayfinder Girls operates in 157 countries and has four distinct programs:

- Trailfinder: for girls ages 7 to 10
- Wayfinder: for girls ages 11 to 13
- Trailblazer: for girls ages 14 to 16
- Waymaker: for girls ages 17+

The Wayfinder Girls have six regional centers, with Dux Manor also functioning as the worldwide headquarters.

- *Dux Manor* in London, England (whose logo is shown below)
- *Tristar Lodge* in Colorado, United States of America
- *Te Manawa o te Tuakoi Tonga* in Rotorua, New Zealand

- *Nayati* in Mumbai, India
- *Dari House* in Lagos, Nigeria
- *Zhǐdǎo* in Hong Kong, China

www.wayfindergirls.org

I

BE PREPARED

"Welcome to the apocalypse!" the sign declared in large, cheerful red letters. "Please register here."

I sucked in a long, deep breath. Surely the best thing to do when *always* fearing the worst was to attend an "apocalypse" training camp. And better yet, a fun camp run by the Wayfinder Girls at Dux Manor, a three-storied hostel and activity center located about a fifteen-minute drive from my home in North London.

Dux Manor seemed more like a place for a royal visit rather than a camp, with the red-brick exterior speaking of age and wealth. The large building, with matching wings on either side of a central entrance, reminded me of the Lego castles I'd built with my younger twin brothers. It was cool that Dux Manor had been converted into a hostel, and it would be a fun place to stay, as long as the rooms weren't haunted.

But the rooms wouldn't be haunted. Dux Manor was the Wayfinder World Center.

Please don't let the rooms be haunted!

"Maggie and Anahira, we have to register over here," my mum declared, doing her best to power walk toward the sign while carrying an oversized blue chilly bin.

I turned to my best friend, Anahira Waititi. "I'll be okay, right?" I'd been to at least three Wayfinder camps before, but this was my first one at Dux Manor.

"I've got you," Anahira replied, flashing me one of her spirited grins.

We followed my mum and joined the back of the line waiting by the sign. Most were Wayfinder Girls, dressed in official yellow-and-black Wayfinder hoodies, with pleated, knee-length black skirts and black leggings. It was nearing the end of the half-term autumn break, and we were all expected to obey our parents' instructions to stay warm. We had more choice over our shoes, as long as they were sneakers. I wore pink light-up Skechers and Anahira had on a pair of black Converse high-tops.

Mum greeted the woman in front of her, and they soon became engrossed in conversation. I quickly stepped back when my mum said "Maggie's special needs". I wasn't keen on sharing my personal struggles with a random adult.

The line moved quickly, with the registered Wayfinder Girls sent to sit at nearby picnic tables with their bags. The adults were sent home after the girls had finished registration.

So the apocalypse will begin without any parental supervision.

A man with a huge dragon tattoo covering his left arm stole my attention. The dragon's tail started just below his shoulder and its head ended just before his wrist. The man wore a black singlet and had long wavy black hair. I watched as he waved goodbye to one of the girls and then turned to leave. My mouth fell open as I saw another dragon tattoo covering his right arm. I stared wide-eyed as he walked away, amazed that anyone had the confidence to display such fantastical tattoos.

As I watched him retreat to the carpark, I caught someone staring at me from a tree. A chill swept through me as I realized the person had green skin and seemed almost part of the tree itself. The person's wide, deep-brown eyes held me momentarily spellbound, as though they belonged to a different world. The eyes narrowed as the green-skinned person lifted a bony, green finger and pointed at me.

I spun around and squeezed Anahira's arm. "Look!"

"What? What is it?" Anahira asked, rubbing the spot where I'd squeezed her arm.

"Someone's watching me," I whispered, pointing in the direction of the tree.

"Where?" Anahira responded, matching my whispered tone while staring in the direction I was pointing. "All I can see is a tree."

I dared to turn my head and look back at the tree. The person with the strange-coloured skin and alien eyes had disappeared.

"It was a person," I insisted in a shaky voice, as the tightness in my chest collapsed into a dull ache. "In the tree. Someone with green skin." Something that wasn't possible, unless they were wearing makeup or something. But how had they vanished?

Anahira glanced at me and then at the tree, and then back at me. "Maybe you're just anxious about camp?"

I stared at the tree. I was definitely feeling anxious, but I tended to feel anxious about everything. Someone *had* been watching me.

Although it did sound crazy, especially the bit about green skin.

Had I somehow imagined it?

Maybe the man with the dragon tattoo had sent my imagination racing?

I squashed my fear about the strange watcher deep below my other worries as we finally reached the registration area. I didn't need to trouble Mum with what I'd seen, or not seen. She'd just start to worry. A Wayfinder leader sat at a table, with a laptop open in front of her. The leader greeted us with a wide smile. "Ah, our lucky last campers. Good morning and welcome to the apocalypse. My name is Meiling. Who do we have here?"

"Margaret Elizabeth Thatcher and Anahira Waititi," my mum responded, speaking on our behalf.

A part of me died as Mum used my full name. I wished she would *stop* doing that. Adults tended to respond with either disgust or pity when they heard my name. It wasn't as if I'd chosen it. My mum named me after two powerful women, but she hadn't considered the unpopularity of my namesake, Margaret Thatcher, the ex-Prime Minister of Great Britain. I couldn't understand why adults disapproved of me simply because of my name, but they did.

It wasn't the same for Anahira. Not only was she tall and athletic, but she shared the same surname as Taika Waititi, the supercool New Zealand film director and actor. Anahira had lived in London for three years, since moving from New Zealand with her family. She once claimed Taika was her uncle, and I hadn't yet worked out whether she was telling the truth or not. She just grinned when I questioned her about it.

Either way, she got broad, welcoming smiles, and I got tight, disapproving stares.

"Well, you are both most welcome," Meiling replied, checking our names on her screen. She gave no indication whether she disliked my name or not, which was a first.

Meiling darted a quick look to her left and to her right, wiggled the index finger of her right hand, and invited us to lean in closer. "Here are your top-secret passes," she whispered, handing over two black lanyards, each holding a laminated name tag. The words *Light the path, Lead the way* were printed in yellow on the lanyards.

The tag displayed my first and last name above the words *Apocalypse Survivalist-in-Training*. At the bottom of the tag were the words *Amazon* and *Special*.

"Not that top-secret really," Meiling added with a grin. "But definitely important. Please wear them at all times. Oh, and here are your room keycards. Don't lose these."

Meiling handed over two keycards. "You're both in the Amazon room, on the second floor. I think you're the only girls to have their own bathroom and shower. Lucky you."

So *Amazon* stood for the room. And I wasn't so sure about lucky. I mean, it was cool to have our own bathroom, but it might make it harder to fit in with the other girls at camp. Most of them would be staying in dorm rooms and having to share a bathroom.

"Margaret," Meiling added, eyeing my name tag. "You have special dietary needs?"

"Please just call me Maggie," I responded, looking again at my tag. So that was the reason for the word *Special*. But why broadcast it to everyone at camp?

"Alright, Maggie," Meiling replied. "What can't you eat?"

I waited for Mum to answer, but Mum instead turned to me and half-nodded. I was supposed to take more responsibility for my food needs or something.

My chin dropped. "I'm allergic to dairy, eggs, kiwifruit, and tree nuts, and I've also got celiac disease, which means I can't eat gluten."

Meiling's eyes went wide. "Oh, you poor thing. Did you say kiwifruit? That's an odd food to be allergic to, isn't it? My friend has problems with peanuts, so I can appreciate what you are going through."

I forced a smile through my clenched teeth. I knew Meiling meant well, but she didn't know what I was going through. I mean, how could she? She didn't have to live with the constant threat of food making her sick. Some food could even send me into anaphylactic shock and cause me to stop breathing.

"We manage the best we can," my mum told Meiling, probably sensing my mood. "Now, I was told I could store Maggie's food somewhere."

"Maggie's food?" Meiling asked, her voice rising in pitch.

"Yes. Maggie can't eat the same food as the other campers."

"Oh, of course. Yes. You have her food with you?"

"Yes, it's all here." My mum indicated the large blue chilly bin she was carrying. "Maggie's food is all fully labeled. As is her chilly bin."

Labeled with warnings like *Don't Touch* and *For Maggie Thatcher ONLY*. Just one more way for me to stand out from everyone else.

"That's good," Meiling said as she stood. "I'll take you inside and get someone to help. Anahira, are you going to wait with the others?"

"I'll go with Maggie if that's alright," Anahira replied, shooting me a reassuring smile.

"Yes, that's fine. You can leave your gear at one of the picnic tables."

We walked onto the grassy lawn and put our duffle bags down at one of the vacant picnic tables, but I held on to my meds bag. It's a small pink bag I use for my asthma inhaler and epi-pen.

I don't go anywhere without my meds bag!

Meiling stood as we returned and addressed the girls waiting by the picnic tables. "I'll be back in a moment." She then turned and led us to the main entrance of Dux Manor.

We entered the reception area. The high ceiling, deep reddish-brown wooden walls, and polished white floor deepened the sense of history and wealth. It reminded me of a museum. On the wall behind the reception desk hung a bright mural displaying the three-star symbol of the Wayfinder Girls: a large four-pointed star with two smaller stars on the upper right. I'd attended Wayfinder programs since I was eight and felt a surge of pride every time I saw the grouping of the three stars.

A Wayfinder leader sat at the reception desk and smiled as we approached.

"Hi, Faatimah," Meiling greeted the leader at the desk. "Any chance you could show…"

Meiling paused as another Wayfinder leader emerged from the room behind the reception area.

"Oh, Lady Marie. Sorry, I didn't mean to bother you."

"No trouble at all, Meiling," the new leader replied as she came around the reception desk. "How may I be of service?"

"I just need someone to show Maggie where to store her food."

"Ah, yes, Margaret Thatcher," the new leader said, shifting her attention to me and reading my name tag. "My name is Lady Marie Studfall, and I'd be delighted to show you a safe place for your food."

Lady Marie Studfall was the most elegant woman I'd ever met. Tall and confident, with hazel eyes and blond hair set in perfect waves. She also had more pins on her Wayfinder uniform than I thought were possible. She must have been the most highly deco-rated leader in Wayfinder history.

"It is a pleasure to meet you, Lady Studfall," my mum declared while trying for some reason to curtsy. "My name is Gwendolyn."

Mum's behavior got super embarrassing when she met important people. Mum must have decided Lady Studfall was *really* important, as she usually just introduces herself as Gwen. She must have also forgotten she held the chilly bin, as she almost fell over.

"Just Lady Marie, please," Lady Marie said as she helped my mum rebalance. "Do you require some assistance with the chilly bin?"

"Oh, no. No, I can manage," Mum replied, her face red. "Thank you."

"Alright." Lady Marie turned her attention to Anahira, noting her name tag. "And you are Anahira Waititi."

"Yes, Lady Marie," Anahira answered smoothly. "Although Ana is pronounced *Un-a*, like Anna from Frozen."

"Oh, I'm terribly sorry, Anahira," Lady Marie responded, pronouncing the name correctly. "Thank you for informing me. Now, if you would care to follow me, I will show you where to store Margaret's food."

Lady Marie nodded toward Meiling, turned to her left, and indicated for us to follow her.

Anahira had just corrected Lady Marie!

I darted a wide-eyed look at Anahira, but she seemed completely unconcerned, paying more attention to the surroundings rather than the adults with us.

We walked down a wide corridor, built with the same high ceiling, reddish-brown walls, and polished white floor as the reception area. On the walls to our right were a series of six framed pictures, one for each of the Wayfinder regional centers; London (England), Colorado (United States of America), Rotorua (New Zealand), Mumbai (India), Lagos (Nigeria), and Hong Kong (China).

I stopped beside the New Zealand one. "What's this supposed to be?" I whispered to Anahira, pointing at the image displayed behind the word "Rotorua."

"It's some mud pools," Anahira whispered back.

"Mud pools?"

Did I hear that correctly?

"Yeah, they're hot and smell like rotten eggs," Anahira replied with a big grin.

No way.

Surely the image celebrating Rotorua would not have been some smelly mud pools? The English picture showed the Tower of London, Colorado had a huge mountain range, Mumbai had some kind of massive arch monument, Lagos had a cool-looking bridge, and Hong Kong showed off its harbor. But New Zealand?

Mud. Hot, smelly, mud.

"Margaret and Anahira," Lady Marie declared, turning back to face us. "If you don't mind, I do have rather a lot to do today."

"Sorry, Lady Marie," Anahira quickly responded.

"Yes, sorry." I ducked my head and moved away from the pictures.

"There is a kitchen for guest use on the first floor," Lady Marie explained as we caught up to her and my mum. "But the Wayfinder Girls are our only guests this weekend, and they will be using the dining room. So Margaret, you can use the entire kitchen for storing and preparing your meals. The kitchen is fully resourced with plates and cutlery, although I assume you will be using all your own equipment?"

"Yes, everything she needs is in here," my mum answered for me, using her chin to indicate the chilly bin.

Lady Marie nodded and then led us to a wide, reddish-brown, wooden staircase. Large portraits of dignified-looking women lined the wall up the entire length of the stairs.

Lady Marie considered the chilly bin. "May I suggest we use the elevator?"

"Yes, thank you, Lady Marie," Mum answered while contorting her body into something resembling a half-curtsy.

The elevator waited just past the staircase. Lady Marie pressed the button on the wall, and the elevator doors opened. The opposite end of the elevator door contained a mirror, with the name and logo of Dux Manor etched in white. The logo featured an old sailing ship with its sails puffed out, straining toward the three-star symbol of the Wayfinder Girls.

Lady Marie and Mum walked into the elevator first, and Anahira and I filed in behind. Lady Marie turned to the control panel, pressed "1," and the elevator doors closed. The elevator carried us up to the first floor. Lady Marie led us out of the open elevator doors, down the hallway, and into a room with a kitchen and small dining area.

"Will this be to your satisfaction?" Lady Marie asked.

"Yes, it is perfect," my mum answered as she placed the chilly bin on a table. "Thank you, Lady Marie." Mum started to curtsy one last time, but thankfully managed to stop herself.

"It is my pleasure," Lady Marie responded. "Now, I must leave you to attend to other matters. Margaret and Anahira, please assemble outside with the other girls after you are finished here. Do not go to your room."

"Yes, Lady Marie," Anahira and I answered in unison as Lady Marie turned and left.

I turned to Anahira, eyebrows raised. "Wow!"

Anahira grinned. "You let her call you Margaret."

"Yes, well, my name sounded really posh when she said it."

"Maggie, please," my mum commented. "There is no need to go gooey-eyed over Lady Marie. She is just a normal person." Mum opened the chilly bin and began taking food out. "Now, will you help me with the food?"

I stepped forward to help but caught the confused look on Anahira's face.

"Gooey-eyed?" Anahira whispered.

I laughed. It was one of Mum's favorite sayings.

"Is something wrong?" Mum said, turning to look at Anahira and me.

"Not at all," I replied, while trying to get Anahira to stop grinning.

"Good," Mum responded. "It's only an overnight camp, so you've got two lunches, one dinner, and one breakfast in here. You've brought plenty of snacks?"

"Yes, there's some in the chilly bin and a few in my duffle bag."

"Good. Let's put your pizza and toasted sandwich in the fridge. Lady Marie said you are the only one using this kitchen, but your food is labeled just in case. Are you sure you're okay with salmon and crackers for your lunch tomorrow?"

"Yes, Mum."

"You're okay with using the oven to heat up your food?"

"Yes, Mum."

"You've got both epi-pens in your meds bag?"

"Yes, Mum," I answered, patting the pink bag hanging at my side.

"You're allowed to use your phone?"

"I think so."

"Well, just ask Lady Marie if there's any problem. She'll sort it out."

"Okay," I responded, quickly covering up the beginnings of a laugh. Mum had somehow made Lady Marie sound like a close family friend.

"I'll look after her, Mrs. Thatcher," Anahira said.

"Thank you, Anahira," Mum responded. "I'm so glad that you're here. Now, Maggie, I'll be with the boys at their football tournament, but call if you need anything."

"Yes, Mum."

"Alright. Well, we should stop wasting time. I'm sure they want to get camp started."

Mum led the way out of the kitchen as Anahira grinned again. Mum was the one taking all the time, fussing over my food needs.

We made it back out to the courtyard, where Mum hugged me goodbye. I glanced at the tree that had hidden the strange watcher, but thankfully, I didn't see any sign of him, or her, or it. Anahira and I went to sit with the other Wayfinder Girls at the picnic tables.

There were about forty girls in total. Most girls smiled as we sat down, although at least two girls stared at us before whispering something to their friends. We had been the last ones to arrive but the first ones to enter Dux Manor, and the question of special treatment could be felt in those whispers. The word *Special* on my nametag didn't help matters much.

We waited a few moments before Lady Marie emerged from within the Manor and walked out to greet us. Meiling and the other leader joined her.

"Good morning," Lady Marie began. "My name is Lady Marie Studfall, and it is my pleasure to welcome you to Dux Manor. You have already met Meiling, but may I also introduce Faatimah to you."

Lady Marie paused to allow Faatimah to smile and wave. Faatimah seemed to be a similar age to Meiling, probably in her early twenties, although it was hard to correctly guess their ages. Take Anahira and me. Despite us both being in Year 8 at Camden School for Girls, Anahira could pass for a Year 11 student, while I could easily find a home within Year 6.

It's really not that easy being short.

"We hope you will enjoy the fun challenges these two days provide because it is important to be prepared, even in times of peace and prosperity," Lady Marie continued. "Of course, the real question these two days will ask of you is, will you survive?"

A wry smile crossed Lady Marie's face as nervous energy rippled through the group of girls, causing an outburst of gasps and giggles.

I ran my hand through my mess of dark curls. Lady Marie had captured the feeling I had going into any situation, whether it was an apocalypse training camp, a school trip, or even when crossing a bridge.

How can I be certain the bridge won't collapse?

Anahira nudged me and smiled. "It's alright, Maggie. We've got this."

Lady Marie raised her hand, silencing the girls. "Your first challenge starts now. Within this courtyard are six objects. Six hidden objects. You must work as a team to find one of these objects. You each have an image of part of the object, but you must find the other girls to complete the image. Within the image is a clue as to its location."

Lady Marie paused again, but this time in response to the confused looks on the faces of the girls, mine included.

"It might be prudent to check the back of your name tags," Lady Marie added.

All of the girls lifted up their lanyards to check the back of their tags. My name tag had a small black shape with a thin strip of yellow on its right edge.

It could be anything.

A quick check of Anahira's tag revealed something looking like two blue fingers.

"Well, I guess that means we're not together," Anahira concluded.

I dropped my head as a heaviness settled in my body. I knew I couldn't have been with Anahira during the whole camp, but I didn't realize we'd be separated so soon.

"And girls," Lady Marie announced, raising her voice. "You have three minutes."

A riot of activity erupted in response to Lady Marie's announcement, with girls rushing to check one another's name tags.

I stood up to participate and did a quick scan around the area. My breath froze as I caught a person watching me from a tree, a person with green skin! The green-skinned person again lifted a bony finger and pointed at me.

Another girl ran up to me and grabbed my attention with the image on her name tag. She had a long red shape, which didn't match mine. She quickly moved on.

I shot a wide-eyed look back at the tree, but the green-skinned person had once again disappeared. I darted a look at the space around the tree, but there was no sign of anyone.

Could they be part of camp?

The Wayfinder Girls weekend camps were always creative and fun, such as the *Jurassic Park* camp I attended last year and the *Mission Possible* camp the year before that, but it seemed I was the only one who could see a green-skinned watcher.

So, they can't be part of the theme.

Another girl rushed up to me, and this time, her object seemed a match, as it had a strip of yellow, the same size as my black-and-yellow object.

"Hey, we match," the girl said with a wide smile. "My name's Kayla. Shall we go find the others?"

I didn't respond, as I was still trying to look past Kayla at the tree.

"Are you alright?" Kayla asked.

I turned my attention to Kayla, who had sparkling dark eyes and long, black, braided hair.

"Yes, sorry. My name's Maggie. Let's go."

Kayla turned to start the search for the other girls who would make up our team. I followed, but my focus was not on the task. There *had* been someone with green skin watching me from the tree. I *hadn't* imagined it.

But who were they, and what did they want?

And why do I get the feeling they meant me harm?

2

THE INVITATION

The first day of challenges had ended and I'd well and truly proven that I wouldn't survive an apocalypse. I got *bitten* in the zombie challenge, *abducted* in the alien challenge, and *infected* in the pandemic challenge. As for the wilderness challenge, let's just say my contribution to my team resulted in the collapse of our all-important shelter.

I don't trust ropes. Or knots. I especially distrust knots!

The food side of camp had gone okay so far, apart from missing out on some fun at lunchtime. I went to my private kitchen, heated up my toasted sandwich, and returned to the dining room. While I was away, the girls had been sorted into new groups of about five or six, and then each person's hands had been tied to the girl on either side of them. The line of girls had to work together to ensure that everyone could eat their lunch.

The activity turned out to be quite funny, as whatever one girl did with her hands affected the others next to her. At one point, a girl announced she needed to go to the bathroom and her whole team had to get up and move with her. Everyone laughed.

Anahira had offered to sit with me, but I couldn't deny her the fun of being involved. I was fine sitting in the corner by myself, eating my warmed-up toasted sandwich.

I hadn't seen anything more of the person with green skin. I didn't even have a chance to tell Anahira about seeing the mysterious watcher a second time. We had been rushed straight into challenges after that starting activity, which proved to be the easiest one of the day. My group's item was a yellow flashlight, which we found quickly. But then we had to move on to the first challenge.

Every challenge had a strict time limit, and we had to stop whether we succeeded or, as in my case, failed. It had all been designed for fun, but it was still a packed program. The only time allowed for breaks were the scheduled mealtimes.

I'd seen Anahira with her group a few times during the afternoon activities and it seemed she was doing well. Anahira even had time to smile and wave, which must have meant she was smashing the challenges.

The same, unfortunately, could not have been said about my group, thanks mainly to the difficulties I had with most of the tasks.

Especially the knots.

The bell for dinner had rung, and I searched for Anahira to let her know I'd be off to reheat my pizza in the private kitchen. I couldn't find her anywhere, so I went to the kitchen by myself. While I waited for my food to heat up, I stared out the window, which offered a view of the front garden and courtyard area, including the infamous tree.

It appeared to be nothing more than a normal tree. But it was somehow home to a person with green skin who had the ability to instantly disappear.

Or not. I guess I could have imagined it. *Twice.*

My sight shifted as I turned back to the kitchen, and I did a double-take. Anahira and Lady Marie were standing together at the far end of the courtyard, and they seemed to be in a serious discussion about something. Anahira kept shaking her head at whatever Lady Marie was saying. I got the impression that Lady Marie did not like Anahira's response.

The timer beeped, and I turned from the window. Stopping the timer, I put on an oven mitt and removed my pizza from the oven. There were four slices, all of them with mushroom and onion on top of a tomato-paste spread, with non-dairy cheese melted throughout. All on a gluten-free pizza base.

Yum!

I transferred the pizza to a plate I'd brought from home, filled up my water bottle, and walked towards the dining room, carrying my dinner, as well as my meds bag.

Anahira was waiting for me just outside the dining room.

"Hi Maggie, sorry. I was going to help you."

"It's okay. It wasn't hard."

"That's good."

"What were you talking about with Lady Marie just now?"

"What?" Anahira replied, taking a step back.

"Lady Marie. I saw you from the window of the kitchen."

"Oh," Anahira responded, dropping her gaze. "It was nothing."

"It looked quite serious."

"No, no. It was nothing. Let's get dinner. I'm starving." Anahira spun around and hurried into the dining room.

I followed Anahira and sat down at a table as Anahira joined the girls lining up to get their dinner. I stared at my best friend. She was hiding something. I was sure of it.

I took a wet wipe from my meds bag and wiped the table. I couldn't have been sure what the last person ate, or whether the table had been cleaned properly, so it was best to make sure it was clean before I started eating. I put the used wet wipe to the side to throw in the bin later. I picked up my pizza to take a bite, but my hand stopped halfway to my mouth.

Anahira had acted strangely when I asked her about talking with Lady Marie. And she had seemed overly keen to line up for dinner.

What is Anahira hiding?

-------- / / -------

I DIDN'T GET A CHANCE TO FIND OUT MORE ABOUT ANAHIRA'S conversation with Lady Marie, as the dining room was too public. Straight after dinner, we had assigned chores to do. Mine was to tidy up and pack away the ropes from the wilderness challenge. I took my plate and cutlery back to the kitchen, kept hold of my drink bottle and meds bag, and then tackled my chores.

After chores, we all met together in the back garden of Dux Manor for the bonfire. As we were in a residential area, we couldn't have a real fire. Instead, we were each given three glow sticks, which we placed together in a large pile to resemble a bonfire.

It looked cool.

We sat around the "fire," and Meiling led us through some songs. She had a good voice. We sang all the favorites, "Campfire's Burning," "Alice the Camel," and the "Meatball" song. It was the best moment of camp.

"May I congratulate you all on your efforts today," Lady Marie began, once the singing had stopped. "The challenges were intended to be difficult, but I hope you all had fun."

Most girls around the campfire smiled or laughed, agreeing with Lady Marie. I tried to join in but couldn't find the same level of enthusiasm for my efforts.

"After we conclude our formalities here, we will sing the Dux Manor song, and you will be presented with a Dux Manor pin."

Even broader smiles greeted Lady Marie's announcement.

"I would like to commend four girls for the outstanding leadership they showed today. I will be recommending them for the next level in their Leadership badges."

Lady Marie paused and studied the group of girls.

Even though I knew that I had no chance of being acknowledged, my heart still beat faster. Every Wayfinder Girl hoped to progress in their badge levels.

"The first three are girls who helped lead their teams to the successful completion of most, if not all, of today's challenges."

Some groups succeeded with the challenges? Wow.

"So congratulations to Samantha Needleton, Razia Rashidi, and Anahira Waititi."

Anahira!

I gave Anahira a hug.

Anahira smiled but only half-heartedly returned my hug.

Something is definitely wrong.

"The fourth Wayfinder Girl helped her team stay on task and motivated them, despite their lack of success. A possibly more difficult leadership skill."

That sounded like my team.

"Congratulations to Kayla Indi," Lady Marie announced.

It *was* my team. Kayla had been the first to find me during the matching activity in the morning, and she had stayed super cheerful and positive throughout the whole day.

"Of course, the most important lesson we can take from today is that we can all learn to be the best versions of ourselves," Lady Marie continued.

Sure. But what is the best version of me?

"Tomorrow will be an exciting day. The challenges have finished, and the adventures begin. You will all be personally invited to participate in an adventure. Your invitation has been placed in an envelope on your pillow in your room."

Wow. That's so cool!

"Please note that it is merely an invitation," Lady Marie continued. "You do not have to accept. There are other alternatives available to you."

For some reason, Lady Marie directed her final words to me. I wasn't sure why, but it seemed relevant to me, somehow.

"But now, let us sing the Dux Manor song in closing." Lady Marie nodded at Meiling.

"Thank you, Lady Marie," Meiling responded. "Dux Manor has its own song, and we would like to sing it to you. Please join in if you know it. We'll sing the first verse to you, and then we can all sing the verse together a few times until you've got it."

Meiling, Faatimah, Lady Marie, and two Wayfinder Girls started singing.

"We strive for good, to be the best.
We will not slumber, we will not rest.
Peace we seek, hope we grow.
Deeds and actions are what we sow.
By helping others, in meeting need,
We choose to serve, we choose to lead.
We guard the path, we light the way,
To peace on Earth, come what may."

"That sounded lovely, well done," Lady Marie declared after we had sung the verse a few times. "We will now distribute the Dux Manor pins. In accepting the pin, you are pledging yourself to uphold the dignity of Dux Manor and declaring that you will always seek peace. Please take a moment to consider whether you are willing to make this pledge."

I focused on the bright glow-stick "fire." I had no problem with upholding the dignity of Dux Manor, although I didn't know how I would do that. I could definitely pledge myself to the idea of peace.

But what on Earth can I do to achieve peace?

It had to start somewhere. So why not with me? Or with the Wayfinder Girls, at least.

"Thank you everyone for treating this seriously." Lady Marie broke the silence. "I am proud of all of you. Please stand."

We all stood as Meiling and Faatimah walked around the circle, handing out pins.

Meiling soon stood before me. "Will you accept this pin?"

"I will," I answered.

Meiling smiled warmly and handed me a pin.

"Thank you," I responded.

Meiling smiled again and moved on.

I stared at the blue-and-white pin. It displayed the same Dux Manor logo on the glass of the elevator. An old sailing ship, its sails puffed out, straining toward the three-star symbol of the Wayfinder Girls. I squeezed it tightly, feeling such a strong connection to the Wayfinder Girls and to Dux Manor.

This is what I want. To belong.

"Alright, girls," Lady Marie concluded. "There is supper available in the dining room, and then it is time for bed. Please feel free to take some glow sticks and don't forget about the invitations awaiting you in your rooms."

The circle of girls broke up with a burst of excited conversation. I turned to Anahira. "Wow."

"Yeah, it's awesome," Anahira replied, staring at her own pin.

"What adventure do you think we're going to get?"

"I'm not sure." Anahira shrugged and turned her head. "Let's get our glow sticks."

It was not like Anahira to dismiss something so exciting. She was definitely hiding something, even if I had no idea what.

"Here you go." Anahira held out three glow sticks.

I hesitated. The glow sticks had been mixed up and the ones Anahira held out to me could have been anyone's. Their previous owners might not have cleaned their hands properly after dinner.

"Oh, right, sorry," Anahira replied. "We don't need them."

"Thank you."

"No worries." Anahira put the glow sticks back. "Let's go."

We followed the rest of the girls to the dining room, where cups of warm cocoa and a platter of chocolate brownies were set out.

I sat at a table as Anahira went to get herself supper. I had placed a small bar of safe dairy-free chocolate in my meds bag ready for supper, and I took it out, planning to eat it with a drink from my water bottle.

Anahira returned with a cup of cocoa and a brownie, wrapped in a white serviette.

"It looks good," I said, as Anahira sat down opposite me.

Anahira took a sip of her cocoa. "How's your chocolate bar?"

"Delicious," I replied, taking a big bite.

Anahira finished her supper, returned her cup, and then left to wash her hands. As soon as Anahira returned, we headed to

Amazon. I was eager to find out what adventure I'd been invited to, even though Anahira seemed to be walking slower than usual.

Sure enough, in our room, we found an envelope on each of our pillows.

I put my water bottle down on the small dresser and sat on my bed, picking up the envelope, which had my name handwritten on the front. I started to open the envelope when I noticed that Anahira had not made any move toward her bed.

"Aren't you going to open yours?" I asked.

"Oh, yes, sure," Anahira responded as she sat on her bed. She picked up her envelope but didn't make any move to open it.

I wasn't sure what was wrong with Anahira, but I couldn't wait any longer. I opened the envelope and pulled out a small piece of paper.

On the paper were written five words. "Come to the Owl room."

I turned the page over but couldn't find anything else written anywhere on the paper. I checked the envelope. It was empty. There was nothing but the five words.

What is going on?

I considered Anahira. She still hadn't opened her envelope but was watching me carefully.

'What does it say?" Anahira asked.

"Come to the Owl room."

Anahira's eyes went wide. "Really?"

"Yes."

Anahira attacked her envelope. She yanked out a piece of paper similar in size to mine. She read the paper and grinned.

"What does it say?" I asked.

Anahira turned her paper toward me.

"Come to the Owl room," I read.

Anahira laughed. "Yes!"

"But what does it mean?"

"It means we have to go to the Owl room."

"The what?"

"The Owl room."

My eyes widened and my breath caught in my throat. "Dux Manor has an Owlery?"

Anahira laughed. "No, it's not Hogwarts. The Owl room is just a name given to a small meeting room. Just like our room is called the Amazon room."

"Oh," I replied, slowly shaking my head.

How does Anahira know about the Owl room?

"Come on," Anahira said, getting up. "Let's go."

"Where?"

"To the Owl room, of course."

"What, now?"

"Yes. That's what the invitation said, isn't it?"

It was the instruction written on the invitation, but I didn't move. Lady Marie had told us that we would get an invitation to an adventure happening tomorrow, *not tonight*. She'd even said that after supper it was time for bed. She hadn't mentioned anything at all about any extra meetings.

"Come on, Maggie," Anahira urged.

I looked up at Anahira. She seemed so excited. So different from how she was acting earlier. But I hunched my shoulders, not sure I should leave my room.

"I've got you," Anahira said, reaching her hand out to me.

I guess it won't do any harm to at least check it out.

"Okay, if you say so," I said, reaching out to hold Anahira's hand and stand up. "Where is this Owl room?"

Anahira grinned. "Follow me."

Anahira led me to a small meeting room with a sofa covered in a bright yellow throw, two yellow bean bags, four armchairs, and a giant world map covering an entire wall. Sitting in the armchairs were three other Wayfinder Girls, one of whom was Kayla Indi.

"Hi, Maggie," Kayla said with one of her typical broad smiles, the kind that stretches from ear to ear.

"Hi, Kayla," I replied. "Did you get a message to come here too?"

"We all did." Kayla indicated the other two girls. "This is Razia Rashidi and Samantha Needleton."

"Just call me Sam," Sam replied, considering me intently.

"Welcome," Razia said, giving a little wave before reaching up to adjust her white hijab.

"I'm Maggie Thatcher," I said in greeting.

"And I'm Anahira Waititi," Anahira said next to me.

We sat on the sofa. "So, do you know what's happening?" I asked.

"Not really," Kayla answered.

"But you all knew where to find this room?"

The other girls all nodded as though it was obvious. I studied them more closely and almost panicked. I was sitting with the four Wayfinder Girls Lady Marie had commended for their leadership. They were the top four girls at camp.

But what am I doing here?

I leaned forward, prepared to get up and leave when Lady Marie strode into the room.

"Good evening," Lady Marie began, not wasting any time. "Thank you all for coming tonight. I realize that it may have been somewhat mystifying but let me assure you, it is of utmost importance."

I had no idea what Lady Marie was talking about, but I edged back onto the sofa, trying my best to avoid drawing any attention.

"I am about to tell you something highly confidential," Lady Marie continued. "But before I say anything more, I need to know that whatever you learn tonight, you will keep it secret."

Keep it secret? Keep what secret?

I turned to Anahira, but she only had eyes for Lady Marie.

"I'm afraid that I must insist," Lady Marie added.

One by one, the other girls made some kind of a declaration, almost as though it had been rehearsed. "I promise to keep anything I learn tonight secret."

Anahira was the last to say the words. She turned to me and nodded.

I glanced at Anahira and then turned to Lady Marie. I still had no idea what was going on, but I surprised myself with the realization that I would have done anything to find out more.

"I promise to keep anything I learn tonight secret," I managed to say.

"Good," Lady Marie responded. "You will soon discover why secrecy is needed."

Lady Marie clasped her hands together and considered each of us in turn. Her gaze lingered on each person, but it lingered longest on me.

"As you know, the Wayfinder Girls exist to empower girls to be their best and to bravely face the challenges that life may bring," Lady Marie explained. "But there is also a hidden purpose. A purpose only a select few know about."

A hidden purpose? What on Earth could that be?

"We are the Earth's protectors, its Guardians," Lady Marie declared.

Lady Marie paused, and again her gaze lingered on me.

"From what?" I asked, unable to hold myself back.

"From other worlds," Lady Marie answered, as calmly as stating that it was nighttime.

I managed to stop myself from laughing. Lady Marie seemed nothing but serious. The other girls, Anahira included, did not appear to treat it as a joke. Not at all.

"There is a secret program run by the Wayfinder Girls," Lady Marie continued. "A program called Guardians. Every five years, we recruit a new team to be trained as a Guardians unit. This year, we are offering each of you a chance to be trained. You will learn about the existence of other worlds and how we protect the Earth."

I couldn't believe what I was hearing. Was it true? A hidden purpose? A secret program? Other worlds?

And an offer to be trained as a member of Guardians? Me? But how could I be a Guardian? It would be a disaster. I'm more likely to cause the end of the Earth rather than protect it.

"That is all I will say on the matter," Lady Marie added. "You will have questions. Your questions will be answered. But first, you must decide whether you want to know more."

Lady Marie removed several blue and red ribbons from her

pocket and placed them on the coffee table in the center of the room.

"Please take one of each color before you leave. If you do not wish to know any more or do not feel able to keep the secrets you will learn, then wear the blue ribbon on your uniform to breakfast. You will have a choice of any of the adventures the other Wayfinder Girls are going on. If, however, you do wish to know more and want to be trained as an elite member of Guardians, then wear the red ribbon to breakfast. Your training will begin tomorrow."

Lady Marie paused and again considered each of us in turn.

"There is no judgment either way. It is entirely up to you. Choose wisely." Lady Marie turned and abruptly left the room.

No one said anything after Lady Marie left, not even Anahira. I barely noticed as one or two of the girls picked up their ribbons and walked out of the room.

I stared at the blue and red ribbons still on the table.

What on Earth am I going to choose?

3
HIDDEN FIGURES

I t took a long time for me to get to sleep, and then I woke up a couple of times in the middle of the night. It wasn't surprising, really, not with everything I'd learned.

I woke up the first time after dreaming about a person with green skin laughing at me from the middle of a tree. It reminded me of the Grinch, more of a sneer than a laugh. I stayed awake for a while, wondering if the person I'd seen watching me had anything to do with the other worlds Lady Marie had mentioned. I hoped not.

The second time I woke up left me feeling even more troubled. I had dreamed about Anahira and Lady Marie talking. Lady Marie asked Anahira if she should consider me as a recruit for the Guardians, and Anahira had shaken her head and laughed like it was the funniest thing she'd ever heard. It took longer for me to get back to sleep after that dream.

But now, here I was, awake and dressed, and staring at the one blue and the one red ribbon I'd taken from the Owl room.

"Can you imagine it?" Anahira said, watching me from a sitting position on her bed.

"What?"

"Learning about other worlds!"

Anahira made it sound like a wonderful adventure, but I wasn't so sure. I struggled to cope with the world I was currently in, let alone trying to deal with any others. I'd probably just discover more food I was allergic to.

"Do you know what you're going to do?" Anahira asked after she picked up on my less-than-enthusiastic response to her statement.

"No," I replied with a sigh. "You?"

"Yeah, I think so."

I knew what Anahira would do. She would choose the red ribbon and join the Guardians. And why not? Unlike me, Anahira was brave and confident, a perfect candidate for the elite Guardians unit.

"It's time for breakfast," Anahira said.

"I know. I need to get my food from the kitchen."

"Do you want some help?"

"No, it's all good."

"I'll see you in the dining room then?" Anahira asked.

"Yeah, I won't be long."

Anahira stood and walked to the door.

"We've got this, Maggie," Anahira insisted before she left the room.

I stared at the door a moment before turning back to look at Anahira's bed. A blue ribbon rested on her pillow.

"Good for you, Anahira," I said to the empty room.

Why couldn't I have the same self-belief as Anahira?

Why couldn't I have the courage to have talked to Anahira about my dreams?

My biggest worry sprang from my second dream, that I wasn't good enough to be in Guardians. I definitely wasn't as good as the other four girls.

Definitely not.

Yet, somehow, I had been invited.

I stared at the blue and red ribbons. It was time to choose. I picked up one of the ribbons and pinned it to my hoodie.

I left the room. I only looked back twice.

· · ·

Breakfast had finished, and there were only the five of us left in the dining room. All five girls with red ribbons pinned to their hoodies.

Anahira was so excited when I'd appeared in the dining room with a red ribbon that she leapt up and gave me a massive hug. We sat down with Kayla, Sam, and Razia. It seemed to be the right thing to do.

Breakfast finished quickly, with adventures starting right away. All of the Wayfinder Girls were wearing ribbons that matched the particular adventure they were doing, and extra Wayfinder leaders had arrived during breakfast to help run the activities.

A group wearing yellow ribbons headed into the city of London to the British Museum and the Churchill War Rooms. Another group wearing green ribbons went to Hampstead Heath for raft building and racing on one of the ponds.

I looked out the window at the morning sunshine, relieved that the raft-building group could dry off if they got wet. They would surely be provided life jackets.

I don't need to worry about them.

Lady Marie walked into the dining room a few moments after all the other girls had left. She considered us a moment and then nodded. "Follow me."

Lady Marie turned and walked out of the dining room, and we leapt up to follow her. She led us to the elevator, and we all walked in as the door opened.

"What are we doing in the elevator?" I whispered to Anahira.

Anahira shrugged. She probably knew as much, or as little, as I did.

Lady Marie removed her Dux Manor pin from the lapel of her jacket and inserted it in a tiny gap at the bottom of the control panel. A small section of the metallic wall next to the panel opened, revealing an illuminated scanner.

My gasp of surprise was echoed by the other girls, and we all pressed forward to try and get a closer look.

Lady Marie returned her pin and placed her left palm on the scanner. In response, a bright green light enveloped her hand. Lady Marie removed her hand, and the scanner returned to its hiding place.

A moment later, the light shining through the glass panel in the ceiling of the elevator changed from white to green, and the elevator moved. Despite the only choice available being to move up, the elevator started going *down*.

I shot a wide-eyed look at Anahira, who grinned in response.

The elevator stopped, and the metallic wall and mirror at the *opposite end* of the elevator doors slid to one side. A large underground space opened out from the elevator, its limits and contents hidden in shadow.

Lady Marie edged forward and walked into the shadowy space. In response, ceiling lights activated, and the entire area lit up. A large rectangular wooden table dominated the center, with a massive digital TV screen imposing itself at the far end of the table. To the right of the table was a lounge area with three black sofas, two rows of wooden lockers, and a single row of wooden benches in-between. To the left of the table was a row of six desks, complete with chairs, computer screens, and cabinets. The desks filled the entire wall, ending just before a door.

Lady Marie turned around to face us. "Welcome to the Guardians' command center."

"Wow!" Kayla exclaimed with a wide grin.

"Not bad," Sam added.

"It is most impressive," Razia commented, eyeing the row of computers.

Kayla, Sam, Razia, and Anahira moved out of the elevator to explore the room, but I stayed where I was. The underground command center did not appeal to me at all.

"Are you alright, Margaret?" Lady Marie asked

The other girls stopped and turned to look at me.

"Is there an emergency exit?" I asked, choosing to ignore the fact that Lady Marie called me Margaret.

Sam started to laugh but stopped when Lady Marie turned to

her, eyebrows raised in a manner that suggested Sam should know better.

"A good question, Margaret," Lady Marie responded, turning her attention back to me. "And an important lesson to begin our training. Guardians Rule #26: One must always make sure of one's own safety."

Only rule number twenty-six? Shouldn't that be rule number one?

Lady Marie studied me long enough to make me feel uncomfortable. "There is a second exit through the door to my right," Lady Marie explained, raising her right arm to indicate the direction behind her. "It leads to a tunnel, which emerges in the garden behind Dux Manor. Through a tree, in fact. There is a bathroom through the door on my left. And behind the TV screen is a fully stocked kitchen."

I nodded in response, but I was far from satisfied. A tunnel which ended in a tree? How is that even possible? An idea struck me like a thunderbolt.

The green-skinned watcher in the tree. Did they come from here?

"Any other questions?" Lady Marie asked.

I had so many questions. But then I considered Anahira and the other girls, who seemed impatient to check out the space. "No," I somehow managed to say.

"Good," Lady Marie replied, turning to include everyone. "Take a moment to explore. We will meet at the table in five minutes."

Lady Marie strolled to one of the lockers. The rest of the girls followed Lady Marie's advice and moved further into the room.

I didn't move. I couldn't stop imagining all the things that could go wrong with being trapped in a secret underground location. What if the elevator stopped working and the exit tunnel got blocked? What if there was a fire? What if the tunnel flooded? What if someone got injured and help couldn't arrive in time? What if...

"Come on, Maggie. I've got you," Anahira encouraged, smiling at me.

I clutched Anahira's hand as I stepped forward. "Thanks."

Anahira knew all about my neurotic impulses and didn't mind one bit.

"No worries. We're all a bit munted, aye," Anahira replied.

I laughed at Anahira's use of the word *munted*. A word I hadn't known until Anahira had used it in class one day. In New Zealand, "munted" meant broken or damaged. While I appreciated the support, I couldn't see how the word applied to Anahira.

"Let's check this place out," Anahira suggested as she led me forward.

"Okay," I replied tentatively, following Anahira. A member of the elite Guardians unit should not have been worried about exploring their own command center.

Anahira led me first to the door leading to the emergency exit. The *exit* was not much more than a narrow tunnel, which sloped upward. Lady Marie claimed it ended in a tree, and as much as I wanted to confirm the fact, I was also worried I'd meet someone with green skin. We didn't go any further into the tunnel.

Anahira and I checked out the rest of the space, investigating the kitchen and bathroom. Both were spacious and modern. It was pretty cool.

"Okay, girls," Lady Marie announced. "Please come and sit down."

We all came and sat around the table. In front of Lady Marie were a pair of glasses, four golden ropes, six small silver discs, and something which looked like a remote control, although it seemed to be made entirely of gold.

"I will allocate these items in a moment," Lady Marie stated. "But first, what questions do you need answered right now?"

I looked around at the others, hoping they might ask just one of the questions plaguing my mind, or at the very least, they would ask a question, *any* question. I didn't want to be the only one with all the questions.

"How does the tree exit work?" Anahira asked.

Oh, Anahira. Thank you!

Lady Marie smiled. "I'm afraid that's something of a mystery. All I can say is that the tree granted entry some time ago. It was our sole means of access to our underground base until we installed the elevator, which then allowed us to improve the entire space."

The tree granted entry? Can this get any weirder?

"How many people know about this place?" Sam asked.

"A good question, Sam," Lady Marie answered. "We train a new Guardians unit every five years, some of whom stay on as leaders. You have already met two of these leaders."

That must be Meiling and Faatimah.

"We are governed by a Council. A group of high-ranking current and ex-Wayfinder leaders. We all work hard to keep our activities hidden from the public. Guardians Rule #7: One must always guard our secrets."

Guarding secrets is more important than being safe? That doesn't sound right.

Lady Marie made it sound like a warning, although I had no idea what would happen to someone who betrayed the Guardians. Surely nothing. It was the Wayfinder Girls, after all. *The Wayfinder Girls!* Committed to caring, supporting, and encouraging girls.

There is nothing to worry about.

"Lady Marie," Anahira asked. "Have you ever seen anyone with green skin?"

I shot a panicked look at Anahira. Why was she mentioning the strange watcher?

Lady Marie considered Anahira for a moment. "I am not aware of any reports of people with green skin. Why do you ask?"

Anahira looked at me, eyebrows raised.

"I thought I saw someone with green skin watching me yesterday," I admitted.

Sam and Kayla laughed, and I shrank down into my chair.

Lady Marie held up her hand. "Another learning opportunity. Guardians Rule #23: One must never scoff at strange sightings."

Okay, so now not scoffing at strange sightings was higher up than keeping safe.

I need to get my hands on one of these rulebooks!

"Please tell me more, Margaret," Lady Marie instructed.

"It was at registration," I responded tentatively. "I saw someone with green skin watching me from a tree. I told Anahira, but when I looked back, they had disappeared."

Lady Marie raised her chin. She brought her right hand up to her face, her index finger tapping on her lip. She stopped tapping, her finger poised in midair. "Did you ever see them again?"

"Yes, Lady Marie. Once more," I answered while catching Sam rolling her eyes. I pressed on, despite the heat rising in my face. "At the start of the first activity."

Anahira looked sharply at me. I hadn't managed to tell her about the second time I'd seen the watcher.

"And they disappeared again?" Lady Marie asked, continuing her questioning.

I nodded.

"Do you think it means anything?" Anahira asked.

"I'm not sure it means anything significant," Lady Marie responded. "Although I cannot be certain about what Margaret believes she saw, I estimate that it will prove harmless. I will raise the matter at the next Guardians Council meeting. Thank you for bringing it to my attention, Anahira."

Lady Marie seemed disappointed in me.

What if I had just imagined it all?

"Now, to the matter at hand," Lady Marie said, indicating the items in front of her. "I have told you that the hidden purpose of the Guardians is to protect the Earth from other worlds. But I have not yet told you how we do this."

I sat up in my chair. Despite my anxiety and fear, I was fascinated by how this all worked. I mean, who wouldn't be?

"You may know that there are six Wayfinder centers throughout the world," Lady Marie continued. "But what you don't know is that they have each been built where the barrier between worlds is at its weakest. Taken together, our six centers form a collective shield, which helps protect the world from interdimensional threats."

Barriers between worlds? Interdimensional threats? Collective shield?

My dad watched a lot of documentaries on conspiracy theories, but this would have blown his mind.

"Now you may be wondering what we can do against such threats," Lady Marie asked.

All five of us nodded, eyes wide.

"Well, it is nothing too dramatic, I can assure you," Lady Marie added. "We simply send them back."

"Back where?" Kayla asked.

"Back to the world they came from," Lady Marie answered.

"We don't harm them, do we?" Razia inquired.

"No, Razia. We send them back to their own world, unharmed."

"How?" Sam asked.

"With these items," Lady Marie declared. "Although how they precisely work is still a bit of a mystery, I'm afraid."

We all stared at the items on the table. They didn't look special, apart from the golden remote control, if that was even what it was. The items didn't look like they could have done anything against interdimensional threats.

"But what do they do?" Anahira asked.

"You will discover what they do when you practice using them," Lady Marie replied. "Anahira, Sam, Razia, and Kayla, you will each be issued golden ropes. Margaret, you will be given six silver discs. Razia, if you are willing, I would like you to have the glasses."

"Glasses?" Razia replied.

"The very latest in smart technology. The glasses can access the internet, including the secret server the Guardians use. They can also record video."

I stared at the black-rimmed glasses. Each side was thicker than a normal pair of glasses, with the left-hand side housing an extra adjustable lens.

"I will gladly wear them, Lady Marie," Razia confirmed.

"Excellent," Lady Marie responded. "I will explain what I can about the glasses, ropes, and discs once we're in the minibus."

"The minibus?" I asked, my voice rising in pitch. "Are we going somewhere?"

"Yes, we can't very well train here. We are going to the Ravenwood campsite in the Chiltern Hills. It's just under an hour's drive, which will allow time for Razia to practice using her new glasses."

I darted a look at the other girls, none of whom seemed at all worried that we were leaving Dux Manor. But that wasn't in the plan for today. The plan my mum approved had only included activities in and around London, nothing that required an hour's drive.

I'd never heard of the Ravenwood campsite. What if it wasn't safe? What if I had an allergic reaction? How close was the nearest hospital? Would medical help reach me in time? How would Mum know where I was? What if we had an accident on the road?

I don't cope well with sudden changes.

"But what are we going to do at Ravenwood?" I asked, not able to hide my concern.

Lady Marie smiled. "We are going to open doorways to other worlds."

4

INTO THE WOODS

Lady Marie drove out of Dux Manor in a yellow eight-seater minibus, with the name and logo of the Wayfinder Girls emblazoned on the outside of the van. We had loaded the minibus with the items we needed, as well as a packed lunch. I'd gathered my salmon and crackers from the small kitchen. My own special lunch.

Razia sat in the front of the minibus, while the rest of us sat in the back.

"You might be wondering why we are using this vehicle," Lady Marie said as we turned out of the Dux Manor driveway. "We have learned that people ask fewer questions if they see Wayfinder Girls going around on official Wayfinder business."

They are probably worried about being asked to make a donation or buy some of the world-famous Wayfinder Pineapple Lumps: chocolate-covered lumps of chewy pineapple.

"Now, sit back and relax," Lady Marie added. "I will explain all I can during the drive."

A short, barked laugh almost escaped my lips. I could try sitting back, but there was little chance of me relaxing. It was scary enough to learn about the existence of other worlds. But to also discover that there were doorways to these worlds that could be opened—that was enough to make me shut myself in my room and never come out.

I was only able to cope because Anahira sat beside me. And because Lady Marie had insisted that we were perfectly safe. She claimed we were embarking on a simple training exercise and that there was absolutely no danger at all.

I didn't hear too much more of Lady Marie's explanations. My mind clamped onto the idea that we would be safe. That it was only training. That Anahira was with me. I really couldn't handle too much more than those three thoughts.

I desperately hoped that they were all true.

※ ※ ※

IT TOOK US THE BEST PART OF AN HOUR TO REACH THE RAVENWOOD campsite, located near a small village called Asheridge. To get there, we traveled on a road that was not much more than a country lane, bordered by trees on both sides.

Apart from some really nice-looking houses, Asheridge seemed to consist only of an old, double-story, red brick building called the Red Raven.

"That is a rather excellent country pub," Lady Marie asserted as we drove past.

Several baskets of pink and purple flowers hung on the outside wall of the Red Raven, and three green picnic tables sat on the lawn outside the pub. It looked very inviting.

I should ask Lady Marie to drop me off here.

I could wait at one of the tables while the others dealt with other worlds. But the opportunity passed quickly, and I hadn't had the courage to ask anyway.

The number of trees increased as we left the Red Raven behind, and we soon turned into a driveway almost hidden from the road by trees.

We stopped at a gate, shut with a chain and padlock.

"Razia, would you mind opening the gate?" Lady Marie asked as she handed Razia a key. "Please lock it after I drive through."

Razia nodded and got out of the minibus.

A small wooden sign on the side of the driveway contained the name 'Ravenwood' in crooked, hand-painted white lettering. It looked creepy.

Razia unlocked and opened the gate. Lady Marie drove forward and waited for Razia to get back in the minibus.

"Did you lock it?" Lady Marie asked.

"Yes, Lady Marie," Razia answered and handed back the key.

"That's good. We don't want any extra visitors today."

Extra visitors?

Does that mean we were expecting some visitors? But where would those visitors come from? They wouldn't come from other worlds, would they?

I grabbed Anahira's hand, squeezing tightly.

"It's okay. We've got this," Anahira whispered.

I nodded, but I didn't let go of Anahira's hand.

Lady Marie drove forward. We followed the driveway as it curved to the left, past another gate, which led to a single building on the edge of a large area of grassland. We continued to the end of the long driveway, before stopping in a parking area, next to a wide and dense section of woodland.

"Welcome to the Ravenwood campsite," Lady Marie proclaimed as she parked the van. "An ideal spot for backwoods camping. And, when occasion dictates, perfect for Guardians training."

Lady Marie got out of the minibus and indicated for us to join her. One by one, we left the minibus and huddled together in a group.

"There is a bathroom available," Lady Marie announced. "May I suggest you make use of it, while I release a drone."

"A drone?" Sam asked.

"I have booked the full use of this facility for the day, even though we will be here no more than three hours, but it is prudent to ensure that what we do is hidden from any prying eyes. Guardians Rule #17: one must ensure the area is clear before one begins training."

Rule #17? So what is Rule #1? I really need to know.

Of more immediate concern was the need to check if the area was clear. Was that to make sure no one else saw what we did? Or was it to make sure no one else got hurt in case something went wrong?

"Quickly now, girls. Please use the bathroom if you need to," Lady Marie said as she indicated a small wooden cabin, a short walk from the car parking area.

We took Lady Marie's advice, although I think most of us just wanted to walk off the long drive and explore the area, making full use of the bright, sunny autumn day.

We were definitely in the countryside. Long stretches of rolling green fields could be glimpsed through gaps in the trees.

Lady Marie was standing at the back of the minibus when we returned. "The drone's thermal imaging sensors are active. They will sync with Razia's glasses and alert us in case of any intruders. Razia, please confirm that the link is active."

Razia reached up to adjust her glasses. "It is active, Lady Marie. I have thermal imaging from the drone. There are a lot of very small heat signatures, probably birds, and something that might be a fox or a badger. There are some deer in the neighboring woods, but the area we are in is mostly clear. I cannot detect any other people."

"Good. Alright then, girls, please collect your ropes," Lady Marie responded, unzipping a large black carry bag she had retrieved from the back of the minibus.

The other girls stepped forward one-by-one and collected a golden rope.

"Maggie," Lady Marie added, opening a small black case. "Your discs."

I stepped forward and took the six small silver discs out of the case.

Lady Marie put the bag and case in the back of the minibus and closed the door. She then turned to face us. "Follow me," she instructed as she walked away.

We followed Lady Marie as she led us into the woods. Tall

beech trees dominated the area, trees with smooth gray bark and huge domed crowns. I knew the trees from my Woodland Wayfinder badge I completed two years ago—level three!

After a short walk along a path through the woodland, we reached a clearing of sorts, a large flat space bordered on all sides by beech trees. The branches of the trees stretched out high above us, forming a kind of a roof covering. It seemed almost like a natural room inside the woods, with a thick reddish-brown carpet of fallen leaves and beechnut husks.

"Here we are," Lady Marie proclaimed as she brought us to a stop. "Now, Anahira and Kayla, please line up on my right. Razia and Sam, to my left. Margaret, stand with me."

We all moved to do as Lady Marie instructed. She positioned us so that we stood in a semi-circle. I took up the center position with Lady Marie.

"You may be feeling nervous, but please know there is no need for any concern," Lady Marie encouraged us. "We have been doing this for many years and there have never been any mishaps. Simply follow my lead."

I clenched my fist, as though squeezing an invisible stress ball, and started patting the meds bag hanging by my side.

"You all good, Maggie?" Anahira asked.

I turned to Anahira and shook my head.

"Alright, girls. Let us begin," Lady Marie announced.

Lady Marie lifted up the golden device that we first saw in the Guardians' command center. She adjusted a few settings and looked up expectantly.

"Here it is, our first doorway."

I followed Lady Marie's gaze and blinked. I wasn't certain what I expected, but it wasn't exactly what I was seeing.

The "doorway" wasn't really much of a door, more like a shimmering of the air a short distance in front of us. It looked like a small pool of water standing upright.

A vertical pool of water that defied gravity.

And might not have been anything at all like water.

The view through the doorway showed nothing more than an

orange sea. Or at least, it could have been a sea. Peering through the doorway was like trying to see through a wall of mist. The only thing visible was a flat and featureless expanse of orange.

Lady Marie left the doorway open for maybe a minute. It was hard to tell with my heart thumping in my chest and my palms starting to sweat. But nothing happened. Lady Marie adjusted another setting on the golden device and the doorway disappeared, as though it had never existed.

I breathed a sigh of relief as the world returned to normal.

"Is that it?" Sam asked.

"That was indeed your first viewing of another world," Lady Marie answered.

"But it was just a bunch of orange," Sam protested.

"Yes, Sam. But orange not of this world," Lady Marie concluded.

Sam frowned but didn't say anything more.

"Razia, did you capture the encounter?" Lady Marie asked.

"Yes, Lady Marie," Razia responded. "I have the whole encounter recorded."

Encounter?

If a view of a whole lot of orange qualified as an encounter with other worlds, then I guess I didn't need to be so worried. Certainly better than the slimy, six-eyed monster I'd imagined, one with a row of razor-sharp teeth and long, clammy, black tentacles.

"Alright, girls. That was just to get us started. We find it best to begin slowly," Lady Marie explained. "This next one should be a little more exciting."

Okay. I'm not out of the woods yet.

Lady Marie adjusted the golden device.

The air shimmered again, and another vertical pool of not-water appeared. The doorway this time revealed a rocky terrain studded with what looked like white spires or possibly trees. It was hard to tell.

Lady Marie again left the doorway open for a minute or so, and this time, there was movement detected on the other side.

"Excellent," Lady Marie declared. "Just what I was hoping for. Kayla and Sam, can you please have your ropes ready for use?"

I tensed, but what emerged through the doorway could have been mistaken as a child's stuffed animal. It was small and furry, with a hooked nose and a tail that stood up like an antenna. Its wide eyes stared up at me as it tentatively shuffled through the doorway.

"Kayla, your rope please," Lady Marie instructed.

Kayla threw the end of her rope quite gently, but it quickly latched onto the little intruder and twined itself around the center of its body. The creature stopped, turned its head, and considered the rope. It didn't seem like it was hurt, but it could no longer move.

"Margaret, your turn."

I stared at Lady Marie and then back at the creature.

"You simply need one of your silver discs to touch the creature."

I looked down at the silver discs.

How can physical contact with the creature do anything?

"Margaret, please either throw a disc on the creature or place one on its fur. It's perfectly safe. But if you continue to dawdle, it may well invite its friends to join us."

I warily stepped forward, reached out, and dropped a disc on the creature's thick yellow fur. The fur immediately sprang up as though blown by a strong wind and the creature was sucked back through the doorway, which closed with a loud *pop*.

I spun around to Lady Marie. "I didn't hurt it, did I?"

"No, you just sent it back to its own world."

I studied the area the creature had walked through. There was no sign it had even been there. The doorway and my disc had gone. But somehow, Kayla still had her rope.

"How?" I asked.

"A bit of a mystery there, too, I'm afraid," Lady Marie admitted. "You see, we didn't create the items we are using. They were gifted to us as part of a treaty arrangement."

A treaty arrangement?

"A treaty with who?" Anahira asked.

Lady Marie waved her hand in the air. "We are getting a bit ahead of ourselves. But let's just say that the items we use to defend the Earth are not of this world. They were gifted to us by the inhabitants of another world, a world that sought our help in defending the pathways between worlds."

It sounded way too fantastical to be true. But here we were.

"So, is that it?" Sam asked again. "We protect the Earth from too much orange or invasion from walking stuffed animals?"

"Please, Sam," Lady Marie responded. "You are merely at the start of your training. There is much still to learn."

Sam didn't look very impressed, but she nodded.

"Alright," Lady Marie declared. "Let's try one more time before we take a break. We may need more than one rope."

That didn't sound promising. Would we need more than one rope because there would be more than one creature, or was Lady Marie expecting a creature that would be too big for just one rope? Neither option sounded good. Although, to be fair, the first two encounters with other worlds had gone okay.

"Alright, girls. Here we go." Lady Marie finished adjusting the golden device.

The air shimmered in front of us, and the vertical pool of not-water revealed a lush and dense green landscape.

"Stand ready, girls. Some things can move quickly," Lady Marie ordered.

I plucked another one of the silver discs out of my left hand and squeezed it with my right hand, ready for use. I focused on the doorway.

Let's get this over with.

Something like a dark wave swept across the doorway, and the view abruptly changed. A barren and gray stretch of wasteland replaced the previous green landscape.

"Is that supposed to happen?" I asked, turning sharply to Lady Marie.

Lady Marie didn't respond, choosing instead to stare at her golden device.

"Lady Marie?"

Lady Marie still didn't respond, her focus entirely on the device.

"There's something moving in there," Anahira pointed out.

"Something big," Sam added.

"More than one," Razia confirmed.

Lady Marie looked up, her normally serene features masked in worry. She darted a look at her device and repeatedly pressed on one particular spot. She shook her head and then looked back at the doorway. "Right, girls. We've got a live one. Stand ready."

I faced the doorway as the other girls tightened their grip on their ropes.

"Steady now, girls," Lady Marie instructed, as her usual poise and calmness returned.

A guttural roar sounded from the other side of the doorway. I tensed and shot a quick look at Anahira, who glanced at me and nodded. "We've got this."

But the *thing* that broke through the doorway didn't seem to be easily *got*. It was huge. I mean, really, really big. Its height was matched by its massive torso, forearms, and forelegs. It was wearing some kind of weathered armor, like what an ancient human warrior might have worn, and it held a thick wooden club in its right hand. Completing the "I'm so scary" look were its bear-like claws and two horns protruding out of its huge, hairy head.

The bear-man-creature-thing roared and raised its arms in apparent triumph.

We all stepped back. That club looked like it could have caused some serious damage.

"Stand your ground," Lady Marie commanded, doing her best to rally us. "Use the ropes. Now!"

As one, the girls holding the ropes released them. From my right, a rope whipped around the creature's left leg and another around its left arm. The same happened on my left. The girls clung to the ropes with both hands, valiantly struggling to stay upright.

The creature howled as its progress was halted.

"Now, Margaret," Lady Marie instructed. "Throw a disc!"

I took aim, pulled back my right arm and threw one of the silver discs.

The disc sailed high and wide, completely missing its target.

That's just great.

"Again, Margaret."

I grabbed another silver disc, steadied myself and threw. The disc bounced off one of the creature's horns and dropped harmlessly to the ground. The creature barely noticed the touch of the disc but wrestled instead to free itself from the golden ropes.

The discs aren't working. Why not?

"Margaret. Focus."

I picked another silver disc. One of only *three* left. I took aim and threw. But in its struggle, the creature ducked its head and the disc missed its target yet again.

The creature redoubled its efforts against the ropes. It flexed its powerful muscles and managed to free its arms, causing two of the girls to stumble.

The creature roared in triumph as a second creature appeared in the doorway.

Oh great! Just how many of these things are there?

"Margaret!"

I stared at the pleading face of Lady Marie and then back at the creature, which was about to break free from the last two ropes.

The creature fixed me with a ravenous gaze and roared again.

I flinched and threw the second-to-last silver disc. It flew straight into the creature's mouth. The creature instinctively chomped down on the disc, and its eyes widened in surprise. It briefly strained against some kind of fierce wind-like force and was sucked back through the doorway, causing the second creature to hastily retreat.

The doorway closed with a loud *bang*, almost like a fat firecracker going off, leaving the beech woodland and countryside as quiet and undisturbed as when we had first arrived.

I stared open-mouthed at the space the doorway had occupied and struggled to control my rapidly increasing breath. I turned wide-eyed to the rest of my unit, who seemed just as shocked as I was.

All apart from Sam, who folded her arms and turned to Lady Marie.

"Will we get a badge for this?"

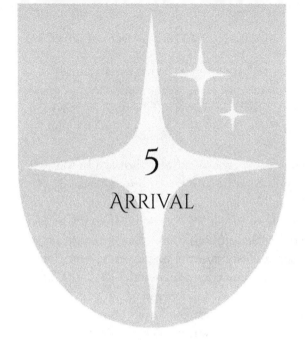

5
ARRIVAL

I reached into my meds bag and grabbed my inhaler and spacer. My hands shook as I lifted the spacer to my mouth, pressed my inhaler, and took two long, deep breaths.

"Well done, Margaret. Bit of a close call, but you got there in the end."

I looked past my spacer to the now-serene face of Lady Marie, although she did shoot a questioning look at the golden device she still held in her hands.

"Was that supposed to happen?" I asked, returning my inhaler and spacer to my meds bag.

"No, Margaret," Lady Marie answered while lowering the golden device. "I'm terribly sorry, but that was most definitely not supposed to happen."

I noted the one silver disc I'd managed *not* to throw. I'd used four of the discs. *Four.* What would have happened if I'd missed with all of the discs?

"Lady Marie?" I asked, trying to avoid the direction my thoughts were taking me.

"Yes, Margaret?"

"Can you please just call me Maggie?"

Lady Marie smiled. "Yes, alright, Maggie it is."

"Thank you," I answered. "What went wrong?"

"I'm not terribly sure, I'm afraid. I'm not certain how we encountered that creature. It might well be the most dangerous visitor anyone in Guardians has thus far dealt with."

Visitor?

I didn't know what kind of visitors Lady Marie was used to, but surely none of them wanted to remove anyone's head with a large club.

I probably needed a few more puffs from my inhaler.

"Ka pai, Maggie. It's all good," Anahira said.

I turned to Anahira, who, despite everything, looked calm and composed. Her brown eyes shone brightly as she stepped forward and gave me a hug, saying more in action than words ever could. I broke from the hug and caught the reactions from the rest of my unit.

Kayla grinned. "We knew you could do it."

"Well done, Maggie," Razia added. "It wasn't an easy task."

Sam nodded, although her frown revealed that she was not impressed.

"Alright, girls, first things first," Lady Marie said as she gathered us close together. "Is everyone okay?"

Anahira and Kayla both answered, "Yes."

Razia nodded and Sam gave the thumbs up.

"Maggie?" Lady Marie inquired.

"I'm okay, I think. I'm sorry I missed."

"Nonsense. That creature was enough to put anyone off their aim," Lady Marie stated.

Lady Marie was being kind. No one else would have been so wasteful.

"The important thing is that we are all safe," Lady Marie added. "I cannot state how sorry I am about what just transpired. It has never happened before; I can assure you."

Lady Marie couldn't have assured me of anything at the moment. Hadn't she claimed we wouldn't be in any danger? So what on Earth had just happened?

"What even was that thing?" Anahira asked.

"A very good question, Anahira. What do you think, Razia?"

"I believe it may have been a Bugbear, Lady Marie," Razia stated calmly while reaching up to hold her glasses. "I did a quick search of the Guardians' database and managed to find several references to similar creatures in some Old Welsh and Old Scots accounts. I will need to do further investigation, but the Bugbear was certainly dangerous."

Dangerous? It wanted to eat us for lunch!

"Did you get enough footage?"

"Yes, Lady Marie. I'll cross-check it back at Dux Manor."

"Good. Thank you, Razia. Well done."

Razia had taken to the smartglasses as though she'd been using them her entire life.

Lady Marie considered us carefully. "Congratulations to all of you. You have achieved something that no one else within Guardians has yet accomplished. You can now be confident the items work, despite the apparent malfunction with my device. How did the ropes feel?"

"Almost as an extension of our thoughts," Anahira answered, eyes widening.

"Yeah. We imagined what we wanted the ropes to do, and they obeyed," Sam added.

"We didn't even have to tie knots," Kayla boasted with another broad smile.

"But did we lose connection with two of the ropes?" Lady Marie asked.

There were murmurs, but no one answered Lady Marie. Kayla and Razia dropped their heads. It must have been their ropes the so-called Bugbear had shaken off. Neither of them should have been upset. I only had the job of throwing the discs because I was hopeless with ropes. And knots!

"It is alright, girls. We are here to learn," Lady Marie encouraged.

"And get badges," Sam suggested.

"Yes, thank you, Sam. Due to that last encounter, I have no

hesitation in awarding you all the Earth Defender Level 1 badge. A feat you can be especially proud of. Well done."

Lady Marie's announcement was met with broad smiles from all the girls—except me. My actions hadn't merited a badge.

"I'll issue your badges back at Dux Manor. But, of course, you won't be able to display them anywhere or show them to anyone."

"Keep it secret. Keep it safe," I whispered.

"What was that, Maggie?" Lady Marie asked.

"Oh, nothing really, Lady Marie, just something Gandalf said."

"Gandalf? The wizard?" Lady Marie clarified.

"Oh, no. Not another Harry Potter fanatic," Sam complained.

"That's Dumbledore, not Gandalf," Anahira corrected Sam, before I could.

"Whatever," Sam replied.

"Girls, please," Lady Marie chimed in. "Gandalf's words are spot-on. Thank you, Maggie. Secret and safe. That's what we must be. No one can discuss what they've done or seen here today. No one. Not even with your parents or siblings."

"Or boyfriends," Kayla added quickly, provoking giggles from the other girls.

"Quite," Lady Marie replied, raising an eyebrow.

"But girlfriends are okay," Kayla continued, with another broad smile, and another burst of laughter from the girls.

"Yes, thank you, Kayla," Lady Marie responded. "I cannot stress to you enough just how important it is that we keep the knowledge of what happened today secret and safe. We do so to protect the other worlds. Do you understand?"

We looked around at each other and nodded, although I wasn't sure I understood.

We do so to protect the other worlds? Protect them from what?

"To be honest, I don't think anyone would believe me if I told them," Anahira added.

"That is in all likelihood true, but let us not tempt others with the knowledge of other worlds," Lady Marie responded.

Yeah, who would believe that girls involved in a secret program run by the respected Wayfinder Girls were attacked by a creature from another world, after the doorway to the creature's world was opened as part of a training exercise.

I struggled to believe it myself.

"Alright, girls," Lady Marie announced. "I think we should take a well-earned break. Let's leave the area spotless, shall we? Guardians Rule #15: One must always leave a place better than one found it. Maggie, will you kindly gather the discs?"

I ducked my head and walked away, embarrassed by the reminder of my poor throwing ability. The discs apparently only left our world if they made contact with something from another world, but that required some basic coordination. A thing I was not blessed with.

Anahira would have helped me collect the fallen discs, but it was my task to complete. All I needed to do was to find a flash of silver amongst the fallen leaves and beechnut husks.

I managed to find two of the discs easily enough, the one that had hit the Bugbear's horn and the one that had just missed. I added them to the one disc I hadn't thrown and looked around for the first disc. I couldn't see it anywhere.

I tried to relive that first wild throw. Understandably wild, given I faced a savage creature from another world. But a wild throw, nonetheless.

I moved further away and searched the ground. How far did I actually throw the disc?

"Is this what you be lookin' for?"

I looked up and gasped. Appearing out of nowhere stood two of the strangest "people" I had ever seen. They were about my height and had long, silver hair and pointed ears. One of them held my missing disc in their right hand. I stared at the raised disc and then darted a glance behind me. Lady Marie and the others had left the clearing, presumably to store their items in the minibus.

I'm on my own.

I turned back, surprised that I hadn't felt the need to run away. Instead, I felt oddly calm. I discovered the two strangers arguing with each other.

"Of course she's lookin' for that. We watched her pick up them others."

"I don't need you to be tellin' me what we saw. I was bein' polite, I was."

"Polite, was it? You've terrified the poor wee mite."

"I suppose you would have done better, mun?"

"I would've used me old charm."

"Charm? What charm?'

"Don't you be startin' that again."

"I'm not bein' funny. My charm's brighter than yours."

I had no idea what they were arguing about, but I was feeling unnaturally relaxed and curious. The strangers' long, silver hair was tied back from their foreheads with a thin golden band, each housing a gem, one blue, the other green. They were brown-skinned, with bright eyes matching the color of their gems. They were dressed in brown trousers, brown boots, and green capes, which somehow seemed appropriate, but I wasn't so sure about the football shirts. That I recognized them as football shirts was the fault of my football-mad family. I simply couldn't escape the madness at home. And so I identified, without even trying, a Barcelona shirt and a Manchester United shirt.

I really didn't know why they were wearing football shirts. They didn't seem anything like typical football fans. In fact, there was nothing typical about them at all.

"Excuse me," I said, injecting myself into their conversation. "Who are you?"

The two strangers ceased their bickering and turned toward me. Their eyes shone with an intense light as they both bowed.

"Why, I'm Tylwyth," the blue-eyed one declared after completing his bow.

"And I'm Teg," the green-eyed one added with a smile.

I had the distinct impression that their names were supposed to mean something to me, but they didn't—not at all.

Tylwyth and Teg waited expectantly and not knowing what else to do, I introduced myself with a bow of my own.

"I'm Maggie. Maggie Thatcher."

"A pleasure to meet you, Maggie. Maggie Thatcher," Tylwyth replied.

"An honor indeed, like," Teg added.

Like what?

Nothing more came from the one called Teg. Instead, the strangers stared at me expectantly.

"Can I have my disc back, please?"

Neither Tylwyth nor Teg responded. I didn't know how or why, but they both radiated disappointment.

"I'm sorry," I quickly added, not certain I really was. "It's just that I…"

"No need to apologize," Tylwyth interrupted, raising his hand. "Many things are lost."

"Too many," Teg bemoaned.

I had no idea what they were talking about, but Tylwyth held the silver disc in his hand, so maybe he meant the disc.

"You'd be wantin' this disc then?" Tylwyth asked, noticing my attention on the disc.

"Yes, please," I answered.

"You'll have to trade, you will."

"Trade?"

"Aye. Trade," Teg confirmed.

"But I've got nothing to trade."

"Ah, but you do," Tylwyth responded.

"What?"

"You'll be gettin' the Iron Lady to help us."

"The fate of our two worlds depends on it," Teg added.

Our *two* worlds. So Tylwyth and Teg were not from my world. Not a surprise really, given the silver hair and pointed ears. Although, why the football shirts?

"Okay, but who is this Iron Lady?"

"She'd be an Avenger, like Iron Man, but you'd surely be knowin' that," Tylwyth replied.

I barely managed to stop myself from laughing out loud. Tylwyth and Teg didn't look like they were being funny. Not at all. But I felt like I was in the middle of a very weird dream.

"But Iron Man is a fictional character," I explained.

Tylwyth and Teg now looked at me as if I was the one being funny.

"Now don't you be testin' our patience, Maggie Thatcher," Tylwyth declared.

"Next you'll be tellin' us all the others are fictional too. But we've been watchin', we have. We've, like, seen them all," Teg added.

"But Iron Man exists only in Marvel comics and movies. Just like Captain America, the Incredible Hulk, Starlord, and Groot. They're not real."

"Now we know for sure you're fibbin', Maggie Thatcher," Tylwyth responded, tilting his head. "Groot is real. He's same as the Maximus Grootisa folk we have back home."

"They are rippin' good at football," Teg added. "Especially goalkeepin'."

I stared at Tylwyth and Teg in open-mouthed astonishment.

Just where are Tylwyth and Teg from?

"Aye. They should be banned from the Cup competition. It gives the Dryads an unfair advantage," Tylwyth told Teg, taking advantage of my silence.

"You don't need to be tellin' me that. I already know, mun," Teg replied.

"I'm just makin' my point, is all."

"Next, you'll be tellin' me that cringin' nonsense about Messi bein' the only one who could score against the Maximus Grootisa keepers."

"He'd do better than Ronaldo."

"You're dreamin', like. Ronaldo would score way more."

I was so absorbed in Tylwyth and Teg's conversation that I took a moment to realize that someone was calling my name. I turned around to discover Lady Marie and the rest of my unit close by. They were watching me cautiously. Anahira started to move toward me, but Lady Marie put out an arm and held her back.

"Are you alright, Maggie?" Lady Marie asked.

I completed one of my standard self-examinations. "Yes, I

think so."

"Who were you talking to?" Lady Marie inquired.

I turned my head to see Tylwyth and Teg still absorbed in animated conversation. I pointed at them and turned back to Lady Marie, but I could tell by the confused looks that no one in my unit could see the strange visitors.

Apparently, I was the only one who could see or hear Tylwyth and Teg.

"Maggie, there's no one there," Lady Marie stated calmly.

"Yes, there is," I insisted, ignoring the idea I might have been going crazy.

Lady Marie turned to Razia. "What can the drone tell us?"

Razia reached up to adjust her glasses. "The drone is only reading five heat signatures in this area large enough to be human."

Only five heat signatures? But that would mean Tylwyth and Teg were not real.

"Razia, please use the extra lens on your glasses and see if you can locate anything that might support Maggie's claims," Lady Marie instructed.

"Who's there, Maggie?" Lady Marie asked, folding her arms and turning her attention towards me. "Another green-skinned person?"

"No, Lady Marie," I responded, feeling increasingly foolish. "There are two people, or creatures, or something. Their names are Tylwyth and Teg."

A look of panic replaced the disbelief on Lady Marie's face.

"Tylwyth and Teg? They gave you those precise names?" Lady Marie fired back at me.

I nodded as my embarrassment gave way to confusion. Surely Tylwyth and Teg were harmless, or at least not as big a threat as the Bugbear we'd just faced.

"What are they doing? Quickly now," Lady Marie insisted.

"They are arguing whether Messi or Ronaldo would score the most goals against Groot."

Lady Marie seemed completely lost for words.

"Groot is a Marvel character, but Tylwyth and Teg claim to know a real Groot-like species where they come from. Messi and Ronaldo are…"

"I do happen to know who Messi and Ronaldo are, thank you," interrupted Lady Marie, shaking off her bewilderment. "Did Tylwyth and Teg ask you for anything? Anything at all?"

"They want me to get the Iron Lady to help them."

Lady Marie appeared even more taken aback by what I'd just said, but I wasn't sure why.

"They don't mean you, do they, Lady Marie?" Maggie asked.

"No, definitely not me," Lady Marie answered emphatically. She then focused her attention on Razia. "Have you located them?"

Razia nodded while holding her glasses. The extra lens made her look like a jeweler. "I have them. It took a while, but I managed to adjust the lenses to the right setting."

"And?" Lady Marie urged.

"They are over there." Razia pointed. "They are fairly short, dressed mostly in brown and green, and some kind of sports shirts. They appear to be arguing with each other."

"Are there any more of them?" Lady Marie asked.

Razia scanned the area with her glasses. "No," she eventually replied.

Lady Marie seemed relieved. She turned her attention back to me. "Did they give you anything, Maggie, or did you agree to anything?"

"No, they said they wanted to trade but I never agreed to…"

"Well, that's not bein' true, Maggie Thatcher, is it now?"

The gasps of surprise from the others was all I needed to know that Tylwyth and Teg had made themselves visible to everyone.

Lady Marie stepped forward and curtsied as though she was greeting the queen. "It is an honor to meet you. May I ask your names?"

Hang on. Hadn't I already told Lady Marie their names?

But Tylwyth and Teg both grinned in response.

"Why, I'm Tylwyth."

"And I'm Teg."

"Be welcome, Master Tylwyth and Master Teg. I am Lady Marie Studfall."

Tylwyth considered Lady Marie a moment. "'Tis an ancient name, Lady."

"A name deserving of its full honor," Teg added.

Lady Marie inclined her head. "I am Lady Marie Rosemary Millicent Ward Studfall."

Both Tylwyth and Teg bowed in response.

I stared at Lady Marie. My middle name of Elizabeth was burden enough. So how did Lady Marie cope with *three* middle names? And *Millicent*? Wow.

Just how did Tylwyth and Teg know about Lady Marie's full name?

"Would you care for a drink?" Lady Marie continued. "I'm afraid we don't have milk, but we do have tea."

Milk? Why offer them milk? They're not children, are they?

"'Tis a shame. I would've liked me a drop of milk, I would," Teg answered.

"Now, don't you be dishonorin' our welcome," Tylwyth responded, talking directly to Teg. "'Tis good to see that the old ways are not entirely forgotten."

"Aye, 'tis that."

"A drop of tea then," Tylwyth told Lady Marie. "If it's not too much trouble."

"It is no trouble at all," Lady Marie responded calmly.

Lady Marie turned to Anahira and Kayla. "Would you kindly go and pour three cups of tea from the flask in my bag? You'll find it in the back of the minibus. There should be enough cups. Please bring the cups of tea to me."

Anahira shot me a sympathetic look and then she and Kayla left, while the rest of us stood in awkward silence. Lady Marie maintained a polite smile, with Tylwyth and Teg doing their best to appear content, but there was an underlying tension in the air. I really didn't know what to make of Lady Marie's offer of tea, only that it seemed the right thing to do.

Anahira and Kayla eventually returned, intently focused on the cups in their hands. Anahira took the two cups she carried to Lady Marie, who chose one of the cups and turned toward Tylwyth and Teg. They walked forward to accept the cups.

As Teg accepted the tea, Tylwyth brushed past me.

Tylwyth then stepped up to Lady Marie to accept the second cup of tea.

Kayla gave the last cup of tea to Lady Marie and, as though it had been rehearsed, all three drank at the same time.

"That's a nice drop of tea, that is," Teg purred over his cup.

"Very nice," Tylwyth agreed.

"I am glad," Lady Marie responded.

Tylwyth nodded and drank the remainder of his tea, as did Teg and Lady Marie.

Lady Marie then gathered their cups and handed them back to Anahira and Kayla. She turned to Tylwyth and Teg. "Now, how may we be of service?"

"Our need is great," Tylwyth began somberly. "Our regent, Queen Aylwyin, is threatened by Prince Draikern, a dark prince who seeks to rule in her place. If he succeeds, then the doorways into your world we protect will be abandoned, and you will be attacked."

"The doorways you protect?"

"Aye, Lady Studfall. Or is that also forgotten?"

Lady Marie considered Tylwyth without responding. Tylwyth's news certainly sounded serious, although I still didn't know what world Tylwyth was talking about.

"We might have lost knowledge of some things," Lady Marie finally answered. "But the fair dealings between our two peoples live long in the memory. I am unsure how I may be of service, but if it is in my power, I will aid you in whatever way I can."

Tylwyth and Teg both responded by bowing to Lady Marie.

"We thank you for your kind offer, we do," Tylwyth declared, after completing his bow. "But we have already bound one to our cause."

Lady Marie started to turn in my direction but then snapped back to Tylwyth and Teg. "Who is it you have bound?"

"Why, we've bound one of your kind," Tylwyth responded.

"Who do you mean?" Lady Marie verged on insisting.

"Maggie. Maggie Thatcher," Tylwyth pronounced, pointing at me.

My heart skipped a beat.

"But I didn't..."

"Quiet, Maggie," Lady Marie interrupted before continuing her questioning of Tylwyth. "There has been no exchange or agreement."

"Ah. But there has."

"May I inquire as to the nature of this agreement?"

"Maggie agreed for the Iron Lady to help us."

"But we didn't trade," I burst out, despite the warning look from Lady Marie. "You never gave me back my..."

With a sickening thought, I stared at my hand. Four small silver discs stared back. Tylwyth must have slipped the missing disc into my hand just before he got his tea.

"But that's not fair. I never..."

"A bargain has been made," Tylwyth interrupted. "Maggie is ours until our deed is done."

I turned quickly to Lady Marie. "I didn't agree to..."

Lady Marie raised her hand, cutting me off. "I'm afraid that a bargain has indeed been made, Maggie. Tylwyth and Teg are from Faerie. We cannot undo what has been done. You are bound to them now."

I stared wide-eyed at Lady Marie, unable to mask my shock. Did she just say that Tylwyth and Teg were from Fairy? At least that was what I thought she said. Tylwyth and Teg certainly didn't look anything like fairies. Not the type I'd seen in children's stories anyway. And they came from a world that had beings like Groot. And Dryads, whatever they were.

Another world.

The thought hit me like a sledgehammer. Tylwyth and Teg were from another world. And I'd been tricked into helping them.

I caught the silly grins on the faces of Tylwyth and Teg.

Just what mess have I gotten myself into?

6

THE TWO PRINCES

"What did they want again, Maggie?" Anahira asked.

We were sitting on wooden benches in another part of the Ravenwood campsite, in a shaded area designed for group meetings. The space almost looked like a large, open-air chapel, with a tall entryway and a circular fence.

"They needed Minyid and Olaf," I replied. After speaking with Lady Marie, Tylwyth and Teg had walked over to me, told me what they needed, and then promptly disappeared.

"Minyid and Olaf?" Anahira clarified.

"Yeah. Have you ever heard of them?"

"No, sorry, Maggie," Anahira responded. "Did they give you any clues?"

I shook my head and tried imitating the high-pitched voice of Teg. "We'll be needin' Minyid and Olaf. It's rippin' important."

Anahira smiled. "Not bad. But was that really all they said?"

I nodded. Tylwyth and Teg hadn't provided any more than that. I didn't know who Minyid and Olaf were, what they did, or where I could find them, and I certainly didn't have any idea how I could possibly help creatures from Faerie.

Faerie.

Lady Marie claimed it was the proper name for Tylwyth and

Teg's world and that they were known as the Fae—and they were nothing like the fairies in children's stories. No. The Fae were tricksy, supernatural beings who were very powerful and should have been treated with caution and respect. And the Fae could apparently avoid being detected by human-made technology. That was why Tylwyth and Teg hadn't been picked up by the drone.

"Maggie, why did you stay when they first appeared?" Anahira asked. "Why didn't you run away and find us?"

I'd wondered about that myself. Why hadn't I fled as soon as I'd seen Tylwyth and Teg?

"I just felt really calm," I replied. "Calmer than I've felt in a long time."

"They must have charmed you," Lady Marie asserted.

Charmed me? That's not good, is it? Will they make me do things I don't want to do?

"It's all good, Maggie. We've got you," Anahira insisted, likely picking up on the anxious look in my eyes.

"You should have asked them what they meant," Sam interjected.

"I would have," I answered. "But they disappeared before I could ask. They seemed to think I would know what they were talking about, but I have no idea."

"I still think they are important people, probably royalty," Kayla suggested.

"What, you mean *Prince* Minyid and *Prince* Olaf?" Sam said with a smirk.

"Yeah. Wouldn't you like to meet a prince?" Kayla responded with a broad grin.

"No," Sam concluded, a little more testily than necessary.

"Girls, please. Let's keep things civil, shall we?" Lady Marie insisted. "Do you have anything, Razia?"

"Not really, Lady Marie," Razia answered, reaching up to adjust her glasses. "There is no reference to anyone called Minyid, and I'm afraid the main references to anyone called Olaf are from the Disney movie, *Frozen*."

"Oh, great. Not another Disney flick," Sam responded.

"Hey," I retorted. "*Frozen* is awesome. It's not just…"

"Let it go, please, Maggie," Lady Marie interrupted. "I think now is a good time to take a break and get something to eat."

Despite everything that had happened, I couldn't stop a smile spreading across my face. Did Lady Marie really just say "let it go" in reference to *Frozen*? Did she do it deliberately?

Surely not.

I tried reading Lady Marie's expression, but there was no evidence her "let it go" comment was anything more than pure coincidence.

"The packed lunch is in the minibus," Lady Marie continued, oblivious to my suspicion she was a closet *Frozen* fan. "Maggie, I take it you have your own lunch?"

"Yes, Lady Marie," I replied, coming painfully back to my non-Disney reality.

"Alright, girls. Let's take about half an hour to eat and relax. We'll drive back to Dux Manor after lunch."

Kayla, Razia, and Sam stood up and headed toward the minibus.

Lady Marie smiled at me, and then followed the three girls.

"C'mon, Maggie, let's get lunch," Anahira encouraged, after seeing that I hadn't moved.

"Okay," I responded, getting to my feet, although I wasn't feeling very hungry.

I walked next to Anahira and tried to make sense of what had happened to me. The trouble was, it made no sense at all, and I had no idea where to start looking for Minyid and Olaf.

Are they connected to the Iron Lady?

That was how this whole mess started, arguing with Tylwyth and Teg about the reality of Marvel characters. It had seemed like a joke at the time, but I certainly wasn't laughing now.

Who are Minyid and Olaf? Who is the Iron Lady? And how can I possibly do anything to help?

My dealings with Tylwyth and Teg had almost made me forget the fight with the Bugbear.

Almost.

I would prefer not to know that such terrifying creatures were waiting to try and force their way into our world. Waiting near doors protected by the world of Faerie.

At least for now.

I shuddered and searched for any sign of my newfound friends. Or should I call them "masters"? I wasn't sure.

I looked up to see the other girls getting their lunches out of the minibus. My lunch consisted of a packet of rice crackers and a tin of salmon. I wasn't sure what Anahira was having, though we'd eat together, and then after lunch, travel back to Dux Manor, where hopefully I'd get some answers.

* * *

THE DRIVE BACK TO LONDON PASSED QUICKLY. I'D KEPT A LOOKOUT for Tylwyth and Teg, but I hadn't spotted them anywhere. I wasn't sure where they'd gone or how they'd managed to get there.

They are probably checking out Wembley Stadium.

I couldn't quite match creatures of Faerie with football fandom, but it was just my luck to get landed with both. I wasn't like Anahira, who played both netball *and* volleyball for our school. I really didn't get sports.

Of course, I was proud that Osgood and Zola, my younger twin brothers, had both made the Chelsea football academy, but why did it take so much of everyone's time and attention? Training, games, drills, and seemingly endless tournaments. Any of my activities seemed insignificant in light of the boys' football careers.

Careers.

They were only ten years old.

I slumped back in my chair and sighed, staring out the window of the minibus.

What would Osgood and Zola make of Tylwyth and Teg?

They'd probably just argue about who was the best football team.

We soon arrived back at Dux Manor, and I found myself again walking through the front entrance into the reception area.

Lady Marie smiled warmly at Faatimah, who was again seated behind the reception desk.

"Welcome back, Lady Marie. I hope you had a good trip."

"It was certainly eventful," Lady Marie responded. "Any messages?"

"No. It's been very quiet."

"I'll need to report to the Council, but after I've seen to the girls."

"Later tonight?"

"Yes, that will work. Thank you."

"No problem, Lady Marie. I'll make the arrangements."

Lady Marie smiled. "Come along, girls. We have much to do."

We followed Lady Marie as she headed for the elevator. Faatimah smiled as I walked past, but I could barely manage a half-smile in return.

We entered the elevator, and Lady Marie activated the hidden scanner. The elevator soon moved down to the secret underground base the Guardians called home.

"Alright, girls. Please return the ropes to the appropriate locker and help put anything else away," Lady Marie announced. "Razia, you may keep the glasses for now. It would be good for you to master how they work. If you have enough time, please see if you can find any more information about Minyid and Olaf. We'll meet together at the table in twenty minutes."

My unit scattered in response.

"Maggie, a word, please."

I followed Lady Marie to the lounge area. Lady Marie sat on a sofa and patted the seat next to her, inviting me to sit.

"How are you feeling, Maggie?"

"Okay, I guess, Lady Marie."

"I'm afraid that's simply not good enough."

I sighed. "It feels like I'm in a dream. Or a nightmare. First the Bugbear, then Tylwyth and Teg, and then finding out they are from Faerie, and I am bound to them. I don't know what that means, or what I'm supposed to do. I don't know who Minyid and Olaf are. I don't know how we can find them, or what to do even if we do find them." I shook my head and stared at the floor. "I don't even know…" I trailed off, unable to finish.

Lady Marie gently lifted my chin. "It's alright, Maggie. You can tell me."

"I don't even know why you offered me a place in Guardians," I answered, ignoring the tears starting to form in my eyes.

"That is nowhere near as important as the fact you accepted," Lady Marie responded, smiling gently.

"But…" I paused, not really wanting to know for sure, but needing to press on. "It's because of Anahira, isn't it?"

Lady Marie sighed. "Anahira would have refused the invitation if I had not also invited you, yes."

I knew it. That was why Anahira had acted so strangely last night.

"Yet Tylwyth and Teg chose you," Lady Marie said softly.

"They chose me? What are you talking about?"

"They sought you out."

My eyes widened. "How do you know that?"

"The Iron Lady."

"What about her?"

"Your namesake, Margaret Thatcher, the ex-Prime Minister of Great Britain, was commonly referred to as the Iron Lady."

"She was?" I hadn't known that.

"Yes, Maggie. A Soviet journalist was the first to call her the Iron Lady, but it was a name that stuck. There was even a movie about her with that exact title."

"Okay, but what does that mean for me?" I wasn't sure how a movie about a former Prime Minister had anything to do with me.

"When Tylwyth and Teg asked you to get the Iron Lady to help them, they already knew your name. They must have already made the connection."

Tylwyth and Teg believed me to be the Iron Lady? But that's absurd.

"But they said she was an Avenger, like Iron Man."

Lady Marie's eyes narrowed. "An Avenger?"

"Like in the Marvel movies."

"Oh, right, the Marvel movies," Lady Marie responded. "I'm

not a huge fan, as I'm rather busy dealing with real threats from other worlds, but I do hear they are most entertaining. The only Iron Lady I am aware of, however, is the ex-Prime Minister. Which means that Tylwyth and Teg specifically sought your help."

"But what help can I possibly give to creatures from Faerie?"

Lady Marie placed a hand on my shoulder. "I'm not sure, Maggie. But maybe they see strength in you that you don't yet see in yourself."

I couldn't help but grimace. I didn't know what strength Lady Marie was talking about, and I didn't think being sought out by creatures of Faerie was a good thing at all.

"But they tricked me, Lady Marie," I complained. "How can we even trust them?"

"I'm not certain they meant any harm when tricking you, Maggie."

Didn't mean any harm? But they bound me to their cause.

"The motives of the Fae are somewhat difficult for us to understand," Lady Marie explained, after possibly seeing the confusion on my face. "But I don't think they would deem the act of binding humans to their cause as bad. We must remember they are from another world, and they would probably deem it wise to seek help from an inhabitant of this world."

"But couldn't they have just asked for help?"

"Yes, well, I understand that they might regard humans as somewhat untrustworthy and thus believe they have to trick us into helping them."

They think we are untrustworthy?

"I'm afraid we can't ignore their warning about the threat to their world and ours," Lady Marie added. "I'll see what the Council of Guardians have to say tonight, but regardless of what Tylwyth and Teg's real motives are, we will act with honor and will trust in the ancient treaties."

Ancient treaties? What ancient treaties?

"Now, you'd best sort out your items," Lady Marie instructed, removing her hand from my shoulder.

I stayed put. Partly because I still struggled to understand everything that was happening to me and partly because I wanted to hear more about the ancient treaties. Did the existence of treaties mean that there had been previous contact with the world of Faerie?

"Quickly, Maggie. Time is passing." Lady Marie stood and briskly walked to one of the desks on the left side of the room.

Okay, so finding out more about these treaties would have to wait. I instead had to store the silver discs in their designated locker and help tidy up.

I packed the discs away, checked my meds bag, and then looked around to see if anything else needed tidying, but everything seemed sorted.

"Okay, girls," Lady Marie called. "Time's up. Let's gather together."

We all went to the table. I sat next to Anahira.

"I hope you realize how very proud I am of all of you," Lady Marie began. "What we do will not result in any thanks from the world we protect, but we never seek glory for ourselves. Our example is, and will ever be, that of Lady Solana Mapleston, who urged us to live a life in the service of others."

Lady Marie paused and looked at each of us in turn, her hazel eyes shining with intensity. "As the founder of the Wayfinder Girls, Lady Mapleston established the Order of Guardians and began the work that we carry on today."

I sat up in my chair. I'd heard of Lady Mapleston before, all Wayfinder Girls had, but her connection to the Guardians was something new.

"We are who we are because of what Lady Mapleston achieved in the past," Lady Marie continued. "We, and the world, owe her a debt of gratitude."

I recalled Lady Marie's words about ancient treaties and a new question fought for space in my mind. Did Lady Mapleston sign these treaties? Might that mean she had contact with the world of Faerie?

I leaned forward, hoping Lady Marie's next words might provide some answers or at least some insight into the life of Lady

Solana Mapleston. But Lady Marie had apparently finished talking about Lady Mapleston, for she withdrew five badges from her jacket pocket and placed them on the table.

"The Earth Defender Level 1 badge is not given out lightly. It is hard won. You have not only earned the right to receive the badge, but you have also earned the right to receive it with pride." Lady Marie paused, examining each of us in turn. "You were not supposed to encounter anything like the, what was it again, Razia, a Bugbear?"

"Yes, Lady Marie. At least, that is my best guess," Razia responded.

"Right. You were not supposed to encounter anything even remotely resembling the Bugbear that appeared in our world, but you all held your nerve splendidly."

I looked down, my cheeks burning. I hadn't really held my nerve at all.

"Yes, Maggie, even you," Lady Marie added.

I raised my head, catching the encouraging smile from Anahira.

"We were certainly not supposed to encounter creatures from Faerie. Such an encounter was unthinkable. But it has happened, and now we must stand with Maggie. Whatever is to come, we must face it together."

I looked around at the others and felt a surge of hope as everyone met my gaze and nodded.

Lady Marie stood and beckoned us forward one by one. With a practiced formality and grace, Lady Marie picked a badge off the table and placed it in the open hand of the girl standing silent before her. Then she smiled and embraced each girl.

I received my badge and fought back tears. Lady Marie smiled as she embraced me and my tears almost burst out. I stepped back, gripped my badge in both hands, and stared at it in wonder. The badge was circular in shape and forest green in color. It featured an image of the Earth, with a golden shield superimposed on its right-hand side. The center of the shield displayed the classic three-star crest of the Wayfinder Girls. Underneath the image of the world was written "DEF 1."

The badge proved I belonged, as a Guardian.

"It's cool, aye." Anahira came and stood next to me.

"It really is," I replied, my gaze riveted on the badge.

"Okay, girls, gather around." Lady Marie ushered us into a circle. "It is just about time to head back up. We must gather before the other Wayfinder girls return from their adventures, and then we'll have a final clean-up and hold a ceremony to officially end camp. You will definitely need to hide your badges from the rest of the girls."

I held onto my badge even more tightly. It was such a shame we couldn't display them.

"Excuse me, Lady Marie," Razia asked. "But what adventure do we explain we were on. If anyone asks?"

Lady Marie smiled. "A very good question, Razia. Please let them know that you went to the Ravenwood campsite for field-work. You can honestly say you examined flora and fauna that you'd never seen before."

Razia and I smiled, Kayla and Anahira laughed, and even Sam grinned.

"Now in closing, let us sing the Dux Manor song," Lady Marie enthused.

We stood in a tight circle and sang.

"We strive for good, to be the best.
We will not slumber, we will not rest.
Peace we seek, hope we grow.
Actions and deeds are what we sow.
By helping others, in meeting need,
We choose to serve, we choose to lead.
We guard the path, we light the way,
To peace on Earth, come what may."

THE OTHERS BROKE FROM THE CIRCLE TO GATHER THEIR THINGS, BUT I remained still. I'd learnt the Dux Manor song the night before, but I only now realized the importance of the words.

We guard the path; we light the way.

Was the song more than it seemed? Did the words actually reveal the purpose and mission of the Guardians? To guard the path, the path to other worlds. And to light the way in keeping them safe from threats.

To peace on Earth.

There it was. The goal of the Guardians. To protect the Earth from threats both known and unknown. But I'd encountered just one of those threats, and it had nearly ruined me. Tylwyth and Teg claimed that greater threats were trying to break into our world. Threats that might easily overcome any defense the Guardians could muster. So how can we ever claim to light the way to peace on Earth?

There's no way I can help protect the Earth.

I can't even tie a knot.

7
HOME ALONE

"You sure you'll be okay, Maggie?" Anahira asked as she walked to my front door and placed the blue chilly bin she'd been carrying on the ground.

"I'll be fine. Thanks, Anahira," I replied, placing my duffle bag on top of the chilly bin.

"You could come have dinner with us. Mum won't mind."

"Thanks, but I'm okay. I've got some leftovers. I'll message you later."

"Alright, later then." Anahira hugged me goodbye before walking back to her mum, who was waiting in the car, with the driver's window down.

"Thanks again, Mrs. Waititi," I called out.

"No problem, Maggie. Take care."

Both Anahira and her mum waved goodbye as they left me standing on the narrow front patio outside my house. The rest of my family were due to return home a bit late, victorious from the boys' football tournament if Mum's text message was anything to go by. So I'd be home alone for a little while longer.

My home was fairly typical for the Kentish Town area, a three-level Victorian-era home squashed in amongst its neighbors as though they were a row of books. I'd love to live in one of the book-end homes, but my house was still pretty cool. The dark magenta front door stood out nicely against the white stone, a splash of color amongst the uniform row of white-stone houses.

I took the house key out of my meds bag, unlocked the door, and slowly pushed it open, hoping that I wouldn't find something weird like a person with green skin watching me from an armchair or an oversized Bugbear lurking in a corner.

Everything seemed normal, so I edged further in, just past the doorway. The lounge filled up the space to my left, with a large sofa the same color as the door contrasting nicely with the white ceiling and walls, at least those not taken up with bookshelves and display cabinets filled with football trophies. I waited a moment, listening intently for any strange noises, but everything appeared to be okay.

I brought my duffle bag and the chilly bin inside, shut and locked the front door, and hung my meds bag in its customary position next to the door. I left the chilly bin by the door to deal with later and walked to the staircase opposite the entryway. My room sat on the second floor, next to my parents' room, with the boys' rooms on the floor above. The twins each had their own room, which ensured the house stayed fairly peaceful. A small study completed the third floor, with the family bathroom on the second floor, next to my room. A smaller bathroom stood next to the staircase on the ground floor. The lower bathroom saw a lot of use, as it serviced the busiest place in the house: the kitchen and dining area that opened up to the rear patio garden.

My bedroom window overlooked the garden. The patio was fully paved and fenced, with thick flowering hedges bursting with yellow, orange, and red on all three sides. I knew the flowers as Black-Eyed Susans, and we had a few different types, including Enchanted Flame, Little Henry, and Prairie Glow. The brightly coloured hedges created a cocoon of space and gave the garden an almost magical quality. I especially liked the patio area when the sun shone brightly, which it was doing right now.

I decided to drop my duffle bag in my room and then head out to the back patio to enjoy the last bit of sunshine. It was a good place to sit and think.

I'd just dropped my duffle bag on my bed when I heard a loud crash from downstairs.

I froze.

There's someone in the house.

It must have been an intruder as my family was not due home for a while yet. It could have been the green-skinned person, or a Bugbear, or even an ax murderer. I had feared being attacked by an ax murderer for some time now.

I scanned my room. There was little to aid me in a fight against an ax-wielding maniac, but I grabbed the yellow flashlight out of the drawer of my bedside cabinet. Maybe I could whack it on the intruder's head and make a getaway.

Another crash from downstairs made me pause. Should I call the police? If I did call them, would they arrive in time?

I put the flashlight down on the bedside cabinet, picked up my duffle bag, and unzipped the pocket, reaching in to get my phone. It wasn't there. I unzipped the other pocket and felt inside. It wasn't in there either. I opened the whole bag and dumped the contents on my bed. Nothing but clothes, toiletries, and my unicorn soft toy.

Where is it? Where's my phone?

Lady Marie had required all phones to remain behind at Dux Manor when we'd gone to the Ravenwood campsite. All phones, that was, except mine. My food allergies meant I always had to have my phone on me in case of emergencies. Or, as it happened today, I'd kept my phone in my meds bag.

The meds bag hanging by the front door!

I stared at the mess on my bed and then stared at the flashlight on the cabinet.

The flashlight will have to do.

I picked up the flashlight. I had to go downstairs, either to confront the intruder or retrieve my phone from my meds bag. Or flee the house. The last option made the most sense to me, but that still meant I had to make it down the stairs.

I left my room and stood at the top of the stairs leading down to the lounge.

How could a few steps seem so awfully long?

I squeezed the flashlight and placed my right foot on the first step. I paused, listening for any sign that I'd been heard. The house was silent. So I put my left foot down. I repeated the action on the second step. Still no noise. I lifted my right foot to place it on the third step when another crash, followed by a yell, echoed through the house.

I bolted down the remaining steps and rushed to the door. I turned the lock and placed my hand on the door handle.

"Alright, Maggie. What's occurrin'?"

"You be goin' somewhere in a hurry, like."

My shoulders sagged, and I released the door handle. The *intruders* were Tylwyth and Teg, not an ax murderer after all.

But is that a good thing? How did they even know where I lived?

I turned around to see Tylwyth sprawled over the sofa and Teg reclining in one of the two armchairs. Tylwyth held a tub of Ben & Jerry's Chocolate Fudge Brownie ice cream and Teg grasped a two-liter bottle of milk. Tylwyth scooped out the ice cream *with his hands* and Teg had milk dripping down his face as he drank *straight from the bottle.*

"No!" I yelled, as a lifetime of protective impulses smashed all other concerns. Of all the foods I was allergic to, dairy was the most lethal. "Don't you know anything about cross-contamination?"

"Cross what?" Tylwyth asked.

"The Contanim nation," Teg answered. "Must be one of the human kingdoms. One of the angry ones."

"No. It is not a nation or a kingdom," I declared, my voice betraying my rising frustration. "It is about infecting other surfaces with food I'm allergic to."

Both Tylwyth and Teg stared at me blankly. Tylwyth stuck his fingers into the tub of ice cream and Teg lifted up the bottle to swig more milk.

"No!" I insisted, holding the flashlight up for effect. "Go to the kitchen."

Tylwyth and Teg paused in their actions and looked at each other.

I pointed the flashlight toward the kitchen. "Now!"

Both Tylwyth and Teg dropped their heads and got up from their seats. They mumbled something I couldn't quite hear and shuffled off to the kitchen.

I stared after them. My eyes widened. Had I really just told off creatures from Faerie? And had they actually obeyed?

Is it possible?

I turned back to the front door and locked it. I stood at the door a moment, wondering whether I needed my inhaler. I decided probably not, which was a surprise. I took another moment to compose myself and then walked through the lounge into the kitchen and dining area. I took one step into the kitchen and immediately regretted following Tylwyth and Teg.

The source of the crashes I'd heard earlier lay starkly revealed, with the contents of several open cupboards scattered all over the floor and the island bench. Cereal boxes, pickle jars, and carefully labeled plastic containers lay empty and abandoned, their edible treasures littered all over the place.

I counted the broken remains of at least three plates and two mugs, including my dad's favorite, "Not all heroes wear capes" superhero dad mug. It was a disaster.

How on Earth am I going to explain this mess to my parents?

I had a reputation for dropping things, but this would have been a record, even for me.

I looked up from surveying the wreckage to consider Tylwyth and Teg, who stood next to the bench, both looking like guilty golden retrievers caught with a half-chewed pair of their owner's favorite slippers.

"We were gettin' a mite hungry," Tylwyth explained.

"But we might have overdone it," Teg added.

I stared at the two folk from Faerie and then stared at the chaos surrounding them. I couldn't believe it. It was like having two extra brothers.

"Well, you are going to have to clean it all up. You can start by putting the ice cream and milk on the bench."

"But I haven't finished," Tylwyth complained.

"Couldn't we do it later?" Teg added.

"No, you will do it now," I insisted.

Tylwyth and Teg again mumbled something under their breath, but they placed the milk and ice cream on the bench.

Tylwyth then flashed me a broad grin and promptly disappeared. I opened my mouth to protest when I noticed the mess on the floor start to stir. Then, almost in the blink of an eye, all the mess vanished. *All of it.* The only items in sight were the milk and ice cream standing on the bench.

Tylwyth popped back into view. "Alright, Maggie, proper tidy now."

"Proper tidy indeed," Teg added.

"You can close your mouth now, if you like, Maggie," Tylwyth suggested.

I snapped my mouth shut and glared at Tylwyth. I put the flashlight on the kitchen bench and turned to the now-closed cupboards.

When did they close?

I threw open a cupboard door, finding the cereal boxes which only moments ago had lain abandoned on the floor. I tested one of the boxes. It was full. Another cupboard revealed the plastic containers in perfect stacks, all full, all with their labels facing outwards. Yet another cupboard revealed a row of pickle jars, all sealed and untouched. The last cupboard revealed my father's favorite mug, standing in pride of place amongst the other mugs, and shining as if brand new.

I closed the cupboard doors and turned back to Tylwyth and Teg. "That's cheating."

"Now, Maggie. Don't be like that. I did what you asked, I did," Tylwyth responded.

"Everythin' in its proper place and shinin' like new," Teg added.

"Yes. Well. Thank you," I replied after another check of the room. "But you should never have made the mess in the first place. This is my home."

"For that we are mighty sorry," Tylwyth said with a bow.

"Aye. Real sorry, like," Teg said, also bowing.

I was again surprised by Tylwyth and Teg's actions. They seemed genuinely sorry for making a mess. Maybe they'd broken some rule I wasn't aware of.

"It's alright. If you want something to eat, all you have to do is ask," I added.

Tylwyth and Teg both grinned and reached for the milk and ice cream.

"But you will use a glass for the milk, and a bowl and spoon for the ice cream."

Teg looked disappointed but Tylwyth nodded and fetched the necessary items, locating them as easily as though he'd lived in my house his whole life. He poured a glass of milk for Teg and scooped out a heap of ice cream for himself, before putting the milk and ice cream away in the fridge and freezer. He even seemed to know that the items went on the unsafe shelf in the fridge; the shelf where anything unsafe for me to eat was kept separate.

"You will eat and drink them outside." I pointed to the rear patio garden.

Tylwyth and Teg both sheepishly nodded. And they did what I said. Even though I was the one supposedly bound to them.

I watched Tylwyth and Teg retreat to the garden and took a deep breath. How was I ever going to cope with having them in my life?

I really needed something to eat. It might help calm my nerves.

I went to the sink and carefully washed my hands before turning to the fridge to get myself some food. A shout from the rear garden made me pause. I turned back to see Teg rush inside.

"Danger, Maggie. Stay inside."

"What? What is it?"

"Gnomes!"

"Gnomes?"

"Aye, gnomes. Where there's two, there'll be hundreds of the nasty little brutes. Consume everythin' they do."

"But they're just garden ornaments."

"Garden orna-whats?"

"Garden ornaments. They're not real. They're just for decoration."

Teg stared at me in open-mouthed astonishment. He shook his head. "You decorate your garden with fake gnomes?"

"Yes, why?"

"Oh, nothin', mun. You'd just better hope that no real gnomes see that. They'd be mighty angry, they would. You wouldn't like a horde of angry gnomes."

"No?"

"No. They love to dig. They don't know how to stop. They'd be so angry they'd keep diggin' until every livin' thing has been dug up."

"Every living thing?"

"Aye."

"That doesn't sound good."

"It's not. Oh, we'd better tell Tylwyth. He's fixin' on sendin' them back to their own world."

"But they belong to my mum. We got them for her last Christmas."

Teg again gave me an open-mouth stare. "You give fake gnomes as gifts?"

"Yes, well, my mum likes them."

Teg shook his head. "You're mad. She's mad. Maybe you all deserve what's comin'."

My eyes went wide. "What do you mean? What's coming?" But Teg had already turned his back and returned to the garden, calling out to Tylwyth. I caught something about "mad humans" and "fake gnomes."

I stared after Teg and ran my hand through my hair. *Maybe you deserve what's coming.* Another riddle. Or maybe it was related to Minyid and Olaf. Whoever they were.

I took a long breath and turned back to the fridge. I needed to eat. I opened the fridge door and took out the container carefully labeled "Bean mix for Maggie." It was a few days old but should have been fine once it had been reheated. I carefully set about combining the ingredients for my favorite bean nachos meal: corn chips, reheated bean mix, vegan sour cream, and grated non-dairy cheese. I took my time, making sure everything was done right and finishing everything off nicely under the grill.

I transferred my meal to a plate, added a fork from the cutlery drawer, and got a glass of water. I then carried the plate and glass out to the rear patio garden.

"Alright, Maggie?" Tylwyth said in greeting. Although I noticed that he was still keeping a wary eye on the two garden gnomes.

"Need any help?" Teg added.

"I'll be fine. Thank you," I replied, as I made my way to the outside table and put down my plate and glass. I sat in a chair and started to eat.

"What's that then?" Teg asked.

"Bean nachos," I replied.

"You can eat that?"

"Yes."

"It doesn't have any of that cross Contanim nation stuff then?"

"No. It's completely vegan."

"Oh, right. Good."

"Vegan means there's no meat products, right, Maggie?" Tylwyth added.

"Nothing derived from animals."

"Right. So no milk or ice cream then."

"Not dairy, no."

"You poor wee mite," Teg added.

"I can have milk and ice cream from soy or coconut."

"Soy or coconut?" Teg replied, shaking his head.

"It's quite good really."

"If you say so, Maggie," Teg responded.

"What happens if you do have dairy?" Tylwyth asked.

"I can go into anaphylactic shock and stop breathing."

"Oh," Tylwyth responded, looking uncomfortable.

"It's alright. I'm used to it. I've been dealing with it my whole life."

"You're very brave," Tylwyth declared.

"Brave?" I asked while scooping up a handful of nachos.

"Aye. For most people, bein' around food is not a life-or-death situation," Tylwyth added.

I didn't feel very brave. In fact, most of the time I just felt scared. But here I was, sitting in the rear garden with two creatures from Faerie and chatting away like everything was normal.

But it isn't, is it?

"Now, about these two people I'm supposed to find for you," I began.

"People? What people?" Teg responded.

"Minyid and Olaf."

Tylwyth and Teg looked at each other and then burst out laughing.

"What's so funny?"

"The Mynydd o Olau is not a person," Tylwyth answered.

"Mynydd o Olau?"

"Aye," Teg responded. "'Tis a powerful talisman. A relic of ancient magic."

"It's called Mynydd o Olau?"

"You might know it by another name," Tylwyth added.

"What other name?"

Tylwyth and Teg looked at each other and then, in perfect unison, they said, "The Mountain of Light."

I stared at Tylwyth and Teg and ran my hand through my hair. "What? You want me to find a mountain made up of light?"

"Now, Maggie. Don't be gettin' all worked up. It shouldn't be all that hard," Tylwyth responded. "It's not an *actual* mountain."

"Aye. 'Twas stolen from our world and we thought it lost. But we now know it is in your world. You've got till All Hallows Eve to get it for us," Teg added.

"I have until All Hallows Eve to give you the Mountain of Light?" I clarified.

"That's it, Maggie," Tylwyth stated matter-of-factly. "Or else our worlds are doomed."

I stared at Tylwyth and somehow managed not to scream. Did all the creatures of Faerie speak in riddles? I've never heard of All Hallows Eve, and I have no idea where to find this so-called Mountain of Light. How on Earth was I supposed to find something that had been stolen from the world of Faerie?

I opened my mouth to ask for more information when I heard a shout from the front door. "Hi, Maggie, we're home."

I darted a quick look at Tylwyth and Teg, who both responded with wide grins. Which I took for meaning they'd keep themselves hidden from my family. The same couldn't have been said for their bowl, spoon, and glass, which I very carefully scooped up and took to the kitchen along with my plate.

I quickly put the dishes in the sink and started aggressively washing my hands just as my mum arrived.

"Oh, there you are, Maggie. How are you doing, love?"

"Good, thanks, Mum." I finished washing my hands, dried them on a hand towel, and gave Mum a hug. "How was the tournament?"

"Oh, I'm sure you'll hear all about the tournament from the boys, but first, tell me about your weekend. Did you have fun?"

Fun? Sure. Fun battling Bugbears and babysitting supernatural creatures from Faerie.

"Yes, it was really good," I replied, feeling a sharp stab of guilt as I couldn't tell my mum what really happened. It's not that I didn't trust her, but I had promised Lady Marie. If Mum discovered what had really happened, she wouldn't let me continue in Guardians, and then I couldn't help Tylwyth and Teg.

"I learnt a lot," I added, with Mum staring at me expectantly.

"Oh, that's nice, dear. Anahira's mum gave you a lift home?"

I nodded.

"That's kind of her. Remind me to thank her, will you?"

"Yes, Mum."

"And you got your dinner?"

"Yes. Thanks, Mum."

"That's good. The boys might…"

Mum was interrupted as my brothers burst into the kitchen.

"Hiya, Maggie," Osgood said, grinning like a Cheshire Cat.

"Hey, Mags," Zola added, also grinning.

I smiled as the boys both went straight to the fridge. "Hi. How was the tournament?"

"Awesome. We won," Zola replied happily.

"Is there anything to eat? I'm starving," Osgood said to Mum, pulling his head from the inside of the fridge and making a face like a puppy dog.

Mum smiled. "Now, boys, we had something to eat on the way home."

"But that was ages ago," Osgood protested.

"Yeah, c'mon, Mum," Zola added.

"Alright, I'll fix you a snack. Go wash your hands first."

"Aww," Zola complained.

"Do we have to?" Osgood added.

"Yes, go." Mum pointed.

"Later, Maggie," Osgood said as he darted out of the room.

"See you, Mags," Zola said, chasing after Osgood.

"Bye," I managed to say, just after the boys had rushed out of the kitchen.

I turned to Mum. "Well, that was very informative."

"They're still really excited. They had a great tournament."

"And there's the Chelsea game to watch," my dad declared as he strode into the kitchen. "We can just fit it in before their bedtime. Hi, Maggie."

"Hi, Dad," I said, giving him a hug. My dad had named my brothers after two Chelsea football legends. I guess it was good that they'd made the Chelsea academy, otherwise their names might have been a bit embarrassing.

"Did your weekend go well?"

"Yes, thanks, Dad."

"Want to watch the game with us?"

I shook my head and smiled. "Maybe next time."

Dad grinned as he got a drink from the fridge. "Next time it is then."

"Don't make a mess," Mum warned Dad.

"Mess? Me? When do I ever make a mess?" Dad responded as he left the kitchen.

Mum rolled her eyes at me and laughed. "When does he not?"

I smiled, wondering what Mum would have thought of the mess Tylwyth and Teg had created. I glanced around, looking for the two Faerie folk. I spotted them walking in from the rear garden.

"Did someone say football?" Tylwyth asked.

"If you can call it football with Chelsea playing," Teg added.

I nodded and shook my head at the same time, almost giving myself whiplash. I don't think I wanted Tylwyth and Teg watching a game with my father and brothers.

Tylwyth and Teg both grinned in response.

"They, like, won't even know we're there," Teg asserted as he walked past.

I stared after them, wondering whether I could stop them if I tried. Mum might have been a bit concerned if I started yelling at the air.

"Are you alright, Maggie?"

I turned back to Mum. "Yes, Mum. I'm fine."

"How's that report going?"

"Report?"

"Yes, that English report you've been working on. It's due tomorrow, isn't it?"

My eyes widened. I'd completely forgotten about my English homework. "Oh, yes. That report. I better go and finish it."

"Alright, hon. I need to get the boys something to eat, but let me know if you need anything."

I nodded and walked out of the kitchen. I hadn't even half-finished that report. It would take an hour or two of intense work to get it done.

The scene which greeted me in the lounge was of my father and brothers focused on the TV and blissfully unaware of their two unseen guests, who were as equally transfixed by the football as the humans were.

I shook my head in wonder as I climbed the stairs to my room. The mystery of the Mountain of Light would have to wait. I had homework to do.

I would have time to sort out the mystery later.

Heaps of time.

Surely.

8

SCHOOL DAZE

I briefly checked my appearance in the mirror. My pink sweatshirt and black leggings looked good and my hair *had* been brushed, regardless of what Mum might say. I grabbed my school bag and rushed down the stairs. I was going to be late, *again*. Anahira stood waiting patiently for me, wearing a plain white T-shirt with blue Nike track pants. She made standing by the open front door seem like a cool sporting moment.

"Hey, Maggie."

"Hi, Anahira. Sorry." My lateness was becoming a habit.

"No worries. We've still got time."

I nodded and grabbed my meds bag. "Bye, Mum," I yelled over my shoulder.

"Bye, Maggie," Mum's voice drifted out from the kitchen. "Have a good day."

There was no need to say goodbye to Dad. He had already taken the boys to school.

Anahira walked out of my house, and I followed, closing the door behind me. We headed off on our usual route to Camden School for Girls, about a ten- to fifteen-minute walk, depending on how fast we went.

"You alright, Maggie?" Anahira asked, looking at me sideways.

"Yeah, I think so."

"You didn't message me last night."

"Yeah, sorry. I had to get the English report done. I almost didn't make it."

Anahira laughed. "The English report?"

"It's important," I insisted.

"As important as saving the world?"

I stopped short and stared at Anahira. "Tylwyth and Teg!"

"Yes, Tylwyth and Teg. Have you heard from them?"

"They were here last night. I left them watching football with my dad and my brothers, and I had that report to finish. I haven't seen them this morning."

"Maggie," Anahira said quite sternly. "Tell me everything."

I darted a quick look around me to make sure no one could overhear us and then told Anahira about Tylwyth and Teg's visit. I spoke in a hushed tone, despite us being alone on the footpath. I told Anahira about my fear of an intruder, finding Tylwyth and Teg consuming milk and ice cream in the lounge, the big mess in the kitchen, me somehow telling them off, the magical clean-up, the gnomes, and the new mystery about Mynydd o Olau: that it wasn't people I was supposed to find but an ancient magical talisman.

I only managed to reveal the name "Mountain of Light" as we neared the main entrance to school, where a large group of girls were gathered, chatting away happily.

"Mountain of Light?" Anahira whispered, eyeing the girls gathered around the school entrance. "That sounds cool. Did they give you any idea where to look?"

"No. My family came home before I could ask," I whispered back. "Then I got distracted by my English report. But I have to get it for them by All Hallows Eve, whenever that is."

I headed toward the main entrance to Camden School for Girls but noticed Anahira hadn't joined me. I turned back. "Anahira, what's wrong?"

Anahira stared at me, "They really said All Hallows Eve?"

"Yes, why?"

"That's Halloween."

"What?"

"Halloween is All Hallows Eve."

I stared wide-eyed at Anahira. "But isn't Halloween on Wednesday?"

"Yes."

"But that's only *two* days away!" I almost shrieked.

"I know. What do we do?"

The school bell rang, and I shuddered. I had *two* days to find a mysterious magical item stolen from the world of Faerie and return it to Tylwyth and Teg. It simply couldn't be done. I stood dumbfounded as other girls moved past me on their way into school.

"Maggie," Anahira said. "MAGGIE!"

Other girls turned to stare at me, but I didn't care. I just wanted to curl up into a corner and pretend that I didn't have to do the impossible.

"Maggie," Anahira said as she reached me and touched my arm.

I looked at Anahira, my mouth as wide open as one of those clown heads at a school fair.

"It's Monday. We've got assembly first and then class. I'll meet you in the library at morning break. We'll contact Lady Marie. She'll know what to do."

I managed to close my mouth and start moving, joining the flow of girls as though I was a piece of driftwood washed along by the tide.

All Hallows Eve is Halloween.

Which was in two days' time. I had to retrieve the so-called Mountain of Light by the end of Halloween, or the world would be doomed.

Great.

I'd spent most of the previous night worrying over the finer points of my English report.

Talk about getting my priorities wrong.

I navigated the full school assembly and my three classes

before break as though in a daze. We had eight periods a day at Camden School for Girls, each one forty minutes long. I lost count of how many times my teachers and classmates asked if I was all right. I managed to assure them I was okay.

Somehow.

It was a relief when the bell signaling the end of the third class rang, and I hurried to the library. Anahira was sitting in a corner and using her phone.

"Anahira," I said as I sat down. "You're not allowed to use that."

"Desperate times, Maggie."

"But we'll get in trouble." I did a quick search for the librarian but couldn't see her anywhere.

"It's too late for that." Anahira nodded at her phone. "I've found the Mountain of Light."

"What," I replied, my voice getting louder despite my fear of getting caught by the librarian. "How?"

"I Googled it."

I shook my head. "Of course. So, what does it say?"

"Look." Anhira turned her screen toward me.

I stared at Anahira's phone. On her screen was a picture of two very expensive-looking crowns. Both were purple in color with one encased in gold and the other encased in silver. The crowns were covered in diamonds and other jewels and rested on red cushions with gold trim. In front of the crowns laid two golden poles with diamonds at their tips.

"Are those the Crown Jewels?" I asked Anahira, my eyes widening and my voice getting even louder.

"Yes," Anahira replied, pulling her phone down.

"Why are you showing me a picture of the Crown Jewels?"

"Why do you think?"

I leaned forward. "No!"

"Yes. At least, I think that's what Aunty Google is telling me."

I usually smiled when Anahira referred to Google as "Aunty" but not this time. Not if Anahira was saying what I thought she was saying.

"The Crown Jewels of England are the Mountain of Light!" I exclaimed.

"Girls!" A voice sounded from behind a row of books. "Inside voices, please." The grey-haired librarian poked her head around the display books at the end of the row.

"Sorry, Miss," Anahira replied, quickly covering her phone.

The librarian nodded and moved back down the row of books.

"Do you think the librarian heard us?" I asked, my hand resting on my chest as my breathing came in short, rapid bursts.

"She definitely heard you," Anahira responded with a grin while checking her phone.

"I wasn't talking loudly," I insisted.

"You don't have an inside voice," Anahira replied. "But it's all good. You also talk quite fast, and I don't think the librarian would have made sense of what you said."

I've often been told I talk loudly and fast by a few people, including my mum and my English teacher, but I don't sound loud to me. As for talking fast, it's just that everyone else talks too slowly.

"Is the Mountain of Light really the Crown Jewels of England?" I asked, trying very hard to keep my voice to a whisper.

"Just one of the diamonds, I think." Anahira scrolled up and read off the screen. "The Koh-i-Noor diamond."

"Koh-i-Noor?"

"It's a Persian name," Anahira clarified. "The English translation is…"

"Mountain of Light." I finished Anahira's sentence.

Anahira nodded.

"So, all we have to do is get one of the Crown Jewels of England and hand it over to Tylwyth and Teg."

Anahira nodded again.

One of the Crown Jewels? How on Earth could I get one of the Crown Jewels?

"Do you think the queen will give it to us if we just ask nicely?"

Anahira frowned. "Probably not."

I sighed. "So what do we do?"

"I've already messaged Lady Marie."

"What?" My voice rose in volume, despite my best attempts to keep it under control. "What did you say?"

"It's alright. I just said we know what T and T want and that they need it by Halloween. I used the crown emoji."

"The crown emoji?"

"Yeah. Do you think she'll understand?"

"Hopefully." Lady Marie was very smart. She'd probably make the connection, but I wasn't sure how familiar she was with emojis.

The school bell rang. It sounded like a signal for the end of the world.

"C'mon, Maggie," Anahira said, while getting to her feet.

"What?"

"We've got Geography."

I got up and followed Anahira to our Geography class. Only one of two that we had together. I liked Geography. It was interesting and practical, and Anahira and I could do projects together. Projects we could even self-select, after getting approval from our teacher, Miss Harvey.

"Do you think Miss Harvey would let us do a project on other worlds?" I asked Anahira as we walked down the corridor.

Anahira turned to me and shook her head. "No. What are you saying?"

I repeated the words I'd just said in my head and laughed nervously. "Sorry. I'm a bit distracted."

"Yeah, I know. We've got this, Maggie."

I nodded but couldn't share Anahira's confidence. We had to somehow get this Koh-i-Noor diamond from the Crown Jewels and give it to Tylwyth and Teg. We only had two days in which to do it. Getting Miss Harvey's permission to do our project on other worlds did not sound all that far-fetched in comparison.

We entered the classroom and took our assigned seats at the front of the class, near the door. Miss Harvey was a cheerful and encouraging teacher who loved Geography. She was standing at the front of the class and gave us a tight smile as we sat down. I realized we were the last students to arrive in class.

"Sorry, Miss," Anahira said.

Miss Harvey nodded, letting the matter slide for now. Miss Harvey would have done something if our lateness was repeated because lateness was not tolerated at our school. It said so on the large poster next to the whiteboard, part of the Seven Rules in the classroom for learning. Of course, I could rightly claim to Miss Harvey that my lateness was due to supernatural creatures from the world of Faerie, who wanted me to steal a diamond from the queen.

I let out a short, barked laugh, causing both Anahira and Miss Harvey, and presumably, everyone in the class, to stare at me.

"Sorry, Miss," I quickly added, my face red.

"Something you'd like to share, Maggie?" Miss Harvey asked.

"No, Miss Harvey." Something I would most definitely not like to share.

Miss Harvey stared at me for what seemed like forever. "Well, do I have *your* permission to start the lesson?"

I nodded, sheepishly.

"Why thank you, Maggie." Miss Harvey turned her attention to the class. "Welcome back. I hope you had a great Autumn break. A wonderful time of the year, don't you think? Now, I've put the learning tasks for this week on Google Classroom, and I'd like to get your projects confirmed today if possible. Please use the tasks I've uploaded as a guide. I'll come around and talk to you individually this session, just after I've completed the roll."

Miss Harvey turned around and was about to sit at her desk when she noticed that all of the students, including Anahira and me, had not made any move to do what she had asked.

"Come on, girls. Break time is over. You don't need my permission to start."

A wave of sound flooded the classroom as all of the students retrieved their laptops from their school bags.

I pulled out my laptop and placed it on my desk, logging on to the school network. I opened the Geography Google Classroom page and found the learning tasks Miss Harvey had posted. The tasks would normally hold my attention, especially as they were project-related, but I had other things on my mind. I couldn't resist opening another tab and searching for the Crown Jewels. I started scrolling and reading.

"Maggie," Anahira whispered. "What are you doing?"

I checked on what the rest of the class was doing. Miss Harvey had started her conversations on the other side of the room. If she held to her usual pattern, we would be the last ones she spoke with. Not just because of our location in the room, but also because we were regarded as good students and could be trusted to do our work.

Mostly.

"I can't focus on anything else," I whispered back. "Miss Harvey is going to be busy with other students."

Anahira glanced at Miss Harvey and nodded.

I returned to the screen. The Crown Jewels sparkled so brilliantly, they could have been magicked up by the Fairy Godmother in Cinderella. They were on display at the Tower of London. So they would be easy to view. Of course, being on display meant that security was absolutely world-class. The Tower of London was an ancient and intimidating fortress. Maybe it would be better to have searched "How to steal the Crown Jewels." There's probably a helpful YouTube clip about it. I started to type the words.

"Maggie. Anahira."

My head shot up to find Miss Harvey standing in front of us. She hadn't followed her normal pattern at all but had seemingly chosen us as the second group to discuss the project with. I sat up straight and gave my full attention to Miss Harvey. Hopefully, she wouldn't notice what was on my screen.

"I had just popped back to my laptop to update details about Helen and Mira's project," Miss Harvey indicated the two girls on the other side of the room, "when I noticed an email from our principal, Ms. Brinsden. She wants to see you both in her office. Now, I'm afraid. She said the matter was quite urgent."

Anahira and I shot each other a quick sideways glance. We returned our attention to Miss Harvey.

"You'd better go. Ms. Brinsden said to take your bags with you."

My head drooped as I shot Anahira another quick glance. She had already started to pack her things. I did the same as Miss Harvey returned her attention to the rest of the class.

I finished packing and stood up. I followed Anahira out of the class and tried not to read too much in the concerned look Miss Harvey gave me.

I finished packing my things and stood up. I followed Anahira out of the class and tried not to read too much in the concerned look Miss Harvey gave me.

We walked down the corridor together without talking. My thoughts were racing. How on Earth did Ms. Brinsden know? Would we be expelled? Would the police be called in? How would I tell my parents?

"Anahira, I…"

"It's alright, Maggie," Anahira responded quietly but firmly. "There's no way Ms. Brinsden can know anything. It must be about something else."

"What? There's nothing else she would want to see us both about, is there?"

"I don't know. There must be something."

I wasn't convinced. Somehow Ms. Brinsden knew about our discussion concerning the Crown Jewels. Maybe the surveillance in the school was much better than I thought it was. Or maybe the British Intelligence services were monitoring all communication in the same way that the FBI were checking for the word "bomb," only the British were more concerned about the words "Crown Jewels."

Yes, that sounded right.

We kept quiet as we made our way to the administration center. I had not been in Ms. Brinsden's office before. I don't think Anahira had either.

We arrived outside the principal's office and were greeted by the principal's assistant, Mrs. Joyce, according to the nameplate on her desk. She peered at us through wide-rimmed black glasses which had an attached chain of beaded pearls. "Maggie Thatcher and Anahira Waititi, is it? I've been told to expect you."

We both nodded.

"Well, fancy a name like that. No pressure, Maggie."

I half-smiled, but I didn't say anything in response.

"Ms. Brinsden wants to meet you outside the front entrance. She is waiting for you there." Mrs. Joyce almost sounded like she didn't believe what she was saying.

Anahira and I both stared at her.

"Outside. Now, please," Mrs. Joyce insisted.

"Thank you, Miss," Anahira said, as she turned around.

I nodded and followed Anahira. "Outside? Why is she meeting us outside?"

"I don't know," Anahira whispered. "But let's not talk about it here."

I glanced to my left and right. We were leaving the administration area and were on our way to the reception area and no one was paying much attention to us.

"Do you think they are still recording us?" I whispered back, not really sure who I meant. British Intelligence, probably.

Anahira turned to me and shook her head.

I couldn't tell if Anahira meant "no" or "don't talk," but I stopped asking questions. We walked to the reception area and were greeted by one of the receptionists.

"Maggie and Anahira?"

We both nodded.

"Ms. Brinsden is waiting for you outside. She has already signed you out."

"Thanks, Miss," Anahira replied and walked toward the front entrance.

I nodded again and followed Anahira, although I was really starting to panic. The principal had already signed us out. Why would she have done that? That couldn't have been good, could it?

We must be in way more trouble than I realized.

9
HISTORY LESSONS

I followed Anahira out of the front entrance of Camden School for Girls and found our principal waiting for us at one of the outside tables. Ms. Brinsden was the very definition of prim and proper, both in the full-length skirts she wore and the stiff formality she used when speaking at assemblies. I'd only ever seen Ms. Brinsden with a stern and serious expression, but she smiled as she beckoned for us to join her.

I glanced nervously at Anahira, who shrugged and walked over to Ms. Brinsden. I sucked in a deep breath and reluctantly followed. We sat down in the seats opposite our principal.

"Maggie and Anahira, my apologies. You must be wondering what all the fuss is about."

We both nodded.

Just what is going on?

"Yes, I can only imagine," Ms. Brinsden continued. "However, Lady Marie informed me of the severity of your situation and encouraged me to take all measures necessary."

"Lady Marie?" I asked tentatively.

"You know Lady Marie?" Anahira asked right on top of me.

"Yes, well, we work quite closely together when the need

arises. She is sending her car around to pick you up. I wanted to make sure you got away okay."

"You *work* with Lady Marie?" I asked, shaking my head.

"Yes, well. You're not the only one with a few secrets." Ms. Brinsden turned her head as an old silver Rolls-Royce with tinted windows drove up to the parking bay. "Ah. Here is your ride. You had better get going."

Anahira and I stared at the car and then back at Ms. Brinsden.

"Don't worry about school. I'll cover for your absence today. I will personally be in contact with your parents, although I don't yet know what to report, but I'll consult with Lady Marie about a valid excuse."

I nodded, too bewildered to speak.

Ms. Brinsden stood and considered us intently. "Light the path. Lead the way." She returned to the school without a backward glance.

"Light the path. Lead the way," I whispered quickly. "That's the Wayfinder motto."

"What?" Anahira whispered back.

"The Wayfinder motto. Ms. Brinsden must be in Guardians."

"Oh. Wow," Anahira replied, staring after our principal.

A car horn sounded, and we turned to see the back door of the Rolls-Royce swing open.

"I guess we'd better go." Anahira stood and moved toward the car.

"Is it safe?" I asked nervously.

"It's a Rolls-Royce, one of the best cars ever made. Of course, it's safe," Anahira declared excitedly as she got into the car.

I shook my head. Just because a Rolls-Royce was a really expensive car didn't mean it was safe. It was quite old and it had *tinted* windows. That was a bit dodgy, wasn't it? But I didn't really have much choice, so I followed Anahira into the back of the car. I settled into the brown leather seat next to Anahira as the door closed behind me. I didn't shut it.

"Anahira!" I almost shouted.

"What?"

"Where's the driver?"

"There doesn't appear to be one," Anahira responded calmly.

"What? No driver? Then how did the car get here?"

"It must be a self-driving car."

I stared in horror at Anahira. "Self-driving?"

"Yes, cool, aye."

My breath increased in pace. "I can't."

"Maggie. It will be alright."

"No, I can't. I can't go." I moved to open the door.

Anahira gently touched my arm. "It will be okay, Maggie. Lady Marie would never put us in any danger."

"But what about that thing with the Bugbear?" I protested.

"Alright," Anahira corrected herself. "Lady Marie would not intentionally put us in any danger."

I turned to Anahira. My breathing came in short, sharp bursts. "Are you sure?"

"Yes. Trust me. Trust Lady Marie."

As though in response, the car radio activated, and the voice of Lady Marie was heard. "Hello, girls. Sorry about all the drama, but I had to quickly respond to your message, which I esteem to be quite urgent and has some relevance to the queen. Well done, by the way, Anahira, quite clever. Now, you are perfectly safe. The car will bring you to Dux Manor where we have much to discuss. I'm bringing the whole unit together on this. And, don't worry, I'll make sure your parents are notified. So, sit back, strap on your seat belts, and enjoy the ride. Oh, and when you arrive, please use the garden entrance. The meeting rooms are currently being used for a seminar. I'll text Anahira the instructions. See you soon."

The radio stopped and the seat belt light on the dashboard started blinking. I turned to Anahira, and she smiled in response.

"It'll be okay, Maggie."

I reluctantly nodded, and we clicked our seat belts in place.

The yellow indicator light on the dashboard started to flash, suggesting that the car was about to pull out onto the road.

"Oh, Anahira," I said as I tried to steady my breathing. "I hope you are right."

"Maggie. We will be fine. You can trust Lady Marie."

I nodded again, but I was still not sure. I clenched both my hands as the Rolls-Royce pulled out onto the road. I started tapping the fingers of my right hand against my leg with ever-increasing speed. Anahira reached out and grabbed my hand, holding it tight.

"It's okay, Maggie. I've got you."

I turned to Anahira. "Thank you."

"Just think how cool this is. We are in a self-driving Rolls-Royce. It's incredible."

It was cool. I just wish I didn't have to experience it myself. Well, not until full and proper safety tests had been conducted, and thousands of kilometers had been driven. No, hundreds of thousands of kilometers.

Millions.

"Maggie?"

"Okay. Yes, it is cool. It does seem like a smooth ride."

"Very smooth," Anahira responded. "And very safe."

It appeared so. Most traffic accidents were caused by human error, so theoretically, a self-driving car would have been safer.

Theoretically.

The traffic was thankfully lighter than usual, so it didn't take long to reach Dux Manor. I was soon getting out of the Rolls-Royce in the car park of Dux Manor.

"That was amazing," I declared, now safely out of the car.

"Yeah, right," Anahira responded.

I ignored the sarcasm in Anahira's response. "Do you think it is the best car to use for the Guardians?"

Anahira considered the car. "What do you mean?"

"Well, doesn't it, you know, kind of stand out?"

"Yeah, well, maybe that's the point," Anahira responded. "And it is quite old."

"So, no one would ever suspect it of being fully automated?"

"Something like that. They're not that uncommon. Just a bit eccentric."

As eccentric as having to get into a secret underground base by way of a tree.

"We'd better get going." Anahira checked her phone as she moved away from the car.

I hesitated in following Anahira. The last two days had already held more surprises than I could normally cope with, and I was starting to feel lightheaded. It was all getting to be too much. What with the ride in the Rolls-Royce, the thought of the secret underground base, the tree entrance, the Crown Jewels, Halloween, and Tylwyth and Teg. How was I supposed to cope?

Or maybe the person with green skin had me worried; were they still around?

I darted a glance at the tree where I'd first seen the watcher, but it appeared normal. But could the person move from tree to tree? Would they be waiting near the door to the Guardians' base? What would they do if we tried to enter the tree?

"Come on, Maggie," Anahira encouraged, returning to my side and holding her hand out for mine. "I've got you."

I let out a long, slow breath. "Thank you." I took Anahira's hand. I couldn't have done any of this without her.

The tree we needed stood in the rear garden of Dux Manor, part of a large group of trees growing near the neighboring property. We had to walk around Dux Manor in order to get to the trees, but with the seminar underway, most people would be inside soaking up whatever wisdom was being communicated.

We'd look out of place at the seminar, with our school bags and my meds bag. Although, at least we weren't in school uniforms, something Camden School for Girls ditched a long time ago. So, going around the back made sense. It wasn't as if people were barred from walking around Dux Manor. The Wayfinder Girls World Center welcomed all.

I couldn't help but glance around nervously as we walked, especially at the windows that overlooked the garden area. But no one stopped us or called out, and we made it safely to a big old oak tree in the middle of the back garden.

All of the trees were thankfully free of green-skinned watchers.

We moved around to the other side of the tree, so that Dux Manor was completely hidden, and we were shaded from the neighbors by the presence of other large trees and a large, brown, brick wall at the edge of the property.

"What are we supposed to do?" I asked.

"Lady Marie's text said to press this and pull this." Anahira pressed a small knot in the trunk of the tree and at the same time pulled on what seemed like any normal branch. In response, a large portion of the bark of the tree cracked open.

"Now what?"

"Now, we pull the door out further." Anahira got her fingertips into the cracks and pulled. The "door" opened a little bit more.

I joined Anahira and together we pulled open the door. A dark, downward sloping tunnel stretched out from the center of the tree. It was a tight squeeze, especially for Anahira, but we managed to make it into the tunnel. As soon as we stepped inside, a narrow line of yellow lights lit up. The lights were built into the ground of the tunnel, almost like a string of glow sticks lined end to end. Before following the pathway of lights, Anahira turned and closed the door, using handles placed on the inside of the bark.

"Job done," Anahira declared.

"Thanks, Anahira."

"No worries. Let's go."

I was grateful for the lights. I might never have entered if it had been completely dark. The tunnel sloped downward and seemed almost natural as if the Earth had shaped itself around the Guardians' purpose. It didn't take long before we reached the end of the tunnel and stood before the door to the Guardians' command center.

"Are you ready for this?" Anahira said, her hand hovering over the door handle.

"I think so," I replied with a stiff nod. It would be my third time in the secret underground base, and I had just about accepted it was safe.

Anahira opened the door and walked through, holding the door open for me. I shuffled inside, and Anahira shut the door behind me.

"Maggie and Anahira. You're here," Lady Marie greeted us from the large wooden table dominating the center of the space. "Any problems?"

"No problem at all, Lady Marie," Anahira answered, as we walked further into the room. "The car's very cool."

"Yes, well, I know the Americans are making great strides in autonomous vehicles, but one must back British if one can. Quietly, of course. We don't want to make a fuss."

Lady Marie got up from her chair. "Maggie, dear, how are you getting along?"

My shoulders slumped. "I don't know. It's all getting to be a bit much."

"Quite," Lady Marie responded. "Now, the others won't be too far away. Having all five of you live in London has worked out rather nicely for our Guardians unit."

Worked out rather nicely?

I wouldn't have been surprised if it had happened by design.

"How are you able to contact the others?" Anahira asked.

"A good question, Anahira," Lady Marie answered with a smile. "Certainly with the restrictions on phone use in schools, we can't very well just text them."

I darted a quick look at Anahira. She had broken the school rules by using her phone.

"Fortunately, we have other means," Lady Marie continued. "A network of agents committed to our cause, one in each of the schools that the girls attend."

One in each school? Did that mean that the Guardians had been following their potential recruits for a while?

I darted another look at Anahira. It made sense for the Guardians to keep an eye on her. She already had so much to offer and so much potential. But me? I just happened to have been Anahira's friend. One she stuck by, no matter what.

"There are some refreshments in the kitchen," Lady Marie added. "Including something for you, Maggie. Why don't you take a break and get something to eat."

We went to the lockers as Lady Marie returned to the table. I packed my school bag into a locker and considered taking out my water bottle and lunch box. I usually don't eat or drink anything I haven't brought from home, but I needed to trust Lady Marie. So I left my bottle and lunch box in my bag and went to the kitchen area. Though I kept my meds bag with me.

In the kitchen, I found Lady Marie pouring herself a cup of tea and Anahira munching on a bright green apple.

"Maggie, there's a new packet of rice crackers on the bench and a new tub of safe hummus in the fridge. I double-checked the ingredients, but please feel free to check too. Oh, and the glasses have just come out of the dishwasher."

"Thank you, Lady Marie." It seemed that the Guardians leader was one of the few adults, other than my mum, who actually understood food allergies.

"You are most welcome, Maggie. I felt I needed a cup of tea myself."

I smiled and sorted out my own drink and snack. I recognized the brand of both the rice crackers and hummus, but I checked the ingredients just to be certain.

"I didn't know our principal was in Guardians," Anahira said, just before taking a big bite of her apple.

"Yes, well, we tend not to make our involvement public. But given that you know now, it is probably safe to tell you that she is a current member of the Council of Guardians," Lady Marie answered.

"The Council, really?" Anahira sounded impressed.

"Yes," Lady Marie replied, sipping on her tea. "At last night's Council meeting, I revealed the events that transpired yesterday, so Ms. Brinsden was somewhat forewarned that something might happen. Still, she acted with admirable speed and courage. It would not have been easy to break some of the school rules she most steadfastly defends."

Our principal broke the school rules. Wow.

Lady Marie raised a finger. "Please do not share the knowledge of Ms. Brinsden being in Guardians with anyone."

Anahira nodded and took another big bite of her apple.

"Now, please tell me what you have discovered," Lady Marie asked.

I glanced at Anahira and she gestured, encouraging me to take the lead.

"We believe Tylwyth and Teg want a diamond, one of the Crown Jewels," I responded.

Lady Marie took another sip of her tea. "I think you'd better tell me everything, from the beginning."

I gave Lady Marie a full and detailed account of all that had happened since leaving Dux Manor yesterday, although I left out the bit about my fear of an ax murderer.

"Oh, that really is problematic, isn't it?" Lady Marie said when I'd finished.

I nodded vigorously. It was way, way more than problematic.

"You believe it is this Koh-i-Noor diamond they seek?" Lady Marie asked.

"Yes, Lady Marie," I answered.

"I'll get Razia on it straight away. I believe she still has the glasses," Lady Marie responded, putting her tea on the counter and taking out her phone. She typed out a message. "You also believe Tylwyth and Teg need it by Halloween?"

"They said All Hallows Eve," I clarified. "But Anahira says that is..."

"Halloween," Lady Marie finished for me, nodding, and putting her phone away. "Anahira is correct. Halloween is in two days' time. Rather more problematic, wouldn't you say?"

"Yes, Lady Marie," I responded.

"Oh, dear. We do find ourselves in a bit of a pickle, don't we?" Lady Marie concluded, picking up her tea and taking another sip.

A bit of a pickle? That is the understatement of the year!

"Lady Marie," I began hesitantly. "Why are you leaving the fate of the world to a bunch of kids?"

"Sorry, Maggie?" Lady Marie responded.

I glanced at Anahira, who'd almost choked on her apple, and then turned to Lady Marie. "It's just something I've been thinking about. I guess we're not kids, but we're hardly adults. If there really is the threat of invasion by creatures from other worlds, or the possibility of anyone getting hurt, why trust the protection of the Earth to us?"

"A rather good question, Maggie, and one that is not easy to answer. For starters, I think young people are more concerned about the world than many adults. The climate change action is certainly one example of this. Also, young people are not so set in their ways that they can't accept new truths, especially magical ones. It is too great a leap for many adults, believe me. And then, of course, there is the fear that some adults may only see the personal gain from exploiting new worlds."

Lady Marie paused, taking another sip of her tea. She placed the cup on the bench and smiled. "We come to the heart of the reason. The Guardians is a unit of Wayfinder Girls precisely because it was requested by the first world we came into contact with. Or to put it more correctly, that world had been watching us and interacting with us for years, if not centuries, when they made an approach to Lady Mapleston, and our treaty was renewed."

"Our treaty was *renewed*?" I asked, wide-eyed.

"A treaty we think was originally signed with the First Earl of Rosslyn, a resident of a neighboring property when it was called Rosslyn Hall. We are talking well over two hundred years ago. We believe he must have stumbled across the weak barrier between worlds. His name was Alexander Wedderburn and, well, I number amongst his family's descendants."

"You are descended from the man who used to live near here two hundred years ago?" I asked.

That's amazing.

"Actually, Alexander Wedderburn died without any children and his title was passed to his nephew, James St. Bairskine," Lady

Marie explained. "I am a distant relative to the Second Earl of Rosslyn."

"Wow." The names of Lady Marie's ancestors sounded cool.

"Yes, wow," Lady Marie responded, although not really seeming that comfortable using the word. "Of course, my husband, Sir Edmund Studfall, is named after his ancestor Edmund Grey, the First Earl of Kent, way back in 1465."

I shook my head.

1465? That's insane.

"Does he have one of those really long names too?" I asked.

Lady Marie laughed. "Yes, I'm afraid he does. Edmund Charles Henry Grey Studfall."

"Oh, he must be really posh," I replied.

"Quite," Lady Marie responded with a smile. "Now, back to Alexander Wedderburn, if I may. I'm afraid he may have exploited the knowledge he gained from other worlds for his own personal gain. For, soon after being raised to the peerage, he became the Lord High Chancellor of Great Britain. Even the king at the time remarked that Alexander had been the greatest knave in the kingdom."

"Peerage? Knave?" I responded with a slight shake of my head. I loved history, but this was a bit much, even for me.

"My apologies, Maggie. Peerage is the name used to describe nobility, titles, and rank, like duke, earl, and baron. And knave, well, a knave is a somewhat dishonest person. Of course, the First Earl of Rosslyn is not here to defend himself, but he did have a stellar career and a rather infamous reputation."

"Do you think the other world wasn't pleased by his actions?"

"Possibly not. Thus, the reason why the treaty was renewed with the Wayfinder Girls as treaty holders. But we haven't had any firm contact with the other world until now."

Until now?

My eyes widened as I realized what Lady Marie was revealing. Did she mean what I thought she meant?

"Yes, Maggie," Lady Marie responded, probably recognizing

the expression on my face. "The treaty was signed with the world of Faerie. The Fae have been here before."

"Really? How did it go last time?"

Lady Marie grimaced. "Not terribly well, I'm afraid."

I stared at Lady Marie as I felt a hard, tight knot in my stomach. The Fae had been here before, and it had gone badly.

So what will stop it from going badly again?

10

DIAMONDS ARE FOREVER

I sat at the table with the rest of my unit, waiting for Lady Marie to open the meeting. The other girls had started to arrive a few minutes after my chat with Lady Marie, which meant that her attention was focused on greeting them. Razia first, then Kayla and, finally, after about twenty minutes or so, Sam. All three were dressed in similar school uniforms, even though they went to completely different schools. The white blouses, formal skirts, blazers, and ties could have been designed by the same person, despite the wide range of colors.

The knowledge of the Fae's previous visit to our world had troubled me as I waited. Anahira tried to repeatedly tell me that it would be okay, but the words *not terribly well* had taken up permanent residence in my mind.

Just where are Tylwyth and Teg?

I hadn't seen them since last night and had no idea where they spent the night or what they got up to. Maybe they were visiting some of the old places the Fae used to go when they were last here, or maybe they were watching a football game somewhere, or maybe gorging themselves on ice cream at some unsuspecting ice cream parlor.

Yes, that's probably it. Ice cream.

I took a long gulp of water from my drink bottle, which I had retrieved from my school bag. I could have used the glass from the kitchen, but there was something familiar and comforting about my own drink bottle. That's what I definitely needed right now.

"Okay, girls, let's start." Lady Marie sat on the chair at the right-hand side of the table. I sat next to her, with Anahira next to me. Razia sat opposite Lady Marie, with Kayla and Sam completing the row. "Firstly, thank you all for coming. I know you may think you didn't have much choice, but we would never have forced you."

Sam and Kayla glanced in my direction. I was the only one who didn't have a choice, being *bound* to Tylwyth and Teg.

"Secondly, please don't worry about what your school or your parents might say. With the help of one or two in the education circles, we have perfected a reason for our time today. Our unit has been nominated for the Wayfinder World Friendship award."

"Wow," exclaimed Kayla. "That's awesome."

"What's the prize?" Sam asked.

Lady Marie held up her hand. "Sorry, let me please clarify. The award is a cover story, to give us an excuse for why we are meeting here today."

"Oh. So there's not really an award?" Kayla asked, looking heartbroken.

"There will be an award," Lady Marie answered with a tight smile. "It will be called the Wayfinder World Friendship award, but it will be the first time it has ever been awarded."

"What's the award for?" Sam inquired.

"Sorry, I think we're getting a bit off-track," Lady Marie responded. "My husband, Sir Edmund Studfall, has kindly agreed to officially sponsor the new award, but its sole purpose at this time is to give us an excuse to meet here today."

"An excuse?" Anahira asked.

"Yes," Lady Marie answered. "We need time, on very short notice due to an administrative error, to complete stage two of our application for the Wayfinder World Friendship award."

"But there was no stage one?" Sam clarified.

"There was no stage one," Lady Marie confirmed. "We have just made up the award so that we have a reason to meet here today. There will eventually be an award, but we haven't quite worked out all the details. We needed something to tell your parents and your schools, and we think a great excuse is that more time is needed to complete an application for a prestigious international award. The Council has already approved it in principle. Thus, we have used the idea of the award to win the cooperation of your schools and your parents. It has been quite a big undertaking. Do you understand?"

We all nodded.

"Good," Lady Marie continued. "We may be here for some time, so please feel free to contact your parents later in the day but do remember to tell them that we are here to complete our application for the Wayfinder World Friendship award. However, as to the real need in calling this urgent meeting, I hope you'll soon see that it is completely necessary."

Lady Marie then turned to me. "Maggie, could you please update the unit on what has happened since our time together yesterday?"

Had it really only been a day ago?

I told the others everything that had happened since leaving Dux Manor yesterday, again leaving out my fear of an ax murderer. They definitely didn't need to know about that. Kayla smiled at me through the whole account, Sam smirked, and Razia listened intently, every now and then raising a hand to adjust her glasses.

"Thank you, Maggie," Lady Marie said with a smile. "You have had no contact with Tylwyth or Teg today?"

"None. I don't know where they are," I responded.

"And it was Anahira who discovered what Tylwyth and Teg wanted," Lady Marie continued.

"I just Googled it," Anahira admitted.

"Yes, well, it was still helpful. It is what led us to this meeting. We must now decide how we should best proceed, with the approval of the Council of Guardians, of course."

Silence greeted Lady Marie's closing statement. It was quite a lot to take in.

"How do we know it's true?" Sam asked.

"Sorry, Sam. What do you mean?" Lady Marie responded.

"The only one who can confirm what Tylwyth and Teg claim they want is Maggie. How do we know she just doesn't want to steal the Crown Jewels?"

I flashed Sam a wide-eyed stare. "You think *I'm* a jewel thief?"

"You could be. I'm just saying it's possible, that's all," Sam replied.

"Thank you, Sam," Lady Marie added quickly. "A valid question, but I'm very happy to speak to Maggie's character. I don't think any of us want any part of the Crown Jewels for our own personal gain."

Sam didn't look altogether convinced. As if I was some international jewel thief using the cover of the Guardians, a *secret* Wayfinder Girls program, and Tylwyth and Teg—two supernatural beings from the world of *Faerie*—to attempt to steal the Crown Jewels of England.

Ridiculous.

"Now, I asked Razia to do some research into the Koh-i-Noor diamond. It is the diamond also known as the Mountain of Light, and one that Tylwyth and Teg claim to be an important magical artifact stolen from their world," Lady Marie continued. "I believe the results are somewhat fascinating. Razia?"

"Thank you, Lady Marie. The Koh-i-Noor diamond was once one of the largest diamonds ever discovered. It was claimed to be unearthed in India over seven hundred years ago, although it is not clear exactly where or when it was found. The diamond was the size of a hen's egg, and its value beyond measure. It has been significantly cut down to enhance its brilliance, but it is probably worth more now than it ever was. The diamond has been fought over by rulers of many different nations and, despite forming part of the English Crown Jewels, its ownership is currently claimed by India, Pakistan, and Afghanistan."

"So how did it end up in England?" Kayla asked.

"It was *gifted* to Queen Victoria in 1849 by Duleep Singh, the ten-year-old ruler of the Punjab region, following the second Anglo-Sikh war."

"Why do those other nations claim ownership then, if it was a gift?" Sam retorted.

Razia sighed, a possible indication that this was not an easy explanation for her.

"The Koh-i-Noor diamond had been taken as a spoil of war for many centuries before the English got their hands on it. Some claim that it was stolen before it ever came into the hands of Duleep's father, Ranjit Singh. However, Duleep was only ten years old when he was *forced* to give up the diamond as part of the Last Treaty of Lahore. Five years after gifting it to Queen Victoria, Duleep accused the queen of being the receiver of stolen goods."

"Oh. That's heavy," Kayla admitted.

"Yes. That's not even taking into account the dominating influence of the East India Trading Company, who some say acted like pirates," Razia added.

"Like in the Pirates of the Caribbean." I simply couldn't help myself.

"Yes," Razia replied, shooting me a cold-eyed stare. "Just a little bit more real."

I ducked my head. I hadn't meant to be so insensitive.

"Thank you, Razia." Lady Marie inserted herself into the discussion. "I'm afraid my nation has a somewhat checkered history, and the continued ownership of many items of immense cultural value to other nations is certainly a sore point. Akin, I'm sure, to a sense of colonial looting. We are certainly trying to do better and have passed into law the Holocaust Act, which allows for the return of important cultural objects, but I'm afraid it takes more than just an Act of Parliament to do the right thing."

"Thank you, Lady Marie," Razia replied while reaching up to adjust her hijab. "There is just one more thing, if I may."

"Certainly, Razia. What is it?"

"The Koh-i-Noor diamond is said to be cursed."

"Cursed?" Sam asked. "How?"

"Over the many years of its existence, its owners have suffered in terrible ways, including being blinded, slow-poisoned, tortured to death, burned in oil, threatened with drowning, crowned with molten lead, and assassinated by their own family and closest bodyguards. The diamond seemed to drive everyone mad."

"Almost as if it doesn't belong in our world," I said quietly.

"Yes, it is possible," Razia concluded.

The Koh-i-Noor diamond certainly had a colorful past. Could it actually have been a magical artifact stolen from the world of Faerie? But who would have stolen it?

"So, where does that leave us?" Anahira inquired. "It may be a diamond that the English probably obtained illegally some time ago and should be rightfully in the hands of India or Pakistan or Afghanistan. But Tylwyth and Teg are laying an even older claim on it. Don't we just have to decide whether we should try and give it back to them?"

"Yes, thank you, Anahira," Lady Marie responded. "While the history of the diamond is indeed interesting, we are not trying to right history's wrongs. However, we do need to decide whether we will attempt to obtain one of the current Crown Jewels of England. A most difficult decision, even if it means returning a jewel to its rightful owner."

Silence greeted Lady Marie's announcement.

Kayla stood up. "I pledge to do my best, to be true to my beliefs, to serve the queen, and my community, to help others, and to follow the Wayfinder guidelines." Kayla sat down without saying anything further.

An even deeper silence enveloped the room.

I glanced at Kayla. It was rare to see her without her usual broad smile. I knew the words Kayla spoke all too well. They were the words that every Wayfinder Girl said when they made the Pledge. Central to the Pledge was the queen. So, how could we take something that currently belonged to the queen? We would break the Pledge and would have been anything but Wayfinder Girls.

It seemed that the other members of my unit were having

similar thoughts, for the mood in the room turned gloomy and dark.

"Let's take a break," Lady Marie suggested. "Please have something to eat and drink, and go outside if you need to. But, please remember to use the garden entrance. I'll use the time to confirm we have contacted all of your parents and check whether there are any lingering doubts or questions. Let's meet back here in fifteen minutes. Thank you, everyone."

The unit responded quickly, with the girls seemingly keen to get a break. I didn't see much point in discussing it any further. Kayla had identified the truth of it.

"Maggie?"

I turned to Lady Marie, who remained seated while the others left the table.

"Are you sure Tylwyth and Teg meant the Koh-i-Noor diamond?"

I tried to recall the conversation I had with Tylwyth and Teg. "Actually, no, Lady Marie. They have only talked about the Mountain of Light and claimed it to be a magical artifact. We made the connection to the Koh-i-Noor diamond when Anahira Googled 'Mountain of Light.' Do you think we got it wrong?"

"No, I think we are correct, especially given the unusual history of the diamond. I was simply hoping that there might be an easier solution. But life is never easy, is it?"

"No, it's not," I replied, with a firm shake of my head.

Life is definitely not easy.

"We really need to talk about it with Tylwyth and Teg," Lady Marie suggested.

"But I don't know where they are," I responded.

"Have you tried summoning them?"

Summoning them? Like some kind of magician?

"Can I do that?" I asked while running a hand through my hair.

Lady Marie nodded. "There is a snippet of a very old story, which seems to indicate that it is possible."

"Okay," I replied, briefly raising my arms as though I was

praying or surrendering. "But how am I supposed to summon them?"

"I'm not terribly sure, Maggie. You could simply try calling them."

"Out loud?" My hands dropped to the table, my right hand squeezing my left. I guess Lady Marie did not mean calling them on my phone.

"Maybe. Or maybe just in your head."

In my head? Great!

"Okay," I responded, the fingers of my right hand starting to tap on my left hand. "What should I say?"

Lady Marie got out of her seat and stood next to me, placing her hand on my shoulder. "I think it's all about need. That you desperately need them."

"Which is true," I replied, my fingers tapping out a faster rhythm.

"Yes. I'm afraid that it is." Lady Marie's hand left my shoulder and gently rested on my right hand, quieting my tapping.

"Alright, Lady Marie," I replied, letting out a long breath. "I'll try it."

"Thank you, Maggie. I knew I could count on you." Lady Marie left me alone at the table.

I glanced around. The other members of my unit must have taken Lady Marie's advice and gotten some food or gone outside. That was what I would have done, especially with the Guardians' command center starting to feel very small.

Best to get this summoning thing over with as soon as possible.

"Tylwyth and Teg," I whispered, as the heat rose in my face. "My need is great. I really need you. Please come. I need you urgently. Please."

"What are you doing, Maggie? Talking to yourself again?"

I turned to Anahira, who came and sat down next to me with another bright green apple she must have taken from the kitchen. I often talked to myself, as did my dad. He claimed it was the only way to have an intelligent conversation.

"I was just trying something Lady Marie suggested," I responded.

"Did it work?" Anahira asked, before taking a bite of her apple.

"I don't know," I replied, turning my head to look around the space. The command center was quiet and empty, apart from me and Anahira. There was no sign of the other unit members or Tylwth and Teg. "I don't think it worked."

Anahira nodded. "Pretty heavy stuff, aye."

"Yeah." That was one way of putting it. A betrayal of our pledge as Wayfinder Girls was another way of putting it. Or even the end of the world.

"You know that queen part?" Anahira said after finishing another bite of her apple. "We don't actually say that anymore in New Zealand."

"What?"

"Yeah, the Wayfinder Girls Pledge we say in New Zealand is different."

"It is?" I hadn't known that. It was the first time that Anahira had talked about the Wayfinder Girls rules in her country of birth.

"I pledge, with the help of my God, to be true to myself, to do my best to help my community, and to follow the Wayfinder guidelines."

"Oh, so no mention of the queen at all?" I asked, genuinely surprised.

"No," Anahira responded, her apple momentarily forgotten. "You know that checkered history Lady Marie was talking about?"

"Yeah." Although I wasn't absolutely sure what *checkered* meant. I think it meant that some bad things were done, along with some good, maybe.

"Some pretty bad things happened in New Zealand," Anahira suggested, as though responding to my thoughts.

"Oh." I hadn't known much about the history of New Zealand or the treatment of Māori, the indigenous people there. I really should've asked Anahira more about it.

"Still. It doesn't really matter, does it?" Anahira concluded.

"What do you mean?"

"Well, even if we decided to try and give the Koh-i-Noor diamond back, there is no way we could get access to one of the Crown Jewels. It's impossible. So there's not much point in discussing it." Anahira took another bite of her apple.

That was so true. An impossible task even if we had a lifetime to plan, and we had experienced jewel thieves amongst us. We're talking about the actual Crown Jewels. Kept in the Tower of London, one of the most secure places on Earth.

What are we even thinking?

"Alright, Maggie. What's occurrin'?"

"You'd be needin' us in a hurry, like."

My head snapped up to see Tylwyth and Teg sitting across from me—and eating ice cream, of course! In a cone this time.

Thankfully.

Anahira's gasp of surprise at their sudden appearance let me know that she could see them too.

"Can you get Lady Marie?" I asked Anahira.

Anahira flew out of her seat. I turned back to Tylwyth and Teg, who seemed to be really enjoying their ice creams.

It's good that someone's happy.

Tylwyth and Teg had somehow managed to change since I last saw them. They were no longer wearing football shirts but instead wore green waistcoats over short-sleeved brown shirts. They still wore brown trousers, brown boots, and green capes, and their silver hair was still tied back with thin golden bands, with gems matching the color of their eyes.

"I need to know whether the Mountain of Light is the Koh-i-Noor diamond that is currently part of the Crown Jewels of England," I blurted out, without any kind of greeting.

Both Tylwyth and Teg stopped eating their ice creams.

"Crown Jewels of England?" Tylwyth responded, not appearing to take any offense at my lack of greeting.

"'Tis a strange thing," Teg added.

I sighed.

Yes, it is strange.

Everything about the last day or so was strange. But all I really wanted was a straight answer.

Is that too much to ask?

"Master Tylwyth and Master Teg. Welcome." Lady Marie arrived and immediately took the lead in the conversation.

Both Tylwyth and Teg stood up and bowed, while still somehow managing to hold onto their ice creams.

"Thank you, Lady Studfall," Tylwyth said.

"'Tis an honor," Teg added.

"The honor is mine," Lady Marie responded. "May I get you anything?"

"We are well satisfied." Tylwyth indicated his ice cream.

Lady Marie smiled. "I am glad. I am hoping you will be kind enough to help us with more information about the item you have asked Maggie to obtain for you."

"The Mountain of Light," Tylwyth confirmed.

"We have reason to believe it might be the Koh-i-Noor diamond that is now part of the Crown Jewels of England," Lady Marie responded.

Tylwyth glanced at Lady Marie and took another bite of his ice cream. "You wouldn't by any chance be havin' a picture, would you?"

Lady Marie signaled to Razia who, like the others in my unit, had gathered around the table. Razia reached up to her glasses and adjusted them slightly. In response, the large digital screen positioned at the end of the table turned on. It displayed an image of a purple velvet crown with thick white trim at its base, the "Queen Mother's Crown," according to the words alongside the image. The crown was encased in silver and diamonds, with a thick band of jewels between the white trim and the purple velvet. There were too many diamonds and jewels to count, but the Koh-i-Noor diamond was indicated with an arrow. It sat in the middle of the front cross of the crown and seemed almost too perfect to have been real.

Tylwyth stared at the screen and took another bite of his ice cream. "Aye, that's the Mynydd o Olau. What have you done to it?"

"Done?" Lady Marie asked.

"Aye, done," Teg responded. "It's been butchered."

Lady Marie looked at Teg, then at the screen, then back to Teg. "I believe it was cut to enhance its brilliance and also to make it lighter to wear."

"You cut somethin' that's not yours so that your queen can wear it for decoration?" Teg asked, thrusting his ice cream forward as though it was a weapon.

I quickly leaned back.

Ice cream could do me some real harm.

"Master Teg, I am deeply sorry if this causes offense. The diamond was acquired over one hundred and fifty years ago, and those in power did not know its connection to your world."

"Aye, 'twas stolen," Teg bemoaned, calming himself with another mouthful of ice cream.

"I regret that we have damaged it."

"Damaged it, Lady Studfall?" Tylwyth interjected. "You have only made it more powerful. A thing we did not believe was possible."

There was a pause in the conversation as we absorbed Tylwyth's latest revelation.

More powerful?

Just how did a diamond have power? Or maybe its power was only truly experienced in the world of Faerie. How did they even know it was the right diamond, especially if it had been changed as much as they'd claimed it had?

"You might be wondering about the Mynydd o Olau." Tylwyth broke the silence, shooting me a mischievous look. "It calls to us. We'd not be needin' a picture, but it helps. Its full glory can only be seen in our world."

I gulped.

Did Tylwyth read my thoughts?

"We be needin' it back," Teg added.

"Why don't you just go and take it?" Sam asked abruptly.

Tylwyth turned to Sam. "We cannot. There are rules."

"Rules. What rules?" Sam responded. "You don't seem to..."

"Thank you, Sam," Lady Marie interrupted. "I believe Master Tylwyth refers to the provisions of our treaty."

Tylwyth bowed in response.

"I'm afraid that we are bound by other rules, equally as binding as those contained in our treaty," Lady Marie continued. "We cannot simply take something from our queen. It would go against everything we hold dear."

"So, you refuse to aid us?" Tylwyth said.

"I didn't say that specifically," Lady Marie responded, choosing her words carefully. "I believe with the right approach our queen may be willing to listen to your request. But I'm afraid it will take some time before I can get an audience with Her Majesty."

"We'll be needin' it by All Hallows Eve," Teg insisted.

"Yes, regrettably that's only in two days' time," Lady Marie answered. "I'm afraid that is simply not possible, especially as our queen is currently out of the country."

Tylwyth and Teg stared at Lady Marie and then turned to each other.

"'Tis a shame," Teg declared.

"Aye. A real shame," Tylwyth responded.

"Our world will suffer," Teg asserted.

"And the doorways we protect will be exposed," Tylwyth added.

"Lettin' in creatures far more terrifyin' than those simple Bugbears," Teg suggested.

"Aye, creatures that would make slaves of the humans," Tylwyth agreed.

"But at least we be takin' Maggie back with us when we go," Teg concluded.

"What?" I exclaimed, my voice breaking in panic. "What do you mean?"

"Prince Draikern threatens our queen," Tylwyth answered, turning to me. "He'd be willin' to let your world burn for he cares nothin' for humans. If he were ever to rule, then our protections would collapse, and your world would be lost. Queen Aylwyin must have the power of the Mynydd o Olau to defeat Prince Draikern. It is hers by right. We either return with the diamond or we return with you. You are bound to us until our deed is done."

I stared at Tylwyth in open-mouthed shock.

"I'm sure it won't come to that, Maggie," Lady Marie insisted.

"I'm afraid it will, Lady Studfall," Tylwyth responded, turning to face her. "We must not let Prince Draikern win. Queen Aylwyin needs the Mynydd o Olau or she will fall."

"'Tis for you to decide," Teg added.

"Choose wisely," Tylwyth declared.

Tylwyth and Teg disappeared.

I turned sharply to Lady Marie, who held my gaze. I couldn't tell whether sympathy or sadness was reflected in her eyes. Maybe both. I could however now tell what her previous "not terribly well" comment related to.

The Fae must have taken someone back to the world of Faerie the last time they were here.

And now Tylwyth and Teg will take me.

"We don't know what to do," I declared, not for the first time.

It had been about half an hour since Tylwyth and Teg vanished. Half an hour in which I'd struggled to find any way to avoid being taken to the world of Faerie as... as what? A slave? A ransom? A sacrifice? That last one sounded a bit extreme, but what did I know? It would have been better if I had never found out.

Lady Marie had left to update the Council of Guardians after Teg's ultimatum. She'd only just returned from the conference call, but she hadn't revealed any part of her discussion. She seemed to be waiting to hear our ideas first.

"Can we fight?" Sam asked.

"Sam, I really don't believe violence is any kind of solution," Lady Marie replied patiently. "I also don't know whether it is a fight we could win."

"We could if we had an army," Sam asserted.

"Please, Sam," Lady Marie responded. "Let's search for another solution, shall we?"

Another solution?

We could either return the Koh-i-Noor diamond, an impossible task in its own right, or we could try and convince our queen to help—but we probably wouldn't be able to get an audience with the queen in time. Or we could do nothing. Of course, if we didn't act at all, we would most likely suffer an invasion by creatures of other worlds, and I would be taken away by Tylwyth and Teg to the world of Faerie.

I shuddered as I pictured doorways opening all over the world, admitting terrifying creatures who would attack without warning.

The situation is hopeless.

"Does anyone have any ideas?" Lady Marie asked. "Razia?"

I lifted my head and considered Razia, only now realizing that she had yet to contribute anything to our discussion.

Razia reached up to touch her glasses. "I've been wondering whether it is possible to duplicate the diamond."

I sat up in my chair, giving Razia my full attention. Had she come up with a solution?

"Do you believe that is achievable?" Lady Marie replied.

"Possibly, Lady Marie. Yesterday, I noticed we had an advanced 3D printer. It could be programmed to create a copy of the Koh-i-Noor diamond, although I'm not sure what material we would use."

"I might be able to help on that front," Lady Marie responded. "Over the years we have acquired substances and compounds from other worlds. One of those might work."

"They might. Will I be able to examine them?"

"Certainly, Razia. I'll show you where they are after our meeting concludes here."

"And we give the copy we make to Tylwyth and Teg instead of the Koh-i-Noor diamond," I exclaimed loudly, my words coming out in a rush.

"No, Maggie," Razia explained. "I don't think we would be able to fool Tylwyth and Teg, not if the Koh-i-Noor diamond is as magical as they say it is. The *diamond* we'd create would replace the Koh-i-Noor diamond on the Queen Mother's Crown."

Oh, of course.

I slumped back down in my chair. Razia's suggestion wasn't a solution. Even if we could somehow create an exact copy, there was no way we could get the Koh-i-Noor diamond in the first place.

What a mess.

"It is still a valid idea, Razia," Lady Marie responded. "Something to keep in mind if we ever decide to attempt returning the Koh-i-Noor diamond to the Queen of Faerie. I do realize that even thinking the idea is scandalous, and we would need a way to gain access to the Crown Jewels."

"We just need an army," Sam insisted.

"Yes, thank you, Sam. You have made your point very clear. But even if we had an army, which we don't, we would still need to be comfortable with taking something that currently belongs to our queen, despite the challenge to its ownership status."

Sam shifted in her seat. With all her talk of fighting, she was clearly not comfortable with the idea of acting against the queen. None of us were.

"One other aspect we must consider is the reality of the threat," Lady Marie added.

"The reality of the threat?" I queried.

"I'm sorry, Maggie. I don't at all mean to diminish the threat against you personally, but we must determine how real that threat actually is."

"What are you saying, Lady Marie?" Anahira asked.

"Well, to be completely honest, we actually have very little experience in such matters," Lady Marie replied with a tight smile.

Very little experience? But that means...

"Are you saying that the Guardians haven't before faced a threat from one of the other worlds?" I asked.

Lady Marie nodded. "For the almost one hundred years the Guardians have been in existence, there's been very little to do. Every five years we recruit and train a new Guardians unit, but most girls experience nothing more than the training exercises you participated in yesterday at Ravenwood. At least, the ones *without* the Bugbear. It has simply been a wait-and-watch operation, which made it rather difficult to hold people's attention, despite the obvious initial wonder at new worlds."

"You mean, people get *bored*?" Kayla asked, wide-eyed.

"Yes, well. There's only so much watching and waiting people can do, especially if they're young," Lady Marie explained. "There truly has been very little threat."

"Until now," I pointed out.

"Yes, Maggie. Until now," Lady Marie agreed. "In fact, the Council had discussed scaling down operations, given that nothing seemed to happen. A suggestion was even made that we pass our duty to someone else, although I'm not terribly sure who that would be. It has also been suggested that your unit be the last one recruited. Recent events have thankfully put an end to that idea, but we still find ourselves in a unique position. We have no real experience with the threat we are currently facing. Some Council members are doubtful that the threat is anything to seriously worry about."

Well, that's just great.

It's fine for other people to question the reality of the threat. I mean, they're not the ones bound to Tylwyth and Teg!

"So, the Council thinks we should do nothing?" Anahira asked.

"Not quite," Lady Marie responded. "But certainly nothing as extreme as stealing one of the Crown Jewels. It's not something the Wayfinder Girls should ever consider."

I slumped further down in my chair. Of course that was never going to happen. I mean, how could it?

"It is recommended we stay watchful, but I'm afraid we are not allowed to act in any way against our queen," Lady Marie continued.

"But what does that mean for Maggie?" Anahira asked.

Lady Marie responded with another tight smile. "It means that we need to try and protect Maggie. It means that we try to convince Tylwyth and Teg to allow us more time to seek an audience with our queen. I believe she will be receptive to our plight."

"Will that work?" Kayla asked.

"I hope so, Kayla," Lady Marie responded. "You must

remember that most reports we have concerning the world of Faerie are very old. Our world has radically and fundamentally changed over time. Our science and technology has advanced to the point that it would be considered magical, especially to those living just one hundred years ago. To those older than that, well, let's just say that they would encounter a completely different world."

"So, you're saying that we have advanced so much that we no longer need to worry about threats from other worlds?" Anahira suggested.

"That is certainly an opinion held by at least two senior members of the Council," Lady Marie confirmed.

"But, Lady Marie," Razia interjected. "The thermal imaging on the drone at the Ravenwood campsite failed to pick up the heat signatures of Tylwyth and Teg."

"Yes, Razia. That certainly raises some doubts about our so-called superior technology."

"So, what do we do?" Anahira asked.

Lady Marie sighed. "We protect and prepare as best we can. But we must accept the will of the Council."

Lady Marie cast her gaze around the room and waited until each of us had nodded.

"Good. Now let us turn our attention to how we can best prevent Maggie from being taken away by Tylwyth and Teg."

Yes, that would be nice.

"Maggie, would you be willing to stay with me for a few nights?" Lady Marie asked.

Stay with Lady Marie? I'm not sure I could. What about my allergies?

I opened my mouth to answer when the lights in the command center changed to a bright, flashing red.

Lady Marie immediately stood up and scanned the room.

"What is it? What's wrong?" I asked, my high-pitched voice betraying my panic.

"I think we're under attack," Lady Marie answered, not quite seeming to believe it herself.

Under attack? I felt my heart start to race and shot an anxious glance at the other girls. Who was attacking us? It wasn't Tylwyth and Teg, was it?

Surely not.

"Quickly, girls," Lady Marie instructed. "To arms."

I stared at Lady Marie and then back at the girls, who all looked just as confused as I was.

"What do you mean, Lady Marie?" Anahira asked.

"Get the ropes," Lady Marie answered. "Maggie, get the discs. Hurry!"

I stared at Anahira, and we both scanned the room. Apart from the flashing red light, nothing had changed. Who was attacking us?

"Girls. Move. We are under attack," Lady Marie insisted.

"But Lady Marie, there's nothing here," Anahira replied.

"Not us here, Anahira. Dux Manor is under attack," Lady Marie explained, a frantic edge to her voice.

Dux Manor? Something is attacking Dux Manor? How? Why?

"Girls. Now!" Lady Marie commanded.

We all finally responded and rushed to the lockers to get our equipment. I tried not to panic as I recalled the Bugbear. I didn't know how many silver discs I would need, but I quickly grabbed six. Hopefully, that would be enough. Then I joined the rest of my unit who had gathered around Lady Marie. Each of the other girls was armed with their golden ropes.

Lady Marie checked another golden hand-held device, one which looked like a small sundial, but with odd markings.

"I think… yes, it's happening outside," Lady Marie concluded, without explanation.

"Outside?" Anahira responded. "Something is attacking Dux Manor outside?"

"Yes. We must hurry," Lady Marie answered. "We will use the tunnel. Follow me, girls."

Lady Marie set off for the tunnel, followed by Sam, Razia, and Kayla.

Anahira turned to me. "Are you okay, Maggie?"

"Sure," I responded, even though my heart was racing, and I was having serious difficulty with my breathing. "I've got my inhaler with me." I patted the meds bag at my side.

"I've got you." Anahira grinned, somehow managing to smile in the face of some unknown horror. "Come on, then. Let's find out what's attacking us."

I watched Anahira as she headed for the tunnel. Normally, I would run in the opposite direction, but my life was currently far from normal.

I took a deep breath, adjusted my meds bag, and followed Anahira.

We emerged through the tree at the end of the tunnel and joined the others standing in a tight circle around Lady Marie. It was dark under the shade of the tree, suggesting that it was late in the day, possibly almost sunset.

"Okay, girls, listen closely," Lady Marie instructed. "We don't know what's out there, so we must be ready for anything. Something has broken through the gap between worlds. If we can put one of Maggie's silver discs on whatever it is, the gap should close just as the doorways did yesterday."

Sam looked at me with what seemed like a challenge in her eyes. I responded by clenching my hand around the silver discs.

"Right," Lady Marie continued. "We do have one or two other defensive options, but let's use what you're trained with first. Kayla and Anahira, take the right. Sam and Razia, the left. Maggie and I will come through the center."

"What are we looking for exactly?" Anahira asked.

"I'm not terribly sure, I'm afraid," Lady Marie answered. "Anything out of place. Oh, and don't worry about other people. The seminar finished at two and the Wayfinder staff within Dux Manor will be looked after by Faatimah, who's on reception duty again today. She'll make sure everyone is safe."

Lady Marie, Anahira, and Sam led us forward, keeping to the shadows created by the other trees in the garden.

My gaze darted from left to right.

What if we're being attacked by people with green skin?

I imagined a gang of angry, green-skinned warriors watching us from the surrounding trees. The image made me move closer to Lady Marie.

We reached the edge of the tree line and paused, using the cover of the trees to check out the back of Dux Manor. Everything looked normal.

It was getting dark though, darker than it should really be.

"Alright, girls," Lady Marie whispered. "The threat must be located at the front of Dux Manor. We'll need to move quickly around the side. Stay alert. I'm not sure what we will encounter."

We all nodded in response.

"Let's go. Quickly now!"

We moved onto the grass area and then onto the paving stones bordering Dux Manor. I glanced inside a window, expecting to see something large and scary about to smash through the window and leap at me.

"Dux Manor has its own protections, Maggie," Lady Marie whispered next to me, noting my attention on the window. "If the threat is anywhere, it will be outside."

I turned my head away from the window and focused on the trees and garden area.

Please let the threat not be too big.

"Careful what you be wishin' for, Maggie."

I whipped around to find Tylwyth and Teg sitting at an outside table, with Tylwyth sitting on one of the chairs and Teg lounging *on* the table.

"Aye, 'tis not always size what matters."

I opened my mouth to call Lady Marie, but Tylwyth and Teg disappeared. I turned back to find that the others had made it to the end of the building. I ran to close the distance.

Lady Marie turned to me as I caught up. "Is everything alright, Maggie?"

"I just saw Tylwyth and Teg," I answered, my breath coming in short, sharp bursts.

"Where?"

I pointed at the table behind me.

Lady Marie stared at the now-empty table and shook her head. "I'm afraid we have more to be concerned about than Tylwyth and Teg right now."

We turned the corner and cautiously edged past a hexagon-shaped extension sticking out from Dux Manor. In the strengthening darkness, it was hard to make out finer details but there appeared to be a lot of activity at the flagpole area, near the picnic tables at the front of Dux Manor. Lady Marie signaled for us to move to the cover provided by a tree tucked in tight next to the manor.

We moved forward and tried to make out what was happening around the flagpole. My eyes adjusted to the gloom, and I gasped. There was a truly massive figure standing by the flagpole. A figure easily the height of the pole, although it seemed way too thin for its height, and it appeared to have at least six ridiculously long arms, if the movement at its sides was anything to go by.

What on Earth is it?

"Do you have it, Razia?" Lady Marie asked.

Razia reached up to touch her glasses and shook her head. "Sorry, Lady Marie. It's too dark for the glasses to get a good read of the situation."

"Alright, girls. Just like in your training," Lady Marie instructed. "We may only get one chance at this, so no mistakes."

I couldn't miss a target as big as that one, could I?

"Anahira, Sam. When you are ready," Lady Marie said. "Please lead us out."

Anahira looked at the rest of us and grinned. "Let's do this!"

Anahira and Kayla left the cover of the tree and rushed across the paving stones and the driveway to the right-hand side of the flagpole area. Sam and Razia did the same on the left-hand side. Lady Marie and I hurried into the middle, and I grasped one of the silver discs, ready to throw.

Golden ropes flew out from the right and left of me and quickly attached to the... No! The ropes flew through the air as the mysterious giant figure shattered into hundreds of tiny pieces. The pieces briefly swirled about and then formed three separate clumps, hovering in the air above us.

"Girls, retreat!" Lady Marie yelled.

I turned to Lady Marie and caught a glimpse of something silver in her right hand. It was a silver disc. She must have been carrying one in case I missed.

Oh, that's just great.

I stared dumbfounded at her as Kayla, Razia, and Sam rushed past me. Anahira grabbed my shoulder and spun me around.

"C'mon, Maggie," Anahira yelled as she half-dragged me away.

We had nearly reached the cover of the tree when Anahira cried out in pain. I turned to her and saw a group of the flying creatures shooting some kind of tiny darts. Several hit Anahira on her arms and neck, and she cried out in more pain. I managed to support her on the way back to the others.

"To me. Quickly!" Lady Marie urged us to hurry.

We made the cover of the tree, and Lady Marie used another golden device, almost like a remote for a car, to deploy some kind of screen. The air around us shimmered like it did when a doorway to another world opened, although it didn't form a door, but a cocoon that completely covered us. The darts from the flying creatures somehow bounced off the screen.

"That should keep us safe for the time being," Lady Marie concluded, putting the device away in a pocket. "Now, how are we doing?"

To my shock, I noticed Anahira *bleeding* from several tiny wounds on her neck and arms. Sam was in a similar state, with Kayla and Razia also bleeding from tiny wounds on their neck and hands, but they were nowhere near as bad as Anahira and Sam.

Lady Marie took in the condition of the other girls and gasped. She turned to me. "Maggie?"

I did a quick self-examination. I hadn't been hit anywhere. "I'm okay, Lady Marie."

Lady Marie seemed surprised, but she continued on. "We are safe here for the moment. But, girls, how badly are you hurt?"

"Not too bad, Lady Marie," Anahira replied. "It looks worse than it feels."

"Yeah, we can handle it," Sam added.

Kayla and Razia nodded, but they didn't seem like they were okay at all.

"I'm so sorry, girls," Lady Marie admitted.

I looked at Anahira and she responded with a shaky smile. Always the brave one. I would have been crying by now.

"Razia. Are you able to identify what we're facing?" Lady Marie asked.

Razia reached up to her glasses. She grimaced as she did so. The wounds in her hand must have been quite painful.

I looked out beyond our protective screen and saw a mass of flying figures swarming all around the barrier as though they were a hive of large, angry bees.

"I have them, Lady Marie," Razia said. "They are almost humanoid in shape but also have wings. They look like sprites or pixies but are dressed in darker colors than what we might expect. I think they are shooting darts out of something like a pipe or a flute, although it is too small to fully make out."

Sprites or pixies? We're being attacked by a horde of tiny fairy-like creatures?

"How many, ah, *pixies* are there?" Lady Marie asked.

"Too many to count. Hundreds. Possibly thousands."

Thousands?

What good were golden ropes and silver discs against thousands of armed and angry pixies, if that was indeed what they were?

"What do we do now, Lady Marie?" Anahira asked.

Lady Marie took a moment to answer. "I'm not certain. Nothing like this has ever happened before. I do know that we will need help." Lady Marie took out her phone.

"Who will you call?" Sam asked. "The police?"

"I don't think the police will know what to do either, Sam," Lady Marie responded. "No, I'm going to call another Council member."

Lady Marie turned away to make the call, and I looked back to the protective screen, almost crying out in shock. Tylwyth and Teg stood calmly just on the other side of the screen, in their own cocoon of space.

"It looks like you're havin' a wee bit of trouble," Tylwyth said.

"A wee bit, indeed," Teg added.

Wee bit of trouble?

That was one way of putting it.

"Course, this is only the beginnin'," Tylwyth stated.

"Aye. Maggie won't be likin' it when they grow," Teg said with a grin.

"What do you mean?" I asked.

"They'll get bigger," Tylwyth explained.

"Much, much bigger," Teg added.

That didn't sound good. "When?"

"Soon," Tylwyth suggested.

"Very soon," Teg concluded.

Oh, no.

"What can we do?"

"We, Maggie? I'd thought you decided not to aid us?" Tylwyth responded.

"Please," I pleaded.

Tylwyth exchanged a look with Teg. "Oh, Maggie. You melt our hearts."

"Does that mean you'll help?"

"Aye," Teg replied. "But you'll be havin' to trust us."

I didn't really have a choice, did I?

"Come and join us, Maggie," Tylwyth invited me forward.

Join them? Outside the protective shield?

But I'll be attacked!

"Come on, Maggie." Teg extended a hand right through the screen. The protective barrier acted as though it was a thin layer of water, allowing Teg's hand to pass through. "There's no time."

I didn't know if the screen would allow me to pass through, but I somehow found the courage to take Teg's hand and step forward. My progress was halted with another hand grabbing my arm.

"Maggie!" Anahira exclaimed. "What are you doing?"

I turned back to Anahira and saw all of the others watching me, including Lady Marie, who still had her phone to her ear.

"It's alright, Anahira," I replied, strangely calm. "I've got this."

Anahira let go of my arm. I held tightly to Teg and walked through the shimmering screen, just like Teg's hand had done. I glanced back to see the screen close behind me. Anahira looked like she was about to follow me, her face pressed close to the other side of the screen. I quickly shook my head and turned to Tylwyth and Teg.

Tylwyth grinned. "To the flagpole, Maggie."

"Aye," Teg added. "To the breach."

I made sure I stayed in step with Tylwyth and Teg as they walked across the courtyard. The invading pixies surprisingly left us alone, and we walked unopposed to the flagpole.

The pixies swarmed around the flagpole, with the thickest amount near the base. Razia's count of thousands seemed about right.

"Okay. So now what?'

"You've still got one of those silver discs?" Tylwyth asked.

"They won't work. There's too many of them."

"But you're not goin' to use it on them," Tylwyth responded.

I'm not?

"You're goin' to use it on the flagpole," Teg explained.

The flagpole?

"Aye, Maggie. The flagpole," Teg confirmed.

"Place the disc in the slot at the base of the flagpole," Tylwyth instructed.

"There's a slot?"

"Aye, Maggie. The pole will accept the disc," Teg added.

I stared at Tylwyth and Teg, and they both grinned in response.

The pole will accept the disc.

Like some kind of slot machine? Oh well, what did I have to lose?

I stepped forward.

"Maggie," Tylwyth said. "After placin' the disc, get out, quickly."

"Quickly?"

"Aye," Teg added. "As quick as you can, like."

"Okay," I nervously replied.

I stepped into the circle surrounding the flagpole and tried my best not to freak out. The flapping of the pixies' wings sounded really loud, almost like the beating of hundreds of tiny drums, and I felt small gusts of wind as I edged closer to the pole.

I definitely wouldn't like it if these pixies got bigger.

"Nice pixies," I whispered, as I bent down to the base of the pole. My hand shook as I held the disc out in front of me. Was I just supposed to put it in a specific place? I inched my hand forward and the disc was sucked out of my hand into the pole.

I stared at my empty hand and then remembered I was supposed to get away, *quickly*.

I'd only taken one step backward when the flagpole suddenly dropped as though being pushed from above by a giant hand. The pole descended into the ground like a pin into a pin-cushion. The circular ground around the pole disappeared and I momentarily hung suspended in midair before I started to fall.

I screamed as the invading pixies began falling beside me.

I was being sucked into their world!

My body jerked to a stop and I hung suspended in midair, as though strong arms had just grabbed me. I was pulled backward and yanked away from the sinkhole. I managed to look up just in time to see all the pixies around Dux Manor get swept into the hole as though being washed down a giant drain. Then, with the loudest *pop* I'd ever heard, the flagpole returned to its standing position and the ground became solid again.

I felt sunlight on my face and turned to look around me. The darkness and gloom had disappeared with the pixies. It was still quite some time until sunset.

"Maggie!" Anahira yelled as she ran to me, despite the pain she must have felt from her wounds. "Are you alright?"

"I'm okay," I replied as I struggled to my feet.

Tylwyth and Teg must have somehow saved me from falling into the hole.

Anahira gave me a hug.

"Maggie, thank goodness you're alright," Lady Marie exclaimed as she arrived on the scene. "How on Earth did you know what to do?"

"Tylwyth and Teg told me," I replied.

Lady Marie looked around for Tylwyth and Teg, but they were nowhere in sight. She turned her attention back to me. "The pixies didn't attack you?"

"No, Lady Marie. I think Tylwyth and Teg gave me some form of protection, though I don't know how."

"You are bound to us, Maggie Thatcher," Tylwyth announced as he and Teg suddenly appeared next to me.

"Aye. And they be not pixies, Lady Studfall," Teg added.

Lady Marie stared warily at Tylwyth and Teg. "I thank you, Master Tylwyth and Master Teg, for your kindness in helping Maggie."

Tylwyth and Teg bowed in response.

"We still hold to the treaty, Lady Studfall," Tylwyth responded.

"Aye. Even if others lose faith," Teg added.

Lady Marie did not look pleased.

"'Twas a small matter," Tylwyth continued. "Though those that you wrongly call pixies would have ravaged your world."

"Aye. You might be mistakin' them for brownies," Teg added. "But you couldn't be more wrong. Those devils are mortal enemies to the brownies."

Brownies?

What were Tylwyth and Teg talking about?

"Do you still refuse to aid us, Lady Studfall?" Tylwyth asked.

Lady Marie looked at Tylwyth but remained tight-lipped.

"'Tis a shame," Tylwyth responded. "That attack was one of the weakest."

"Aye. The protections are already fadin', which means Prince Draikern must be gainin' strength. You'll soon be facin' worse attacks," Teg added.

"Far worse," Tylwyth suggested.

"And we won't be here to save you," Teg concluded.

"'Tis a real shame," Tylwyth repeated.

Tylwyth and Teg disappeared.

I really wished they would stop doing that. But when I turned to look at Lady Marie, I realized I had bigger things to worry about.

I've never seen anyone with such a look of fear in their eyes.

12
BEST-LAID PLANS

" **A**lright, girls, how are we feeling?" Lady Marie asked. We were back in the Guardians' command center and had spent the better part of the last half an hour tending to the wounds inflicted by the pixies. Or *not-pixies*. Or whatever they were. Faatimah came down to help, and her experience in first aid proved invaluable.

She also told us that the rest of the Dux Manor staff, the non-Guardians sort, had no idea that anything strange was happening outside. The attack was apparently over in little more than five minutes, but it certainly hadn't felt like it at the time.

"I'm all good, Lady Marie," Anahira answered.

"I'm fine," Sam boasted.

"Good," Lady Marie responded. "Razia? Kayla? Are you okay?"

Razia nodded and Kayla grinned.

"Nothing more than a few insect bites," Kayla concluded.

"Yes, well, I'm glad it was nothing more," Lady Marie responded.

"It wasn't your fault, Lady Marie," Anahira said.

Lady Marie grimaced. "You are under my care and protection."

"But you've never encountered creatures like that before," I added.

"That is precisely what concerns me the most," Lady Marie replied.

We fell silent as we watched Lady Marie in an apparent state of unease.

"I am sorry, girls. I never thought I would put you in danger when I recruited you."

"It's all good, Lady Marie," Anahira asserted.

Lady Marie smiled, but her smile lacked conviction. "I'm afraid that it isn't all good, not at all, but I do appreciate the sentiment. I am extremely proud of the way you are all handling this. Especially you, Maggie."

"Me?" I asked, surprised at being singled out.

"If it wasn't for your bravery, we would have been defeated."

My bravery.

Had I heard Lady Marie correctly?

"It took a lot of courage to do what you did," Lady Marie continued. "We all owe you a debt of gratitude."

I looked around at the other girls and found them smiling, even Sam.

"But I really didn't do anything."

"You put yourself in danger in order to protect the rest of us."

"But Tylwyth and Teg did most of it."

"No, Maggie. You did," Lady Marie responded. "And we thank you. Tylwyth and Teg certainly helped, but you acted with great courage and bravery."

Had I really done that?

"That will certainly do for today, girls," Lady Marie added. "I will need to urgently report on recent events to the Council and fear it will be a long meeting. Given the attack we need to decide what our next steps are. Now, if you can, please arrange for your parents to come and pick you up. I can organize a ride for anyone who needs it."

Anahira grinned, but I didn't think I wanted another ride in a self-driven Rolls-Royce. Not because it was unsafe. Just because, well, I could have done without any more excitement for the day.

"Please remember the reason why we met together today, to prepare our application for the Wayfinder World Friendship award. I fear we may need one more day."

"What are you saying, Lady Marie?" Anahira asked.

"We may have to ask your parents and your school for one more day to complete our application," Lady Marie responded.

"But…" Kayla started to say.

"Yes, Kayla. But what we really need is time to respond to the threat to our world," Lady Marie stated. "I will confirm later tonight when I have discussed the matter with the Council. Just be ready to convince your parents we will need an extra day."

Another school day would be taken up with the business of the Guardians.

* * *

"Good morning, girls," Lady Marie opened the meeting. "How are we feeling?"

It was 9 A.M. on Tuesday morning, and we'd gathered once more around the table in the secret Guardians' command center. Everyone was looking better than they did yesterday, which meant the wounds must have healed well.

The other girls had all responded positively to Lady Marie's welcome.

"I'm okay," I replied.

"I'm glad," Lady Marie responded. "I trust that you were able to answer any questions about the Wayfinder World Friendship award?"

I glanced at Anahira. My mum had dropped Anahira and me off this morning, just like she had picked us up from Dux Manor yesterday. She'd been very interested in hearing more about the award. Somehow, Anahira and I managed to make the Wayfinder World Friendship award sound not only real but also highly sought after, even though Mum had never heard of it before. Mum was most impressed with Anahira's account of how prestigious the award was in New Zealand, with the Prime Minister personally presenting the award. That had sealed it for my mum. She was very impressed with the New Zealand Prime Minister.

"Razia? Any problems?" Lady Marie asked, noting that Razia had dropped her head.

"I do understand the need for secrecy, Lady Marie, but I did not like lying to my parents."

Oh, yes.

With everything that was going on, I somehow passed over the fact that I too hadn't been honest. I didn't like lying to my parents either. Keeping certain things secret, like the Guardians, was a bit different than telling an outright lie.

"I understand, and I sincerely apologize," Lady Marie admitted. "Honesty, integrity, and trustworthiness are ideals we strive for within Wayfinder Girls and yes, within Guardians, as much as we are able. Please note that there is now an official Wayfinder World Friendship award, something my husband and I were able to enact last night, so you have not necessarily been lying. A bit of a stretch, I know, but there it is."

Why *was* the award discussed last night? Surely there were one or two more urgent matters.

"Thank you, Lady Marie," Razia answered, although she still did not look comfortable.

"There's something else, isn't there, Razia?" Lady Marie inquired.

"My parents are unhappy about me missing school. They reluctantly allowed me to come today but insist I must go back to school tomorrow."

"Yes, I was going to come to that. The Council agrees with Razia's parents. You will all be going back to school tomorrow. Which means the only time we have for planning and preparation is today."

"Sorry, Lady Marie, but planning and preparation for what?" Anahira asked.

Lady Marie took a long, slow breath. "We come to the matter at hand. You know I attended an emergency Council meeting last night. What you don't know is that we weren't the only ones to be attacked yesterday."

"Who else was attacked?" Sam asked, sitting forward in her seat.

"Across the world, there were three other Wayfinder regional centers that suffered some kind of attack, Tristar Lodge in the United States of America, Te Whare Aratai in New Zealand, and Dari House in Nigeria."

I shot a look at Anahira. Mention of New Zealand had caused her face to knot in concern. She probably had family still living there. I hope no one was hurt.

"Is everyone okay?" Kayla asked, eyes wide.

"Thankfully, yes, Kayla," Lady Marie answered. "By all accounts, we suffered the worst attack here. All of the other attacks involved solitary creatures who were quickly sent back to their worlds using the golden ropes and silver discs."

"Hang on, so there are other Guardians teams?" Sam asked, frowning.

"Not precisely, Sam," Lady Marie responded. "We have ex-Guardians placed as leaders at each of our regional centers, but none of the centers are as fully equipped as we are here. And none have secret underground bases, I can assure you. Each center has a limited supply of ropes and discs. We are fortunate indeed that the right people were able to respond to the threats. It is certainly not something anyone had ever anticipated happening."

"It was a coordinated surprise attack," Sam concluded.

"Indeed it was, Sam," Lady Marie confirmed.

"Do you have any details about the creatures that broke through the doorways?" Razia asked.

"Only vague reports at this stage, Razia," Lady Marie answered. "One report seems to indicate that the otherworldly creature was not overly aggressive, but instead appeared disoriented and confused. We are still waiting for more details to emerge. I am simply grateful that the matter was swiftly dealt with and that no one was hurt."

Which was not the case with the attack we suffered with the pixies, or not-pixies.

"What does this all mean, Lady Marie?" I asked.

"It could mean one of two things, Maggie," Lady Marie replied, taking considerable care over her words. "The Faerie Queen might well be losing her fight against Prince Draikern, meaning that the doorways between worlds are becoming increasingly unprotected, or…"

Lady Marie fell silent.

"Or what, Lady Marie?" Anahira prompted.

"Or the creatures were deliberately allowed into our world as a warning," Lady Marie answered.

A warning? But who would do such a thing?

"Tylwyth and Teg," I gasped, answering my own unspoken question.

Lady Marie nodded. "Yes, Maggie. The attacks happened just after we informed Tylwyth and Teg we couldn't get the Koh-i-Noor diamond. Was that mere coincidence, or something else?"

It did seem connected, unfortunately.

"Is it also a coincidence that the worst attack happened at Dux Manor?" Lady Marie continued. "An attack defeated with Tylwyth and Teg's help."

"So, you do think it was a warning?" I asked. "That Tylwyth and Teg deliberately allowed creatures into our world to attack us?"

Lady Marie sighed. "It appears to be the most likely scenario."

"But what about the ancient treaties?" I protested. "If it wasn't for Tylwyth and Teg's help, we would have failed to protect Dux Manor. Who knows what damage those pixies or not-pixies could have caused."

I didn't know why I was sticking up for Tylwyth and Teg. I mean, they had tricked me into helping them and they had threatened to take me to their world, but I had started to get a bit fond of them both.

"Yes, well. I'm afraid I cannot be certain of anything," Lady

Marie responded. "But you are right, Maggie. Tylwyth and Teg did help us, whatever their motives were."

Their motives?

"You still think they were behind the attack?" I asked.

"I really can't say for sure," Lady Marie admitted. "But warning or not, I'm afraid we can't really take the chance."

"What are you saying, Lady Marie?" Anahira asked.

"The Council of Guardians has reluctantly decided that we must try and return the Koh-i-Noor diamond to the world of Faerie," Lady Marie stated calmly.

We all stared at Lady Marie in shock.

"But that means acting against our queen," Kayla protested.

Lady Marie raised her hand. "I know. The Council deemed that we would actually be defending the queen if we gave the Koh-i-Noor diamond back to its rightful owner."

Kayla turned away and shook her head.

"I realize it is difficult to accept, but there is a tangible threat to our world," Lady Marie continued. "To save the queen and her realm, we may have to take one of her Crown Jewels."

Stunned silence enveloped the unit.

I recalled Razia's detailed explanation of the history of the Koh-i-Noor diamond and how its ownership was claimed by nations other than England, some even going so far as to insist it had been stolen. So, was it okay to return something that had been stolen? But we wouldn't be returning it to another country, we would be returning it to the world of Faerie, a world that was making an even older claim to the diamond.

"But Lady Marie," Anahira said, breaking the silence. "Even if returning the diamond is the right thing to do, there's no way we can do it. It's impossible."

"I'm supposed to give it to Tylwyth and Teg tomorrow," I added. "Tomorrow!"

"Well, yes," Lady Marie replied. "I didn't say it was going to be easy."

Easy? It was nowhere in the same universe as easy.

"To complicate matters further, we only have today to plan. It is back to school for you all tomorrow," Lady Marie explained.

I stared at Lady Marie in amazement. We only had one day to come up with a plan to get one of the Crown Jewels and return it to the Faerie Queen.

Well, that's just perfect.

"Now, I fully understand anyone's reluctance to proceed with such a plan. I will happily release you from this task. You will still remain in Guardians, but you will not have to act against your values and beliefs," Lady Marie asserted. "Do you understand?"

I glanced at the other girls, feeling guilty that I was the one responsible for this situation. Only Anahira returned my gaze.

"So, who is willing to continue?"

Anahira's hand shot up first, then Sam's. Razia reached up to adjust her hijab before she, too, raised her hand. Kayla frowned, looking around at the others.

"I guess if you are sure we'll be saving the queen and her realm," Kayla said as she raised her hand.

"And the rest of the world!" Anahira added.

"The Koh-i-Noor diamond doesn't even belong to England," Razia stated calmly, although the break in her voice betrayed emotion she rarely showed.

I glanced at Razia. I couldn't tell if she was angry or sad, maybe both, but she certainly didn't seem to believe that England had the sole right to the diamond.

"Thank you," Lady Marie said as she looked at the raised hands. "I do appreciate it is not an easy decision. The Council debated it at great length, but it is still difficult to accept."

"Will we get a badge for it?" Sam asked.

Lady Marie turned to Sam, and it seemed she was about to explode, just like Mr. Solon, my chemistry teacher at school, but instead, Lady Marie burst out laughing.

"Oh, Sam," Lady Marie stated. "You are a delight. Do you really think we have a *'Stealing the Crown Jewels'* badge we could award you?"

"Something like that," Sam replied.

We all laughed, even Sam. The awkward laughter covered our shared anxiety.

"Right. Well, thank you, Sam. I needed that," Lady Marie added.

Sam grinned, which was very unlike her.

"We must now get to work," Lady Marie asserted. "Razia, do you still think we would be able to make a duplicate of the Koh-i-Noor diamond?"

"Yes. I think it might work, Lady Marie. I'll need to find the right material."

"I'll show you where to look," Lady Marie responded. "Can I ask Kayla to help you?"

"Yes, that would be good."

Lady Marie turned to Kayla. "Is that okay?"

"Sure. I'm great with bling," Kayla said with a wide grin.

"Yes, thank you," Lady Marie answered with a tight smile. "Anahira and Sam, can I ask you to please get as much information as you can about the security at the Tower of London?"

Anahira and Sam looked at each other and nodded.

"Good. Well, let's meet back together in one hour and report on our progress."

"But what about me, Lady Marie?" I asked.

Lady Marie turned to me. "I'm afraid we'll need Tylwyth and Teg's help on this. I'll gather all of the resources I can, but we won't be able to succeed without magical assistance."

Which meant I had to try and summon them again.

"Alright, girls," Lady Marie stated, concluding the meeting. "Do your best. The fate of the world is in your hands."

The fate of the world? That's not good. I really don't cope well with pressure.

⚜ ⚜ ⚜

"Who would like to begin?" Lady Marie asked. "Razia?"

An hour had passed, and we were all due to report back. I had nothing to say. Despite my best efforts, Tylwyth and Teg had not shown up. I'd tried everything. Asking out loud, asking in my head, whispering, shouting. I even tried singing at one point.

Singing!

I'd tried it in every space inside and also outside in the garden. But no response. Nothing at all.

We're never going to be able to pull this off.

"Thank you, Lady Marie," Razia responded. "Kayla and I have tried several different materials, and I think we have found one that will work, although we won't know until we have tested it fully."

"Will you be able to make it in time?" Lady Marie inquired.

"Yes, Lady Marie. We will resume testing after this meeting. We may have to adjust the programming of the 3D printer to get it absolutely right, but we should have a duplicate ready in time. We can run the printer overnight or even tomorrow, if necessary, right?"

"Yes, I can look after it, as long as you show me how."

Razia nodded, and Kayla grinned.

"Anahira? Sam?" Lady Marie continued. "What do you have for us?"

Anahira indicated for Sam to go first.

"I focused on the guards," Sam responded. "It's a bit of a worry. I mean, I've been to the Tower of London before, a few years ago with my cousins, and the guards were cool to look at, but I never realized just how many there were."

I'd never been to the Tower myself, but I guessed the guards were like the ones outside Buckingham Palace, dressed in bold uniforms and taking their jobs very seriously.

"Anyway," Sam continued. "The Tower of London is an ancient fortress, palace, prison, and active barracks all in one. There are at least thirty-seven permanent guards, called Yeoman Warders, who live there with their families in something called the Waterloo Block. All of these guards have come from the British Armed Forces. In addition, there is the Tower Guard, made up of twenty-two soldiers from the British Army. They put a Field Marshal or General in charge, someone called the Constable of the Tower, and the second-in-charge is called the Lieutenant of the Tower and is also an Army officer."

That sounded like a lot of guards. And they were all soldiers, not your typical security guards. Sam was right when she said we needed an army; it sounded like there was already an army protecting the Tower.

"Very good, Sam," Lady Marie responded. "My husband happens to know the current Constable of the Tower; they served together in the past. Is there anything else?"

"Oh, yes, Lady Marie," Sam added, not dwelling on the status of Sir Edmund Studfall. "I was just describing the military guards. There is also a security team like you'd expect at a bank or at the airport. There is a Chief Security Officer, a Site Security Manager, and a Control Room. There are patrols and bag searches and security-pass systems. The lot."

It should be really easy, then.

"Oh, and there are also ravens," Sam said.

"Ravens?" Kayla asked. "Like, as in birds?"

"About seven or eight at the moment," Sam answered. "Looked after by another guard, someone called the Ravenmaster. There's some legend claiming that there must be at least six ravens at the Tower, or the Kingdom will fall."

I stared at Sam. She was very sincere in her report, but I was struck more and more by the sense of an undercurrent of magic running throughout England. Like the six ravens who protect the Kingdom. Silly superstition or something more?

"Yes, well, we certainly don't want the Kingdom to fall," Lady Marie responded. "That is why we are embarking on this rather desperate act."

Desperate? Lady Marie doesn't hold out too much hope then.

"Thank you, Sam," Lady Marie added. "Anahira?"

"I focused on access to the Tower and the Jewels," Anahira began. "As Sam has said, it's a huge fortress. The White Tower dominates the middle of the inner courtyard, with the Waterloo Block barracks behind it. The Crown Jewels are located in the Jewel House, an underground vault next to the barracks. The

Jewels are on display in the vault, protected by bomb-proof glass and watched by one hundred hidden CCTV cameras."

One hundred hidden cameras? Wow!

"Visitors can view the Crown Jewels by going down into the vault," Anahira continued. "It is quite a narrow staircase and it is quite dimly lit. There is a moving viewing platform that people can stand on to get a closer look, behind the bomb-proof glass. There are more than just crowns on display. There are also orbs, scepters, robes, and dining vessels. It is a huge collection that's supposed to be worth at least three billion pounds."

Three billion pounds? Good grief. How can one family hoard that much wealth?

"Oh, and there are also swords and full suits of armor, including armor for horses, on display in the White Tower," Anahira added.

That's good to know. I could really do with a new suit of armor.

"Thank you, Anahira," Lady Marie responded. "Can you please confirm when visiting times are?"

"Oh, yes, Lady Marie. Visiting hours go to 5:30 P.M. There are Twilight Tours which start at 7 P.M., but you have to book these in advance, and the last one for the year is tomorrow night, and it is fully booked."

Why ask about visiting hours?

Were we just going to visit like tourists, go down to the vault, reach through the glass, and replace the diamond?

Easy.

Although we needed a distraction and a way to avoid the cameras, the armed guards, and the security system. And then a way to get to the diamond, remove it from the crown, and smuggle it out of the Tower of London.

Not so easy then.

"Maggie? Anything to report?" Lady Marie asked.

I glanced at Lady Marie and at the expectant faces of the others.

"Sorry, Lady Marie. I haven't been able to summon Tylwyth or Teg."

"Oh, dear. We really do need their help."

"Yes, but, even if they helped, what can we do?" I protested. "As Sam said earlier, we'd need an army. Or at least a massive distraction, and we don't have..."

I stopped speaking and stared at the corner of the room.

"What is it? Are Tylwyth and Teg here?" Lady Marie asked, following my gaze.

"No, Lady Marie, I'm just remembering something they said, about those pixies, who weren't pixies, but were the enemies of the brownies."

"Yes," Lady Marie answered. "What of it?"

"Who are the brownies?" I wasn't entirely sure why I was asking, but it was something like a crazy hunch.

I mean, why not add a little bit more crazy into the mix?

Lady Marie seemed a little put out by my question. "The brownies that Tylwyth and Teg refer to were, I think, kindly fairy-like creatures who once, a long time ago, did small chores in households when humans were asleep."

Chores? Like cleaning and tidying? Like what Tylwyth and Teg did in my kitchen?

"Are the Girlguiding Brownies named after them?" I asked.

"Well, in a way. Lord Baden-Powell renamed them Brownies after girls had complained about their original name, Rosebuds. He got the name Brownies from a story written by Juliann Ewing in 1870. In the story, two children, Tommy and Betty, learn that they can be helpful brownies instead of being lazy boggarts."

The only boggarts I knew were from Harry Potter, and they weren't lazy.

Scary, yes. But not lazy.

Helpful brownies though, now that was something I could maybe work with.

"Are the Trailfinder troops similar to the Brownies?" I asked.

"You could say that, yes," Lady Marie answered. "As you know, Trailfinder is the name we have given to our program for seven- to ten-year-old girls."

"How many Trailfinder troops do we have in London?"

"Well, I'm not sure it is terribly relevant but there are nearly seventy Trailfinder troops in central London, or over one hundred Trailfinder troops, if you consider greater London."

Each Trailfinder troop had up to twenty-five girls. So if they were over one hundred Trailfinder troops in London, that was a lot of girls.

"Why do you ask, Maggie?" Lady Marie said.

"I think we have found our army."

The other girls looked at me as though I'd lost my mind, but I was fully committed now.

"Lady Marie, do you think your husband could use his influence to convince the Tower of London to allow a special one-off visit? Maybe for tomorrow night?"

Lady Marie considered me, her head tilted and her eyes narrowed. She must have been trying to make sense of what I was saying.

Lady Marie's eyes suddenly widened, and she mouthed a silent *oh*. "Yes, Maggie. I think treating our Trailfinder troops to an enchanting visit to the Tower of London on Halloween might work out well. Although Edmund would have to pull in some pretty big favors."

"Can it be done?" I asked.

"I believe so," Lady Marie answered. "Sir Edmund Studfall is a name very highly regarded within the military. If anyone can do it, he can. Of course, I'd need to convince the Council and the Trailfinder leaders that it's a good idea. All at extremely short notice."

I would leave the details to Lady Marie to sort out. There was more than enough for me to worry about. Just suggesting the idea of visiting the Tower of London had sent my heart racing.

"So, we somehow get some Trailfinder troops a special visit to the Tower on Halloween," Anahira said, catching on. "But how does that help us get the Koh-i-Noor diamond?"

"If I'm right," I responded, my words coming out in a breathless rush, "the guards will be so preoccupied with a horde of screaming and overexcited girls, that it might give us an opportunity to get to the Crown Jewels."

"Why will they be screaming?" Kayla asked, her forehead knotted in concern.

"Oh, just something I saw on Bedknobs and Broomsticks," I answered, surprising myself by how calm I sounded.

"Bedknobs and Broomsticks?" Kayla responded. "What's that?"

"An old Disney movie," I answered.

"Oh, great," Sam responded. "Not again."

"Yes," I replied. "It might just work."

"What might just work?" Sam asked, looking frustrated.

"Well, it all depends on whether Tylwyth and Teg can do what I think they can do."

I turned to Lady Marie, who watched me with almost a sparkle in her eyes, but I didn't know what else to say. It all relied on Tylwyth and Teg.

"Aye. We can be doin' that, Maggie."

The other girls gasped, and I turned to find Tylwyth sitting at the opposite end of the table, with Teg sitting *on* the edge of the table. They had probably been present the whole time.

"We can't touch the Mynydd o Olau directly, mind," Teg explained.

"But we can be gettin' someone in without bein' seen," Tylwyth added.

"Especially if the guards are busy, like," Teg said.

"The ravens will help," Tylwyth asserted.

"Aye, the ravens," Teg concluded.

I didn't know what the ravens had to do with it, but I'd finally gotten the response from Tylwyth and Teg I needed.

Tomorrow, the Trailfinder troops are going to invade the Tower of London.

13
TOWER HEIST

"**A**re you nearly ready?" Mum called up the stairs. "They will be here soon."

"Yes!" I yelled from the bathroom as I studied my reflection in the mirror. I had my full Wayfinder uniform on, a black polo shirt with yellow trim underneath my yellow and black hoodie, with a black skirt and black leggings. It looked good.

I'd been trying to get my hair into some sort of order, but my mess of unruly dark curls refused to cooperate.

Oh well, what is messy hair when you're about to steal one of the Crown Jewels?

I examined my reflection and shook my head. It had been such a painfully slow day. I had to sit through eight periods of school when all I could think about was the Koh-i-Noor diamond and the Tower of London.

Is it really the right thing to do?

I thought so. It made sense, given everything that had happened and the risks of not returning the diamond to its rightful owner, but it still felt wrong. If only the queen hadn't been overseas, Lady Marie might have convinced her to give us the diamond.

Am I crazy to think that it just might work?

That was the really scary part—that it just might work. It wouldn't have been so scary if I knew exactly what Tylwyth and Teg would do, but I didn't. All I had was that they knew what I meant when I talked about Bedknobs and Broomsticks, and they would handle it when the time came. And that they needed me to handle the Koh-i-Noor diamond; they would get me access, *somehow*. Oh, and something about the ravens helping, but how they would help was beyond me.

Of course, if I could have talked to Tylwyth and Teg, I might have discovered more. But I had not seen them since their appearance at Dux Manor yesterday. They had a really irritating habit of disappearing and not responding to any of my summons.

Just like brothers.

So I'd been forced to focus on trivial things such as English, Chemistry, Geography, and even Latin, when all I wanted to do was talk to Tylwyth and Teg, or at least talk to Lady Marie and Anahira about tonight's plan.

School can be so inconvenient sometimes.

"Maggie," Mum called up the stairs again. "I think they're here."

I shot out of the bathroom and flew down the stairs to find Mum peering out of the lounge window at the street.

"Mum? What are you doing?"

Mum turned from the window. "They've got a silver Rolls-Royce."

My heart sank. Surely Lady Marie hadn't sent a self-driving car to pick me up, had she?

There was a polite knock at the door.

I opened the door to find Lady Marie on the doorstep, in her full Wayfinder uniform, decorated with a huge number of pins.

"Good afternoon, Maggie," Lady Marie said in greeting. "Are you ready for this?"

I nodded, reaching for my meds bag hanging in its usual place by the door.

Lady Marie noticed my mum lurking behind me. "Good afternoon, Mrs. Thatcher," Lady Marie said with a smile. "I trust you are well?"

"Oh, very well, thank you, Lady Marie," Mum said, while almost curtsying. "What a wonderful idea, taking the girls to the Tower of London on Halloween. Such fun."

"Yes, well, we have Maggie to thank for the idea."

Mum turned to me. "Maggie, you never told me that."

"Sorry, I must have forgotten."

"Well, aren't you clever."

"She most certainly is," Lady Marie added. "Now, if you don't mind, we have a lot of potentially overexcited Trailfinder troops to look after."

"Oh, yes, I mustn't keep you," Mum replied. "Have a wonderful time, Maggie."

I turned and hugged Mum goodbye. I would either return home after helping to pull off one of the greatest heists in the history of the world, or Mum would get a visit from the police soon after I'd been arrested.

I left my home and followed Lady Marie to the Rolls-Royce. Lady Marie opened the back door of the car for me, and I got in.

"Hi, Maggie," Anahira greeted me from the other seat. "You all good?"

"Sure," I replied, feeling anything but good. "Just a normal day, right?"

Lady Marie got in the passenger seat. "Maggie, I would like to introduce my husband, Sir Edmund Studfall."

"You can just call me Ed," Sir Studfall responded from the driver's seat. He was a gray-haired gentleman with kindly eyes and a quick smile. His hands were resting on the steering wheel, so at least the car was being driven by a human this time.

"It is nice to meet you, Sir Edmund," I responded, not willing to call him Ed. It didn't feel at all right.

"The pleasure is mine. Marie speaks very highly of you."

She does?

"Now," Sir Edmund continued, turning to Lady Marie. "Are *we* ready for this?"

"Yes, dear," Lady Marie responded. "The future of the realm, and possibly the entire world, depends on what happens tonight."

"So, absolutely no pressure then," Sir Edmund replied.

"None whatsoever, dear."

"Alright. To the Tower we go, and may we be forgiven for what we're about to do."

We pulled out of the parking space in front of my house and joined the flow of traffic. It was just after 4 P.M., and it might take us the best part of an hour to get to the Tower of London. We needed to arrive before any of the Trailfinder troops. Our private tour was due to start at 5:30 P.M. and was supposed to finish before 6:30 P.M.

"Lady Marie, how many Trailfinder troops do you think we'll get?" I asked.

"Quite a few, Maggie," Lady Marie answered. "I'm not certain just how many, but after the Council approved our plan, we communicated with all the Trailfinder leaders in London. It was, as I feared, too short notice for many, what with having to get permission from families and sort out transport arrangements. But the attraction of a free visit to the Tower of London, with free transport as well, was too great an incentive for some to turn down."

"Did you say free?" Anahira asked, wide-eyed.

"Yes, well, free to the Trailfinder troops. But at a rather significant cost to us personally, I'm afraid," Lady Marie responded.

"Maybe we could grab another one of those Crown Jewels?" Sir Edmund suggested. "Just to cover the cost."

Lady Marie gave her husband a disapproving glare, and Anahira and I both laughed.

"That's really kind of you," I responded.

"Well, you needed an army," Lady Marie answered matter-of-factly.

"An army indeed," Sir Edmund added. "Although, I may not have been terribly forthcoming about the actual numbers involved when I convinced the Constable of the Tower to agree to the visit."

"Edmund, what are you saying?" Lady Marie asked, almost in the tone of a teacher dealing with a difficult student.

"Well, I may have given the impression that it was only a relatively small group that would be visiting. And for a very special occasion, of course."

"How small?" Lady Marie inquired, continuing the patient-yet-stern-teacher routine.

"A number less than fifty was suggested to me, and I said nothing to dissuade the Constable of the Tower from reaching that conclusion," Sir Edmund admitted.

"So, they will only let fifty Trailfinder girls in?" I asked, my voice betraying my anxiety. I didn't think that would be enough.

"No, Maggie," Sir Studfall answered. "They are simply expecting a group of no more than fifty people. It seemed to be a critical factor in allowing a visit in between their public closing hours and the start of the final Twilight Tour of the year. However, given that permission for the visit comes from the Constable himself, the Yeoman Warders will scramble to accommodate all of the girls that arrive, no matter how many there are."

"How do you know that?" I asked.

"Because, Maggie, the Constable of the Tower is the superior officer, and he will have instructed the Chief Yeoman Warder to accommodate the Trailfinder visit," Sir Edmund explained. "To the Warders, the instruction from the Constable will be treated as an order, and good soldiers always follow orders."

"Oh, okay," I responded. That kinda made sense.

"The nature of the visitors will also be taken into consideration," Sir Edmund added, possibly picking up the lack of conviction in my response. "I happen to know that the Chief Yeoman Warder has two granddaughters who are Trailfinder Girls themselves. He has a very soft spot for our programs and will not want to disappoint any of the girls who arrive."

"Wait," Anahira exclaimed. "The Chief Yeoman Warder is a *grandfather*?"

"Yes, indeed. He has had a long and distinguished career both in the Royal Navy and as a Yeoman Warder. I feel a bit sorry for the man, with all that might happen tonight."

"So it really is an invasion then?" I responded.

"It might even aid your plan, Maggie," Sir Studfall added. "The Warders will be on the back foot from the very beginning."

"But won't they just check with the Constable if more than fifty girls turn up?" Anahira asked.

"The Constable will be unavailable for comment."

"He will?" Anahira said.

"He'll be having a pre-dinner drink with me," Sir Edmund concluded with a grin.

"But won't they just call him?"

"He might just find that his reception is temporarily blocked in my presence."

Anahira turned to me and mouthed the word "how?"

"Those golden devices completely mess with our technology," Sir Edmund continued, after maybe noticing Anahira's response in the rearview mirror. "I happen to be carrying one tonight."

Sir Edmund darted a look at Lady Marie. "Just the small one, dear," he added.

Lady Marie smiled. "You are actually quite clever, you know."

"And don't you forget it," Sir Edmund responded with a laugh.

I smiled, but the idea that the guards wouldn't allow all the Trailfinder troops to enter the Tower of London had been nagging at me. All the golden devices in the world wouldn't matter if we couldn't even get into the Tower.

"Speaking of cleverness, " Lady Marie added. "I think you'll be needing one of the golden devices, too, Maggie."

Lady Marie turned and held out a necklace with a small golden heart. "Put this on, Maggie. It will blur your image on any security footage."

I reached forward, taking the necklace out of Lady Marie's hand. I placed it over my neck, tucking the heart underneath my polo shirt.

"How does it work?" I asked.

"We're not terribly sure, I'm afraid," Lady Marie responded. "But it seems whoever wears this golden pendant cannot be identified on any security cameras. They become little more than a shadow."

"Oh, that's good, I guess." I wasn't sure I wanted to become a shadow. I hadn't really thought too much about the security cameras. They'd be everywhere. With the golden pendant, I wouldn't be identified, but Lady Marie would. And so would Anahira!

My heart started pounding in my chest, beating out a furious rhythm. I turned to Anahira, my eyes wide, and I shook my head.

Anahira reached out and grabbed my hand. I squeezed hers in response.

It's crazy what we're doing. We should call the whole thing off.

But, then again, who knew what might happen? How many lives would be ruined if we didn't succeed tonight?

I stared out the window and noticed that we'd joined the flood of traffic in and around the center of London, slowing our progress. It might take longer than an hour at this rate.

"How will the Trailfinder troops get to the Tower?" I asked, another worry worming its way to the surface of my mind.

"Ah, so you've noticed a potential flaw in our cunning plan?" Sir Edmund responded.

"It's just, you know, the traffic," I replied, not sure if Sir Edmund was making fun or not.

Sir Edmund laughed. "Yes, getting in and out of the city of London is painful, especially at this time of day. Luckily, we've booked space on a couple of City Cruise boats."

"Boats?" I asked.

"The girls and their leaders will be ferried to the Tower Millennium Pier by City Cruises," Sir Edmund explained. "We thought it would be easier for the Trailfinder troops to get to the piers on the edges of London rather than try and drive through the city."

"Kayla and Razia are coming on the first boat, Sam the second one," Lady Marie added. "Just so that we have a Guardians presence on each boat."

"The boats are a good idea," Anahira responded.

"Yes, they are," Sir Edmund agreed. "I am sometimes amazed at my own brilliance." Sir Edmund turned his head to me and winked, and Anahira and I both laughed.

"Edmund," Lady Marie exclaimed. "Let us not get carried away."

"Yes, dear," Sir Edmund responded with another smile.

"Now, Maggie," Lady Marie continued. "Where are Tylwyth and Teg?"

Oh, no. I've been fearing this question.

"Um, I don't know where they are, Lady Marie."

"You don't know?" Lady Marie responded, her voice rising ever so slightly in pitch. "When did you last see them?"

"Yesterday. At Dux Manor."

"You mean, you haven't seen them since our meeting yesterday?"

"No."

"Well, what have they been doing?"

"I don't know." Probably terrorizing ice cream parlors, or possibly stalking football stadiums, or even attacking innocent garden gnomes.

"Well, that is quite problematic," Lady Marie concluded.

"Look on the bright side," Sir Edmund said. "If they don't turn up, then we can just have a nice visit to the Tower and not have to replace anything."

"Yes, thank you, dear," Lady Marie responded. "And then watch helplessly as our world is invaded by Bugbears, and pixies who aren't pixies, and heaven knows what other terrors."

"So, not much of a bright side then?" Sir Edmund clarified.

Lady Marie shook her head.

"Tylwyth and Teg will be there," I insisted, trying to convince myself as much as Lady Marie.

"Yes, Maggie. Let us hope so," Lady Marie responded.

Let's hope so indeed. And let's hope that they know exactly what to do and that they won't put us in any danger.

I didn't remember talking to Tylwyth and Teg about safety, but would they try and protect all of us or would they allow some of us to get into trouble?

As we continued our drive through the congested center of London, a new and sickening worry occurred to me.

What if some of the Trailfinder girls get hurt? I'd never forgive myself. I'm not sure that the safety of the world would be worth it.

⁂

IN THE END, THE DRIVE THROUGH LONDON WAS NOT TOO BAD. WE arrived at the Tower Hotel just after 5 P.M. and parked in the reserved members' section of the car park. Lady Marie and Sir Edmund were members of the hotel, so it made sense to park in the hotel car park. Sir Edmund was meeting the Constable of the Tower at the hotel, in a place called Bar Eleven.

We left the underground car park and walked to the hotel entrance.

"I'm afraid this is where I leave you," Sir Edmund said. "I'd better not be late to meet the Constable. That would be most impolite."

"Yes, dear," Lady Marie agreed. "Do keep him fully entertained."

"Of that, you can have no doubt. Well, all the best then."

Lady Marie and Sir Edmund shared one last look before Sir Edmund turned around and entered the hotel.

"You really are a good man," Lady Marie said quietly, before turning her attention to Anahira and me. "Well, girls, shall we?"

We followed Lady Marie as she walked away from the hotel. It was a short walk from the hotel to the Tower of London, past some of the most iconic scenes in England, including the Tower Bridge. I was, however, not paying much attention to the sights, cloaked as they were in the fading light. No, I was instead struggling to just put one foot in front of the other.

What we're trying to do is madness. It's wrong. It's all wrong. It won't work. Girls will get hurt. Lady Marie will get arrested. We'll all get arrested.

I can't do it.

I stopped and reached into my meds bag for my inhaler. I fumbled around a bit before grabbing my inhaler and spacer. I took two long breaths.

"Maggie? Are you alright?" Lady Marie asked, turning back to me.

I looked past my spacer to Lady Marie, struggling to keep myself together. I shuddered as I returned my inhaler and spacer to my bag.

Lady Marie stepped closer to me and put her hand on my shoulder. "I know, Maggie," she said, trying her best to comfort me. "But it's the only way."

Despite the truth of Lady Marie's words, I couldn't get myself moving again.

"C'mon, Maggie. We've got this," Anahira said, reaching out to squeeze my hand.

I looked at Anahira and sighed. Why couldn't I have been as brave as her?

"C'mon, Maggie," Anahira repeated.

I started to move forward, but then stopped almost immediately.

"Lady Marie, where's the…"

"It's right here, Maggie," Lady Marie replied, patting the pocket of her Wayfinder jacket. "It's alright. I've got this."

Hearing Lady Marie utter one of Anahira's pet sayings broke the hold my fear had over me, and I took another long breath, without the aid of my inhaler.

"But won't you be searched?" My doubts were not so easily defeated.

"A Lady would never be subjected to such a thing," Lady Marie responded with almost a look of disgust. "And, quite besides that, we are not a threat."

"But…"

"Maggie, what my dear husband neglected to mention when he described the plan is that the Tower is a place for families these days. Yes, it has a fierce reputation and yes, there are guards, but the Warders live in the Tower with their families. Children and grandchildren are a welcome part of the place. They might even be having their own Halloween celebrations tonight. We will be welcomed as guests."

"But…"

"Maggie, I know you're worried. I know you're scared. I know you're doubting the entire plan. I am too. But let's not let our fears make the situation worse than it really is. We must try and protect the Earth, no matter the cost. We have a job to do."

We have a job to do.

"How are you, Anahira?" Lady Marie asked.

"I'm all good, Lady Marie," Anahira responded, with almost a defiant look in her eye.

"All good, indeed," Lady Marie replied with a smile.

Lady Marie's use of another of Anahira's sayings made me smile and I started walking.

We have a job to do.

The walk between the River Thames and the Tower of London was impressive, especially with all of the lights starting to come on. There were lots of people on the walkway, some finishing their workday, others venturing out for the evening. But the scene was dominated by the Tower itself, rearing up on my right-hand side. The artificial lights were starting to turn the Tower golden, and the reflection on the water had an almost magical quality. It was a very cool place to visit on Halloween, one that I might even have enjoyed in other circumstances.

Unfortunately, as we passed a family gazing intently at the Tower, I overheard someone talking about the Traitors' Gate, the entrance prisoners accused of treason used in the past.

I stared at the Gate and shuddered.

Is that the entrance I should be using?

I almost stopped walking, but my mind grasped onto Lady Marie's proclamation.

We have a job to do.

I left the Traitors' Gate behind and continued on the path through a cluster of trees. The trees hid the Tower from view, especially given the little natural light that remained, but the Tower's presence was like a hammer in my mind, constantly banging away at what little courage I had left.

I emerged from the shelter of the trees and saw a large group of

Trailfinder girls just beginning to gather together outside the imposing Tower of London shop.

We had only just arrived in time.

Lady Marie strode forward, leaving Anahira and me hurrying to catch up.

There were easily more than fifty Trailfinder girls already gathered, and more were joining them in an almost constant stream. They were all dressed in their yellow and black uniforms and talking in excited high-pitched voices. Several leaders buzzed around the crowd, attempting to impose some sense of order.

Lady Marie started talking with two leaders, quite senior ones, judging by the pins in their uniforms. Although neither had as many pins as Lady Marie.

"Look, there's Kayla and Razia," Anahira said, pointing just to the left of Lady Marie.

We joined Kayla and Razia, standing just a little bit separate from the hyped-up and ever-growing group of Trailfinder girls and their leaders.

"Hi, Razia. Hi, Kayla," Anahira greeted our unit members. "How's it going?"

"It's terrifying," Kayla responded, although she couldn't help grinning.

Razia nodded, while moving to adjust her hijab.

"How are you holding up, Maggie?" Kayla asked.

"I'm terrified," I answered without smiling.

Kayla grinned again. "Are Tylwyth and Teg here yet?"

"No, not yet."

They'd better turn up soon.

Razia looked around while holding her glasses, as though testing my declaration.

"Where's Sam?" Anahira asked.

"She's coming on the next boat," Kayla answered.

"The second boat's not here yet?" I asked, looking at the crowd of girls. There must already have been nearly one hundred girls and leaders gathered.

Maybe they won't let us all in.

"There are only two Trailfinder troops coming on Sam's boat," Razia added, following my gaze. "Most of the girls that are coming are already here."

We would number somewhere close to one hundred and fifty girls and leaders. That was three times more than the Tower was expecting. So, the first test was actually gaining entry.

"Good evening, Razia and Kayla." Lady Marie arrived and greeted the other members of our unit, while also smiling at Anahira and me. "The second boat is just unloading, so it won't be long now. I'll go and speak with the Chief Yeoman Warder and advise him of our numbers. The two senior Trailfinder leaders will join me while you remain here and wait."

Lady Marie joined the two senior leaders and, together, they walked around to the entrance to the Tower. The entrance was called the Middle Tower for some reason I couldn't understand. It certainly wasn't in the middle, but stood alone, not really connected to anything else. But it was the only way we could enter the Tower of London.

The noise and energy levels of the Trailfinder troops increased as they saw their leaders approach the entrance. The noise alone would alert the supervising Warders that they had a much bigger crowd than expected.

"Here's Sam now," Anahira declared while waving.

I couldn't see Sam yet, but I was quite a bit shorter than Anahira. I eventually saw her at the front of a troop of Trailfinder girls dressed up for Halloween. Instead of wearing their official uniforms, the girls were dressed in a bright assortment of home-made costumes, including Disney characters, ghosts, and monsters. There were even a couple of pumpkins.

Sam, however, was wearing her full Wayfinder uniform. I didn't think she would ever consent to wearing a costume.

Sam joined us, and we all greeted each other.

"Interesting costumes," Anahira said, looking at the colorful group.

"Yeah, well, they'd been planning a fun Halloween night for their troop for ages and then got permission to wear their costumes tonight," Sam answered. "It hasn't been a fun trip. They're a very lively lot."

"Aren't they all," Kayla responded with yet another grin.

"So, what's happening?" Sam asked, shaking her head.

"We're waiting for Lady Marie to come back from talking with the Chief Yeoman Warder to see if we're all allowed in," Anahira answered.

Sam looked toward the entrance to the Middle Tower. "Is there a problem?"

"Sir Edmund Studfall gave the impression that we'd have smaller numbers than are actually here," Anahira replied.

"Oh, well, that's just great," Sam responded.

It certainly was not great, but I didn't want to talk with Sam about it right then. I had just noticed Lady Marie return from the entrance to the Middle Tower with a man dressed in an elaborate dark-blue-and-red uniform, complete with a hat the Mad Hatter himself would have been proud of. It looked like a uniform that would easily pass for a Halloween costume.

"Is that the Chief Yeoman Warder?" I asked nobody in particular.

"Let me do a quick ID check," Razia responded while reaching up to touch her glasses. "Yes, that's him." She confirmed after a moment.

"He doesn't look happy," Sam added.

He certainly didn't look happy, although it was hard to tell from this distance. But he was shaking his head and pointing to the crowd of girls. Lady Marie stood quietly at his side with the other two Trailfinder leaders just behind her. I got the impression that Lady Marie was playing the role of a servant pleading with her ruler. Her head bowed, her hands clasped in front of her.

The Chief Yeoman Warder shook his head again and said something to Lady Marie.

Lady Marie responded by lifting her right arm and sweeping it toward the assembled girls, in a left-to-right arc, palm up. She then stepped closer to the Chief Yeoman Warder and said something to him.

The Chief Yeoman Warder looked at Lady Marie and then at the Trailfinder troops. He shook his head and then stormed back into the Tower.

"It looks like he's not going to allow us in," Sam concluded.

As much as I would have liked to argue the point, I feared Sam was right.

We have already failed.

I closed my eyes and sighed. Despite the fact that I struggled about whether we should have been doing this in the first place, I was disappointed. Not just for all the girls who had had their night ruined, but for my unit and for all we'd set out to do.

I didn't know what our failure would cost the world.

But the personal cost of this failure might be too great for me to bear.

14
GONE WITH THE WIND

"Well, that was most uncomfortable," Lady Marie admitted as she rejoined us, waiting outside the Tower shop with the horde of excitable Trailfinder girls.

"What happened, Lady Marie?" Anahira asked.

"I'm afraid my dear husband may have underestimated the seriousness with which the Chief Yeoman Warder takes his responsibilities."

"What do you mean?" Kayla responded.

"He insisted he would only let fifty girls enter the Tower," Lady Marie answered.

I shook my head and turned to look at the girls crowded behind us. So, we might still be allowed in, but we could only take fifty Trailfinder girls with us.

"How do we choose?" I said, not meaning to speak out loud.

"My thoughts exactly, Maggie," Lady Marie added while following my gaze. "Thus, I invited the Chief Yeoman Warder to personally choose the fifty girls that could enter, and then to tell the others they had to go home. Despite all his blustering about being unable to accommodate our numbers, he was simply not willing to disappoint so many girls."

"So, we *are* all going in?" I asked.

"Yes, Maggie," Lady Marie answered. "At least in this part, the plan has succeeded. As we hoped, the Constable of the Tower could not be reached for comment, and so the Chief Yeoman Warder had to make the decision himself. It appears he most certainly has a soft spot for our organization."

So we hadn't failed. Not yet anyway. We were going to enter the Tower of London.

The Tower of London!

To get one of the Crown Jewels and return it to its rightful owner.

I sucked in a very deep breath and clenched my right fist. I could really have used a stress ball right then. Or one of those bubble popper toys.

"How long do we have to wait?" Sam asked.

"Not long, Sam," Lady Marie replied. "The Chief Yeoman Warder will allow us all in, but only in three separate groups for security and safety reasons. He, therefore, has to gather more Warders to act as our hosts and guides. He isn't terribly happy about inconveniencing his staff but nevertheless believes he will find a few willing volunteers."

Lady Marie looked toward the Middle Tower. "Ah, and here he is now."

The Chief Yeoman Warder appeared at the Tower entrance with a team of people dressed in the same dark-blue-and-red uniforms, complete with oversized hats.

Lady Marie turned back to our unit. "Please excuse me as I sort out the groupings."

I watched as Lady Marie talked with the two senior leaders, and soon about three Trailfinder troops headed to the entrance, with most of the girls squealing and laughing. They were greeted by three Warders and then, after being checked in and counted, they disappeared through the gates of the Middle Tower.

The same process was repeated with another group a few minutes later, about four Trailfinder troops this time, as two of the troops were quite small in size.

We would enter with the last group, the two Trailfinder troops that arrived with Sam and one troop that arrived on the first boat.

Which meant we would be with the group dressed in homemade Halloween costumes.

"How are we supposed to separate from the group when we're inside?" Sam asked.

No one answered Sam, but her question sparked off another bout of anxiety in me. I actually didn't know how or when we were going to separate from the Trailfinder troops, or how we were going to prevent the girls from seeing what we were trying to do. Or, indeed, how we were going to hide what we were trying to do from the Warders.

I don't know anything.

"Alright, girls," Lady Marie instructed as she rejoined our unit. "Chins up. Let's go."

We moved to the back of the last Trailfinder troop and walked to the Tower entrance. I moved in a daze, my emotions racing from fear, to worry, to confusion, to guilt, and then back to fear. Everything depended on Tylwyth and Teg.

But can they even be trusted?

Our host, the Chief Yeoman Warder himself, greeted us at the entrance to the Tower. He seemed like a kind older man with a broad smile and a sparkle in his blue eyes. He didn't act anything but pleased to see us. He even said something that made all the other girls laugh, although I couldn't quite share their enthusiasm.

The Chief Yeoman Warder then introduced the two other Warders with him, a man and a woman. I didn't catch either of their names. Up close, I noticed that the Warder uniforms were mostly dark blue with red trimmings, with the letters ER emblazoned on the front in oversized red letters underneath a large red crown. I stared at the crown on the uniform of the nearest Warder. It was clear that the Warders represented the queen, in case I had any doubts about who I was plotting against.

My eyes widened.

It's really happening, isn't it?

The Warders counted the whole group and then checked us in. We walked through the entrance, past two guards standing at attention as though carved from stone. The guards were dressed in red and black with the tallest black hats I had ever seen.

I swallowed a moment of panic. I wasn't expecting guards at the entrance. It could only mean that they knew.

We will be caught.

"It's okay, Maggie," Anahira whispered next to me.

I pulled my attention away from the guards and looked up at Anahira. She always seemed to know when I needed her help.

We walked side-by-side into the Tower of London or, at least, we walked under the Middle Tower and onto a paved stone path that led to a second tower, one connected to the thick outer wall protecting the Tower of London.

The Chief Yeoman Warder led us, with the other two Warders positioning themselves at the rear of the group, just behind Anahira and me. They both smiled at me as they took up positions. I wasn't sure I smiled back.

We moved forward together as one big group, just staying far enough behind the second group of Trailfinder girls so that we were kept separate. The Chief Yeoman Warder stopped us regularly to share some stories from history and to entertain us. His performance seemed to be part stand-up comedian and part history professor. The other girls appeared to be enjoying it, especially the ones in Halloween costumes, but I struggled to pay attention.

The squeals and screams almost reached fever pitch when a place called the Bloody Tower was mentioned. It stuck in my mind because I'd hardly ever heard an adult use the word *bloody* in front of children. It certainly excited the younger girls. I still couldn't make sense of all the words being spoken. Everything was all a bit fuzzy.

Just where are Tylwyth and Teg?

We continued on our tour into the main courtyard and soon encountered the massive White Tower rearing up on our right. We stopped as soon as we had the entire White Tower in view, and our host entertained us with more colorful history. I caught something about William the Conqueror, but I was really struggling to focus.

"Are you alright, Maggie?" Anahira whispered while keeping her attention partly focused on our host.

"Where are they?" I whispered back.

Anahira looked around. "They must be here, somewhere."

I looked around as well. The daylight was fading. The walls, doors, and courtyards within the Tower shone with artificial light, creating a sense of mystery and magic everywhere I looked. Tylwyth and Teg could have been here, watching me even now from the shadows. Maybe they couldn't do anything because we were grouped together with the Trailfinder girls and closely watched by the Warders.

How are we supposed to get away?

The Chief Yeoman Warder finished his storytelling and pointed down the path, indicating where he wanted us to go next. He began to walk forward but his progress was halted when another Warder came rushing up to him, demanding his attention. The new Warder was notable for the black gloves he wore. I hadn't seen any other Warders wear gloves.

The Chief Yeoman Warder turned to our group to excuse himself before turning back to the newcomer. The Warders started talking, with increasingly exaggerated hand-waving from the Warder wearing gloves.

I overheard the female Warder behind me say the word, "Ravenmaster."

"It's the ravens," I whispered to Anahira.

"What?"

"The ravens."

"Ravens?"

"I just heard a Warder talk about the Ravenmaster, and Tylwyth and Teg said the ravens would help."

"Help? How?"

I shrugged. "I have no idea."

The female Warder left her position and joined the Chief Yeoman Warder and the Ravenmaster, who were still in animated conversation. There was a brief discussion and then the female Warder walked back, shaking her head.

The actions of the Warders were noticed by the Trailfinder girls, and there was a noticeable increase in the level of excitement. I strained to hear the words of the female Warder as she returned. I only managed to hear the word "missing."

The ravens are missing?

"I think that Tylwyth and Teg are definitely here, Maggie," Anahira whispered.

"What?"

"Look," Anahira replied, pointing at the side of the White Tower facing the River Thames.

I turned my head in the direction Anahira had indicated, and my eyes went wide as I saw a group of soldiers dressed in steel armor, like from the days of King Arthur. I blinked a few times just to make sure I was seeing clearly. But yes, soldiers clad in full suits of armor were starting to emerge onto the ramp from the White Tower. Three or four soldiers walked under the lights illuminating the entry, their brightly polished armor glistening silver and gold as they turned and marched away. The armored soldiers seemed to move awkwardly, more like robots than humans.

Could it be?

I gasped as I focused on the next soldier to leave the White Tower, only it wasn't a soldier, just a piece of body armor and a helmet, floating in midair. There were no arms or legs. There was no head nor body.

The armor has come alive.

"Bedknobs and Broomsticks," I said, slightly in awe.

Anahira opened her mouth to reply when her words were drowned out by screams from the younger girls, and not just the girls in our group. A company of armored knights, riding on armored horses, came riding down the path from the far end of the courtyard. Actually, riding was not entirely accurate, it was more like they were part of a merry-go-round. The armored horses and knights moved as though frozen in one particular action, bobbing up and down as they progressed down the wide path.

Following the knights were pieces of armor and weaponry, including helmets, body armor, swords, spears, and shields,

marching in formation. Or not really marching, *floating* in formation. The weapons floated in the air alongside the armor in ordered
uniform rows.

The Trailfinder girls in my group were now all yelling and
screaming, though in excitement rather than fear. Some rushed to
surround their leaders, pointing out the armor. Some clung to
their friends. Quite a few, including the whole Trailfinder troop
dressed in Halloween costumes, turned toward the horses and
knights, and screamed in apparent delight like they were on a
rollercoaster.

The leader in charge of the costumed troop, herself dressed in
an elaborate purple and black Maleficent costume, turned to Lady
Marie.

"I don't know how you pulled this off," she yelled over the
noise. "But it is simply wonderful to see enchanted knights on
horseback. What a simply marvelous Halloween!"

Lady Marie nodded, although she couldn't hide her wide-eyed
look of surprise.

Maleficent turned back to her troop of monsters. "Let's get
them, girls."

She and her monsters rushed toward the oncoming knights,
followed almost immediately by the two supervising Warders,
yelling at them to stop.

I stepped forward, worried that the strange knights would ride
into the surging troop, but the knights instead turned to the side
and rode onto the grass, pursued by the screaming, costumed girls.
The armor and weaponry halted in perfect unison, waited for the
girls to rush past, and then continued on their floating march.

The Chief Yeoman Warder stared at the knights in wide-eyed
amazement, but the actions of Maleficent spurred him into action.
He took something out of his pocket and tapped away. Almost
immediately, an alarm sounded throughout the Tower grounds.
The noise of the alarm added to the energy generated by the
younger girls, who started screaming even louder. A thing I hadn't
thought was possible.

In response to the alarm, the courtyard area was flooded with

Warders and members of the Tower Guard. Most of the guards stared open-mouthed at the scene in front of them.

The Chief Yeoman Warder barked out orders, and the Warders and guards responded immediately, moving to intercept the knights and round up the girls.

The whole inner courtyard of the Tower of London descended into a frantic mess of armored knights, screaming girls, and yelling Warders and guards.

The newly arrived Warders started to wrestle with the floating weapons, trying to subdue them, but all they really managed to do was look like circus clowns practicing for their latest routine. The armor simply continued on its relentless journey.

One Warder, both hands clinging to the handle of a large sword floating in midair, was being pulled along by the sword. It looked for a moment as though he was the one leading the march, but the sword was the one in control. The Warder strained to drag the sword down, but his actions had no effect. Two other Warders grabbed the man around his body, trying to anchor him. It worked for a brief moment, until the sword surged forward, dragging all three Warders behind it. The first Warder finally released the handle of the sword, resulting in all three Warders getting dumped unceremoniously to the floor. They lay there as the assorted pieces of armor and weaponry floated over the top of them.

Other Warders and guards chased the armored knights, hands raised in the air, as though they were trying to pacify real horses. It seemed to have the desired effect, until some of the girls managed to get on top of the armor and cling to the back of the knights. At which point the knights shot off in different directions, almost as though giving the girls a ride was the intention of their magical escape all along.

An armored knight trotted past my unit with a Trailfinder girl dressed as Rapunzel sitting in front of the knight on the armored horse. Rapunzel waved at us happily as other costumed Trailfinder girls followed behind, begging for a turn. Two Warders ran behind the troop and yelled for them to get back, while a Guard pleaded, unsuccessfully, for Rapunzel to get off the horse.

We watched as Rapunzel urged the knight to move faster. It somehow obeyed, causing both the begging girls and the worried Warders to run to try and keep up.

"Alright, girls. That's enough," Lady Marie called out.

We all turned to Lady Marie who indicated for the unit to follow her. She led us back to an alcove in a wall jutting out from one of the towers.

We gathered together in the alcove, where the shadows were deepest. We huddled close, almost as a tiny island of calm in the midst of a storm.

"Well, Maggie," Lady Marie began. "I assume we have Tylwyth and Teg to thank for all this commotion?"

It must have been them, although I hadn't seen either Tylwyth or Teg anywhere yet.

"Will the girls be alright?" Kayla asked.

"I believe so," Lady Marie answered. "The animated knights don't appear to want to attack anyone. It simply looks like they are going for a bit of a ride."

A bit of a ride!

I had to love Lady Marie's calm assessment of something as extraordinary as ancient knights coming to life.

"It's not too bad," Sam added, looking around.

"Yes," Lady Marie responded. "The Trailfinder troops will certainly have a story to tell tonight. But we have a job to do."

We inched closer, giving our full attention to Lady Marie.

Lady Marie briefly checked around her and then took out an object from her pocket, wrapped in a white lace handkerchief. She opened the handkerchief and revealed the fake Koh-i-Noor diamond. It caught a shaft of light and glistened brightly.

"Wow," Anahira exclaimed.

"Yes, a very fine job," Lady Marie replied. "Well done, Razia and Kayla."

Razia nodded, and Kayla grinned.

"What happens now, Maggie?" Lady Marie asked.

I shrugged. I had no idea what was supposed to happen next.

"Don't we need to get it to the Jewel House?" Sam asked.

I nodded slowly.

"How are we going to do that then?" Sam continued.

I didn't respond, as I really didn't know.

"The Jewel House is on the opposite side of the courtyard," Anahira said, looking up.

"Yeah, the courtyard currently swarming with Warders and guards," Sam pointed out.

"As well as enchanted armor and Trailfinder troops," Kayla added.

"Can we make it past them?" Lady Marie asked.

We all turned to look at the courtyard. The last line of the floating armor and weaponry was marching out of the courtyard. The armor was being followed by a large group of Warders and guards, trying their best to look like everything was under control. Within the courtyard itself, the chaos was in full swing, with mini battles everywhere. Guards battled to subdue floating bits of weaponry, and Warders struggled to restrain excitable Trailfinder girls. The Chief Yeoman Warder stood at the midway point in the courtyard and appeared to be making a phone call. Probably trying to gather reinforcements.

"Every single available guard must be out here," Sam concluded.

"We cannot get through," Razia confirmed.

"Alright, girls. Let's focus," Lady Marie called us back into our huddle. "We are prevented from making a direct approach to the Jewel House. So, Maggie, how are we going to replace the Koh-i-Noor diamond with this copy?"

I stared at Lady Marie, and then I stared at the fake jewel. I didn't know what to say.

"Alright, Maggie. You'd be wantin' to give me that wee stone." Tylwyth suddenly appeared right next to the fake diamond and urged me to pick it up.

I should have gotten used to Tylwyth and Teg appearing out of nowhere, but I hadn't. My eyes went wide and the breath caught in my mouth.

Lady Marie looked at me quizzically, probably reacting to my change in expression. Which meant Tylwyth had only made himself visible to me.

"C'mon, Maggie," Tylwyth urged. "Time's a wastin'."

I reached out and plucked the fake diamond from Lady Marie's hand. It was surprisingly heavy. Lady Marie nodded as though she was expecting this.

"That's it, Maggie," Tylwyth encouraged. "Teg has been havin' all the fun so far, but now it's my turn."

I looked around for Teg, but Tylwyth shook his head. "He's with the ravens now."

The ravens?

"Alright, Maggie. You'd better be givin' me the stone," Tylwyth continued. "You'll be needin' your hands free for the Mynydd o Olau."

I handed the fake diamond to Tylwyth. The others all gasped as, to their eyes, the entire thing disappeared.

"You ready, Maggie?" Tylwyth added. "We only be havin' a moment."

I wasn't sure I was ready. I wasn't even sure what I was supposed to be ready for.

Tylwyth placed his hand on my shoulder, and the world immediately changed. I found myself in a tight, cramped space. There was glass behind me and the sound of bird wings flapping all around. Bright spotlights made me blink. I squeezed my eyes closed to help me adjust to my new surroundings and when I opened them, I found myself in front of the crown containing the Koh-i-Noor diamond. I was in the Jewel House.

The Jewel House!

The sound of the wings revealed itself as a group of ravens darting in and around the long line of jewels on display. They couldn't really fit in the cramped space and were clearly agitated. I ducked my head as a raven narrowly missed me. I really didn't want to be on the wrong end of those talons.

A particularly large raven approached, its wings outstretched in a feathery embrace. I was certain it winked at me.

Teg?

"It's time," Tylwyth said at my side. "Now, Maggie. Do it."

My right hand shook as I reached out, my fingers hovering in front of the Queen Mother's Crown. The Koh-i-Noor diamond was securely set in the middle of the crown, and I had no clue how to remove it. Didn't I need tools or something? But the tip of one of the large raven's wings touched the top of the crown and the Koh-i-Noor diamond fell into my hand. I pulled my arm away in surprise and somehow managed to hold onto the diamond.

The scraping sound of metal made me turn my head. Coming down the stairs into the Jewel House were three more enchanted knights, all wearing elaborately engraved armor. It made me think of royalty.

Were they here to protect the jewels?

A clicking noise caused me to turn back, and I managed to catch Tylwyth as he finished setting the fake diamond into the vacant slot in the crown.

The world changed again.

I found myself back with my unit on the grounds of the Tower of London.

"Maggie!" Anahira exclaimed, grabbing my shoulder. "Are you okay?"

"What?" I responded.

"You disappeared!" Anahira explained.

I looked around at the concerned faces of my unit. I must have given them all a fright, but I must have only been gone a few seconds at most.

Instead of trying to explain what had just happened, I opened my right hand to reveal the Koh-i-Noor diamond.

"Is that…" Anahira stared at the diamond, unable to finish her sentence.

"No!" Kayla exclaimed, raising a hand to her mouth.

"It is the Koh-i-Noor diamond," Razia confirmed, a hand tightly gripping her glasses.

"As easy as that," Sam concluded with a knowing nod.

The Koh-i-Noor diamond didn't look all that different from the fake diamond Tylwyth had placed in the Queen Mother's Crown, but it felt heavier. It felt hot in my hand and seemed to capture and reflect the light in a much deeper way.

"Here, Maggie," Lady Marie said, handing me the silk handkerchief with as much calmness as though she was handing me a tissue for my runny nose. "Better wrap it up. I'm afraid we're not done yet. We're still in the middle of the Tower grounds, and I fear we may not be able to easily leave."

I accepted the handkerchief and used it to cover the diamond. I then looked around to see that the situation in the Tower grounds was still chaotic. The Warders and Tower Guards were outnumbered by the armored knights, let alone the Trailfinder troops, and there were many battles for control all over the courtyard and grass areas. I wasn't sure who was winning, but at least the girls seemed to be enjoying themselves.

"Alright, Maggie," Tylwyth said, once again appearing in front of me. "Time to go."

"Time to go?" I repeated, my voice rising in pitch. "How?"

Lady Marie looked sharply at me as I said those words. She probably still couldn't see Tylwyth but might suspect who I was talking to.

An oversized raven flew into the tight space in the middle of my unit as Tylwyth placed his hand on my shoulder.

The world changed again. This time I found myself standing on a hill staring out at a massive area of emptiness, a place where the darkening sky completely dominated the landscape, with a fiery orange-and-red glow illuminating the entire horizon for as far as my eyes could see. There was way more sky than land. It just went on and on and on. I had never before seen such a vast and uninterrupted stretch of sky.

Where on Earth has Tylwyth taken me?

15

AT WORLD'S END

As my senses recovered, I realized that others were with me. I turned to discover my entire unit standing in a line. They all looked as shocked as I felt.

"How?" I asked, not really sure if I was asking how we got wherever we were or how they all managed to come with me.

"Lady Marie urged us all to hold onto each other just after you'd said, 'Time to go,'" Anahira responded. "It must have worked."

"Yes," Lady Marie added. "I wasn't going to lose you."

Lose me?

"I suspected Tylwyth and Teg's involvement when you first disappeared," Lady Marie continued. "I didn't want you to be alone again."

"But you never actually saw Tylwyth or Teg?" I asked.

"No, Maggie," Lady Marie answered. "I'm afraid that they only ever intended to take you. We were not part of their plan."

"Only me?" I responded warily. It was not a nice thought.

"But we're all with you now," Anahira declared.

"We've escaped the Tower together," Sam added.

"And we have the Koh-i-Noor diamond," Kayla concluded, clearly not quite believing her own words.

I took a moment to absorb our situation. The last few moments in the Tower of London had rushed by so quickly that it had been hard to keep up. But we'd actually done it. We'd escaped the Tower of London with the mystical Mountain of Light.

But where have we escaped to?

"Where are we?" Kayla asked, echoing my thoughts.

"I believe I might know," Lady Marie replied. "But Razia, will you please confirm?"

Razia reached up to touch her glasses.

"Where?" Kayla asked again.

"Romney Marsh," Lady Marie answered.

"Yes, Romney Marsh," Razia added. "Nearly two hours' drive from London."

We got here in an instant. Wow.

"Why here?" Anahira asked, looking at the emptiness stretching out in front of us.

"I'm afraid I don't really know," Lady Marie answered. "Although I can tell you that we are currently standing on what used to be the edge of England thousands of years ago. All that is before us used to be water. But I can't explain why we are here."

Lady Marie's words prompted me to stare once again at the flat emptiness stretching as far as my eye could see. The bright glow at the horizon was just beginning to soften, the sky starting to come alive with stars. Tiny pinpricks of light.

The stillness and emptiness were unnerving. It felt like the end of the world.

"If I may, Lady Marie," Razia offered. "I believe we are also standing just below the site of an old Roman fort, which was called Portus Lemanis. It was built over seventeen hundred years ago and was one of eleven Shore forts built to defend against Saxon raids. The fort had been built at the head of a wide river."

No one responded to Razia, not even Lady Marie. We didn't need to question whether Razia had her facts right. She didn't speak unless she was certain, and her glasses allowed her access to all the knowledge she needed.

I started to feel a bit light-headed. Only moments ago, I stood in the Jewel House in the Tower of London looking at the Queen Mother's Crown. Now I stood on the remains of an old Roman fort on what used to be the ancient shoreline of England. I held the Koh-i-Noor diamond, a prized mystical relic belonging to the Fae.

I had absolutely no idea what would happen next.

"There is a castle close by," Razia added. "Lympne Castle, built about one thousand years ago. It is further up the hill, some way behind us on the left."

I turned to look in the direction Razia had indicated. I could just make out the lights pooling out from the windows of a very large building. It seemed a fair distance from us, certainly higher than we currently were.

"Are we supposed to go to the castle?" Sam asked.

"I don't think so," Lady Marie answered cautiously. "I can't exactly say why, but I think we are precisely where we need to be."

I turned my attention back to the view in front of us.

So why are we here?

"Maggie!" Anahira blurted out suddenly.

"What?" I asked, turning to face her.

"The diamond. Look!"

I stared at the diamond in my right hand. It was glowing through the silk of the handkerchief. How had I not noticed the light from the diamond? I reached out with my left hand and carefully uncovered the diamond, which glowed brighter in response. A pool of light holding back the growing darkness.

"Wow," Kayla exclaimed. "That's cool."

"It most certainly is," Lady Marie responded. "It seems that the diamond knows this place. Even if we do not."

"Now, you should be knowin', Lady Studfall," Tylwyth said, suddenly appearing in front of me, and looking a bit ragged for some reason.

Lady Marie inclined her head. "Greetings, Master Tylwyth. Are you well?"

Tylwyth bowed in response, although his movements were sluggish. "I'll be fine, thank you, Lady Studfall."

"Will Master Teg be joining us?" Lady Marie asked.

"He'll be needin' a moment or two to recover."

"Recover? From what may I ask?"

"From havin' to bring all of you from London, Lady Studfall," Tylwyth answered, glaring at the members of my unit.

"Well, you must surely know that Maggie is ours," Lady Marie asserted, the determined set of her jaw proving she meant what she said.

"Aye, Lady Studfall. We surely be knowin' that. But we didn't mean no harm. We were goin' to return Maggie as soon as we were done."

"That is good to know," Lady Marie responded. "But we always stick together. Now, if you would be so kind, could you please explain why we are here?"

"We'll be openin' the door to Faerie," Tylwyth explained.

"From here?" Kayla blurted out.

Lady Marie raised her hand in Kayla's direction, indicating for Kayla to keep quiet. "Why here?" Lady Marie asked Tylwyth.

"We be standin' on the old place," Tylwyth responded.

"Yes, we know about the Roman fort."

"'Tis not that! The Romans built on top of the remains of a much older fortress. An ancient place. A place of power."

"What place?" Lady Marie asked.

"Studfall Castle."

Despite her earlier display of authority, Lady Marie seemed completely taken aback by Tylwyth's revelation. She stared at Tylwyth for a moment, looked around her, and shook her head. "There is no such place."

"In that you are wrong, Lady Studfall," Tylwyth declared with a grin.

"Aye. 'Tis as real as you and I," Teg added, suddenly appearing at Tylwyth's side.

Teg looked in a worse state than Tylwyth and seemed to be partly covered in feathers.

Tylwyth turned to Teg. "You've got feathers in your mouth, mun."

"Sorry, like," Teg replied, while spitting out two feathers.

Teg's transformation into a raven at the Tower of London must have come at a cost.

"Hang on. You brought us all here?" Sam asked.

Teg looked at Sam. "Aye. Though not by choice, mind."

"Why didn't you just jump into the Jewel House and jump out again?" Sam continued. "Why go through all that trouble at the Tower?'

"There are rules," Teg answered.

"And protections," Tylwyth added.

"Aye, rules and protections," Teg concluded. "We needed to be in the Tower first, like. We needed a human to invite us in."

"That is all over and done with," Lady Marie stated. "Now, how is the doorway to Faerie opened?"

Tylwyth seemed surprised by Lady Marie's question. He looked at her, then looked at Teg, and then his eyes went wide. He turned sharply and sighed in relief when he saw that the sun had not yet completely set.

"'Tis time," Tylwyth declared.

"Aye. Just in time though, mun," Teg added, also staring at the horizon.

"'Twas to be before sunset," Tylwyth insisted.

"You'd better be gettin' on with it then," Teg pointed out.

"Maggie," Tylwyth said, turning back to face me after glaring at Teg. "There is a large stone pillar near you. Can you feel it?"

"A large stone pillar?" I replied, looking around me. "Shouldn't I be able to see it?"

"It is buried deep in the ground," Tylwyth explained. "You would be able to feel its tip."

I knelt down and felt around the ground with my hands, finding mostly dirt and grass. I explored further and discovered a hard piece of stone jutting out from the soil. The stone felt very rough and cracked. It must have been very old.

"You should be findin' a small gap in the rock," Tylwyth added. "Place the Mynydd O Olau in the gap."

I brought the diamond down and used its light to see the rock more clearly. The gap was there, a hollowed-out bowl, big enough for a hen's egg. I held the diamond over the gap and looked up to Tylwyth, who nodded.

I placed the diamond in the gap. It slipped in easily. I recalled Razia's explanation that the diamond had been cut to smaller than its original size, although Tylwyth and Teg claimed it had been made more powerful. The diamond's light flared for a second and went out. We were blanketed in near-darkness.

I stood up, looking around blindly.

Did I do something wrong?

My eyes had just begun to adjust to the darkness when a beam of dazzling light soared up from the spot where I had placed the diamond. It shot into the air, growing ever brighter, a tall and glowing pillar of light. I turned away from its brightness and noticed another bright beam of light spring into life some distance into the flat nothingness in front of us.

"'Twas an island once," Tylwyth declared, staring at the second pillar of light.

"Aye. A thing of beauty," Teg added.

"Before it was lost," Tylwyth lamented.

The tone Tylwyth used was sorrowful. Hinting at regret and blame. But the loss of the island must have happened thousands of years ago.

Then, all of a sudden, a blast from a musical instrument shattered the stillness.

My breath caught in my mouth as the musical note swept over me. It was not a sound I'd ever heard before. To call it a trumpet blast would have been a gross injustice. The note was crystal clear. It carried with it the sense of soaring through the clouds. Of wonder and gazing at the world from new heights. It suggested that I was something tiny and insignificant in comparison to the hugeness of creation.

The musical note sounded a second time, and Tylwyth and Teg swelled with new energy and strength. Their appearance changed as though they had only been showing us a pale imitation of their true selves. The diamond's light spread out like a giant fan, enveloping Tylwyth and Teg, and the gems on their golden headbands blazed brightly. I longed to keep watching but the intensity of the light forced me to shut my eyes tight.

A third musical note sounded. A note which made the first two notes seem hollow and fake. The power of the note seared through my body. I dropped to my knees and hung my head. I was not worthy to lift my eyes to the purity of the light. I was not even worthy to be in its presence. I was nothing.

I sensed another presence joining us on the hilltop. A presence that dwarfed anything I'd ever known. An entity radiating immense strength and power.

Could it be the Faerie Queen?

"Tylwyth and Teg, you have done well."

The voice was deep, nothing like what I'd imagined a queen to sound like. It gave the impression of a deep pool of water being fed by a waterfall at night, with a full moon reflected on its surface.

"Oh, no!" Tylwyth wailed.

"Prince Draikern, what are you doin' here?" Teg added, his elevated high-pitched voice betraying an extreme level of fear.

"Silence," the voice commanded. "Kneel before me."

Did Teg just say Prince Draikern? The prince Tylwyth and Teg claimed was threatening their queen?

Surely not.

Had Tylwyth and Teg lied to me this whole time? But they seemed just as shocked as I was.

My chest tightened in panic as I realized that we had all been tricked.

"I will take back what is rightfully mine," Prince Draikern proclaimed.

"No!" Tylwyth cried out. "We were servin' Queen Aylwyin!"

"You fools," Prince Draikern replied. "You had strayed too close to the human world, become too obsessed with their pitiful delights. You were so easy to manipulate. You have been serving me, unwittingly, of course, for your wits have deserted you. But you've proved your worth at last. I will claim the Mynydd o Olau and defeat Aylwyin."

Defeat the queen?

The truth hit me like a brick. Prince Draikern planned to rule Faerie. That was why he needed the diamond. I had taken it for him.

What have I done?

I struggled for breath. My hand instinctively reached out for my meds bag, as always hanging by my side. I couldn't sense any of the others of my unit. They must have felt as helpless as I was under the powerful glamor of the prince.

The thud of footsteps signaled the approach of Prince Draikern. His suffocating presence grew ever stronger as he closed in on the place where I'd laid the diamond, an overwhelming malice that made it hard to breathe.

I felt a strong hand touch my head, and I shuddered. The prince held his hand on my head as images invaded my mind: Tylwyth and Teg, believing they'd been specially chosen by their queen to embark on a special mission when it was the prince who had deceived them. The prince, interfering with the doorway that allowed the Bugbear to enter our world. The prince, opening the path for the pixie-like creatures to attack. The prince, watching me through the green-skinned person in the tree at Dux Manor.

The green-skinned person!

Prince Draikern must have chosen me from the very beginning, believing me to be as foolish and weak as Tylwyth and Teg.

More images flooded my mind. Images that seared pain into my chest and caused my legs to shake. Images of brokenness and decay in both the Faerie world and the human world.

All Prince Draikern needed to do was to get his hands on the Mountain of Light.

It is all my fault.

My body shook uncontrollably as the truth became clear. I had failed. I had failed more horribly than I thought possible. My right hand clenched in sudden anger as I realized what I had done, but instead of forming a fist, it grabbed hold of something in my meds bag.

My epi-pen!

Acting purely on instinct, I pulled out my epi-pen and flicked off the cap with my thumb. I plunged my epi-pen into the place where I sensed Prince Draikern was standing.

I somehow made contact with the leg of the prince.

The savage shriek of pain from Prince Draikern nearly made me collapse with fright, but I held onto the epi-pen with every last bit of strength I had.

In a blinding flash I sensed even with my eyes tightly closed, the glamor of the prince was shattered.

I hesitantly opened my eyes, using my hand to try and ward off the brightness of the beam of light still flowing from the stone pillar the diamond sat upon. I could just make out the tall figure of the prince standing next to me. Even without his charm, Prince Draikern radiated immense power.

"Maggie," Tylwyth shouted. "The Mountain of Light!"

The diamond was within reach of the prince. I dropped my epi-pen and lunged for the diamond, my hand reaching it only a moment before the prince's hand.

"Give it to me," Prince Draikern commanded, straightening to his full height as I scrambled to my feet and stepped just beyond his reach.

I didn't have the strength to prevent the prince from taking the diamond. I did the first thing I could think of.

I threw the diamond to Tylwyth.

Or, at least, I threw the diamond in Tylwyth's direction.

Hopefully.

The twin pillars of light collapsed as soon as I had removed the diamond and the only light visible now came from the diamond itself, a glow alerting everyone to its location. It lay on the grass only a few meters away from me.

"Alas, Maggie. I cannot touch it," Tylwyth called out.

"Aye, 'tis forbidden," Teg added.

Prince Draikern turned and made a dash for the diamond.

Anahira got there first. She scooped up the diamond from the grass, backing away quickly.

"LITTLE GIRL!" Prince Draikern roared, reaching for Anahira. "GIVE IT TO ME!"

Anahira threw the diamond to Sam.

Prince Draikern shouted in frustration and lunged for Sam.

Sam threw the diamond to Kayla.

Prince Draikern almost intercepted the throw, his hands swiping at the air.

Kayla threw the diamond to Razia.

The agitated prince leapt at Razia.

Razia threw the diamond to me.

Oh, no.

I caught it. I actually caught it!

Prince Draikern turned his attention to me. "Enough! No more games," he declared, unsheathing a gem-encrusted dagger. "Give the diamond to me."

I stared wide-eyed at the dagger, its sharp edge catching the light from the diamond.

"You'll have to go through me first," Anahira insisted, coming to stand in front of me.

"And us," Lady Marie proclaimed, as the entire Guardians unit gathered around me.

"Aye. We won't be found wantin'," Tylwyth added, as he and Teg took up defensive positions in front of the Guardians.

The eight of us stood together and faced off against the dark Faerie prince.

"Fools!" Prince Draikern sneered. "Whatever you did to me will not last. Even now I can feel my power returning. Soon you will bow before me and beg to give me the diamond."

Prince Draikern spoke true. I could feel his presence growing stronger. It was like being pulled too close to a raging fire. Prince Draikern's glamor would soon overwhelm us all.

— *Maggie Thatcher. Place the diamond on the pillar* —

I shook my head, trying to clear my mind of the voice I'd just heard. Had Prince Draikern already regained his glamor? But it didn't sound like the prince's voice.

— *Do it, Maggie* —

The voice held authority, but kindness as well. I had the clear sense that it didn't mean any harm to me.

— *Quickly, before it's too late* —

Acting on impulse, I turned around and knelt in the grass, hands stretched in front of me, frantically searching for the top of the pillar.

"What are you doing, Maggie?" Anahira whispered.

I didn't answer. Prince Draikern might regain his glamor or attack with his dagger at any moment. Our only defense was obeying a voice I'd just heard in my head.

Desperately hoping that I was not making another terrible mistake, I found the top of the pillar and placed the diamond in the gap in the stone.

A pillar of brilliant light once again soared into the air. The light was almost immediately matched by another pillar of light rising from the place that Tylwyth and Teg claimed was once an island.

A soft and gentle musical note sounded, like from a harp, but a harp that could produce music more crystal clear than anything possible on Earth. It was the noise of children's laughter. Of walking with friends beside a gently flowing stream on a sunny spring day.

Tylwyth and Teg immediately bowed low at the sound.

Another beam of light swept over Prince Draikern. The prince yelled out in pain as the light surrounded him. The images of two tall figures were just visible within the light. They forced the prince to his knees. The jeweled dagger fell from the prince's grasp as his hands were forced to his sides.

A new presence joined us on the hillside, a powerfully calming and reassuring presence. An entity whose likeness I longed to look upon. But I couldn't make out any features. I saw nothing more than a silhouette shrouded in light. It was a more beautiful sight than one I could have ever imagined.

"Maggie Thatcher, I owe you a debt." The voice was the same as the sound in my head, but hearing it out loud was like hearing the most enchanting music, but also more than music. It set a yearning in my heart to hear more. "Humans are indeed a wonder. Strength is found in the strangest of places. I believed the Mynydd o Olau to be forever lost, but I am proven wrong, and many things that have faded can now be restored. Do not fear. Your courage and bravery shine like a star. You have done me and my world a great kindness. One I will not easily forget."

Tears came to my eyes. The words were far too beautiful for me to accept.

"As for you, Tylwyth and Teg," the soothing voice continued. "What am I to do with you? Too long have you lingered between worlds. Too close have you strayed to the humans. We must bring you back and remind you of our ways. Do not be troubled. I am as much to blame for what happened as anyone. Be at peace."

"Thank you, my queen," Tylwyth responded, his head still bowed. "May we say farewell to Maggie?"

My queen? It must be the queen of Faerie!

"You may, but do not linger," the Faerie Queen responded.

Tylwyth lifted up his head. "Oh, Maggie. We are sorry for puttin' you in danger."

"Real sorry, like," Teg added, also raising his head.

"Can you forgive us?" Tylwyth asked.

Forgive them? Who was I to forgive two creatures from Faerie? But both Tywlyth and Teg looked at me with eyes wide open, pleading.

"Of course," I responded, not knowing what else to say.

"Oh, Maggie. You are a wonder," Tylwyth concluded.

"Come. We must leave this place," the Faerie Queen commanded. "It is time for Prince Draikern to face our justice."

Tylwyth and Teg raised their hands in farewell. I started to lift my hand when the light and the presence of the Faerie folk abruptly departed. I immediately felt an almost unbearable sense of loss and stumbled forward, jerking toward the place where the light had vanished.

"Maggie," Anahira called out and grabbed my shoulder, bringing me back to the world.

I shook my head and looked around, my eyes taking a moment to adjust to the darkness. It was too early for the moon to rise, but the stars appeared in greater numbers than I thought possible. I managed to make out the rest of my unit all huddled together. There was no sign of Tylwyth or Teg, or the dark prince.

"Maggie?" Lady Marie inquired.

"I'm okay, Lady Marie," I said, while still clinging tightly to Anahira. "Did you see…" I began, before faltering. How could I truthfully describe what I had just experienced?

"Yes, Maggie," Lady Marie replied quietly. "I believe that was the Faerie Queen."

"What just happened?" I stammered, scarcely believing my own account of events.

"It appears that Tylwyth and Teg had been tricked into obtaining the Mountain of Light for Prince Draikern," Lady Marie answered. "But you somehow managed to thwart his plans. What did you do?"

I looked down at the place where I had been kneeling, shuddering as I remembered the images the prince had stormed my mind with. I turned back to Lady Marie, while still holding on tightly to Anahira. "I stabbed Prince Draikern with my epi-pen."

"You did what?" Lady Marie responded, her voice rising in pitch.

"I used my epi-pen after I realized that the prince had been tricking Tylwyth and Teg."

"The adrenaline from your epi-pen must have been enough to remove Prince Draikern's glamor, at least for a time," Lady Marie concluded.

I was going to need another epi-pen.

How do I explain that to my parents?

"How did you know to summon the queen?" Lady Marie asked.

"She spoke to me," I answered. The absence of her voice was like a hole in my heart.

"That is truly incredible, Maggie," Lady Marie responded. "Without your swift action, the prince would have seized the power of the diamond and defeated the Faerie Queen, leaving our world vulnerable to attack."

"But only because I took the diamond in the first place," I admitted.

"No, Maggie. We removed the Koh-i-Noor diamond," Lady Marie asserted. "A fault and responsibility all Guardians will have to bear, myself more than anyone. I'm afraid I must apologize to you and the entire unit."

"Apologize?" I responded. "What for?"

"We find our way through faith," Lady Marie answered. "But I let fear rule my heart. The attacks we suffered made me scared. Scared for you, Maggie, and for the Guardians unit, and for our world. But my fear almost led to the prince doing the one thing I was most afraid of."

"But we won, didn't we?" Sam responded.

"We saved the world!" Kayla added.

"We did indeed," Lady Marie admitted. "But I was acting out of fear, and for that I am truly sorry. Without Maggie's intervention, my greatest fears would have been realized."

"It's alright, Lady Marie," I said. "It's hard to ignore our fears."

"It is, Maggie. Although I hoped I would know better," Lady Marie admitted. "But all is well now. The threat to the world has been defeated and the diamond has been returned."

"You mean, the Faerie Queen has taken the diamond?" I asked.

"Yes, Maggie. I think you'll find it is no longer here," Lady Marie answered.

I knelt down and searched for the rocky space where I'd placed the diamond.

"Now what do we do?" Sam asked. "How are we supposed to get back to London?"

No answer greeted Sam, and I continued my search. I finally found the top of the pillar and the gap in the stone. As Lady Marie had predicted, the diamond was no longer there, but the space was not empty.

"Lady Marie," I declared as I stood. "I've found something."

"The diamond?" Kayla asked.

"No, something else." I moved closer to the group and held out the object in my palm, but it was too dark to see what it was.

"Anahira, can you get my phone out of my meds bag?" I asked.

Anahira reached into the bag, took out my phone, and turned on the torch setting. The light revealed a golden object. The object had a flat notebook-sized base with tiny bits of gold constantly moving on top, like ripples on a golden lake.

"What is it?" Anahira asked.

"It is another gift from the world of Faerie," Lady Marie answered.

A gift from the queen!

"What does it do?" Sam asked.

"I'm not sure," Lady Marie answered, before looking at me. "May I?"

Lady Marie took the object out of my hand and examined it. Anahira followed with the light. Lady Marie didn't give any indication she knew what the object was supposed to do but at least the mystery of the golden objects had been solved.

They are all gifts from the world of Faerie.

"How are we supposed to get back to the Tower of London?" Sam asked, no longer showing any interest in the golden device.

There was movement on the surface of the object, as though the ripples had responded to Sam's comment. For a moment the ripples had solidified into a shape, like a 3D landscape.

"I think that may have been the Tower of London," Razia suggested.

"Yes, I agree. Well spotted, Razia," Lady Marie replied. "I may know what this object will do, although it is scarcely believable."

I stared at Lady Marie. There were not many things I couldn't believe at this point.

"Please huddle close together," Lady Marie instructed. "Make sure you are all holding on to each other, including me."

We edged closer together until we were all touching, forming a very tight huddle.

Lady Marie held the object in her left hand. "The Tower of London," she declared.

The ripples on the object changed to golden droplets. They

formed an almost perfect 3D replica of the Tower of London, with golden walls and towers rising from a golden base.

"Wow," Sam admitted.

"That's so cool," Anahira added.

It was definitely cool and almost impossible to look away from.

Lady Marie moved her right hand over the object. She pushed her index finger through the golden towers.

The droplets enveloped her hand.

There was a bright golden flash, and the world went dark.

An instant later, we found ourselves back on the grounds of the Tower of London.

16
BACK TO THE FUTURE

I took a moment to get my bearings and looked around. We stood in the same place we had before Tylwyth and Teg transported us to Romney Marsh, in the shadow of the wall jutting out from one of the towers.

"Is everyone alright?" Lady Marie asked quietly.

We all seemed to be okay, although I really didn't know how any one of us would be able to explain what had just happened.

"Are we really back?" Kayla inquired.

"Yes, we are back in the Tower of London," Razia confirmed.

Events at the Tower must have calmed down, if the scene from the courtyard was anything to go by. The inside of the Tower almost resembled a scrap yard, if the *scrap* was brightly polished pieces of ancient armor. The Warders and Tower Guard were reduced to the role of a clean-up crew. They carried the now disenchanted pieces of armor to their proper location. It would take some time to sort everything out.

There was no sign of the Trailfinder girls or leaders.

"Do you think they know?" I asked hesitantly. "About the Koh-i-Noor diamond, I mean."

"I don't think they have any idea," Lady Marie responded.

"They will have a very hard time simply accepting what had happened with the armor."

It certainly seemed that way. The Warders and guards moved as if scarcely believing what they were doing, but there was no sense of panic.

"Alright, girls," Lady Marie instructed. "Time to go. Razia, may I please have the glasses back? I will need the video recordings in my debrief session with the Council of Guardians."

Razia removed the glasses and handed them to Lady Marie.

We followed Lady Marie as she led us out of the shadows by the wall and into the more brightly lit courtyard.

We were soon hailed by a Warder. "Excuse me? Hello?"

I held my breath as a Warder came running up to us.

Is this the moment of truth?

"Are you Lady Marie Studfall?" the Warder asked as he drew near.

Lady Marie stood taller. "Yes, that is who I am." She used as much dignity and poise as she could generate.

"That's a relief. The Chief has been worried sick," the Warder responded.

"The Chief Yeoman Warder?" Lady Marie clarified.

"Yes, Lady Studfall," the Warder replied. "He's waiting at the Middle Tower. We got the rest of your group out safely, but we couldn't find you anywhere."

"Well, here we are now," Lady Marie asserted.

"Yes." The Warder looked as if he wanted to ask another question, but instead walked past us. "I'll lead you out. Please follow me."

Lady Marie considered us intently before she followed the Warder. Her message was clear. *No talking!*

The Warder led us back to the entrance to the Tower of London. There wasn't any armor outside the courtyard. It had most likely already been cleared away. They'd probably wanted to remove all evidence of the night's strange behavior as quickly as possible.

The Chief Yeoman Warder spotted us as we approached the Middle Tower, a look of relief crossing his face. He nodded to the

Warder leading us, who turned around and headed back to the inner courtyard.

"Lady Marie. Thank goodness, you're okay," the Chief Yeoman Warder said in greeting.

"Quite fine, thank you," Lady Marie replied.

"My Warders couldn't find you anywhere."

"I'm afraid we got a bit disoriented, especially with all that was happening."

"Yes, I can't quite believe it myself," the Chief Yeoman Warder responded, although he had a questioning look in his eyes.

"Do you know what happened?" Lady Marie quickly asked, managing to convey the impression that she had absolutely no idea.

The Chief Yeoman Warder shook his head. "I'm completely baffled, I'm afraid. I'm just glad that no one was hurt."

Lady Marie nodded. "Where are the others?"

"They are waiting outside the gift shop. Now, if you may excuse me, I must see to the restoration of the Tower."

Lady Marie nodded, and the Chief Yeoman Warder departed, leaving us to exit the Tower of London. We heard the Trailfinder troops long before we saw them, an overexcited and loud group of girls, all talking over each other about what they had seen.

It was surely a night that no one would ever forget.

☆ ☆ ☆

"So, Tylwyth and Teg had been working for this prince all along?" Sir Edmund Studfall asked from the driver's seat of the Rolls-Royce.

We had wasted little time in sending the younger girls home, including bidding farewell to Razia, Kayla, and Sam. Then we made our way quickly back to the Tower Hotel car park, where Sir Edmund had been waiting. We were on our way home.

"Yes, although not by choice," Lady Marie answered. "It seems they were tricked into believing they were on a mission for their queen."

"Maggie, you really stabbed the Fae prince with your epi-pen?" Sir Edmund asked, unable to conceal his amazement.

"It was all I could think to do," I replied.

"A genius move, Maggie. Very brave," Sir Edmund responded. "Epi-pens will need to become standard issue for all Guardians operatives!"

We all laughed, although I'd never doubted the life-saving power of my epi-pen.

"What about the guards at the Tower?" Anahira asked. "Have you heard anything?"

"Not a whisper," Sir Edmund replied. "I don't think they will ever be able to explain what happened tonight, regardless of how many official inquiries are completed. And, of course, there is nothing actually missing."

"But, won't they discover the diamond is a fake?" Anahira responded.

"Maybe, Anahira. But the Crown Jewels very rarely leave their display cabinet these days, and there are rather a lot of them. The jewels are cleaned every year, but it will take a keen eye to detect the fake, and only if the diamond is removed. There is no reason for that to happen. They will likely be more concerned about how the ravens got into the Jewel House."

"I guess they won't accept magic as a reason," I noted.

"No, Maggie. Magic is definitely not in the handbook for the modern British soldier," Sir Edmund replied.

That's a handbook I would like to read.

"They would also be hard-pressed to explain why their technology malfunctioned," Sir Edmund continued. "The golden devices are quite discreet."

The golden devices!

I reached up, took off the necklace, and held out my hand. "Lady Marie, you'll need this back."

"Thank you, Maggie," Lady Marie replied, picking the necklace out of my hand. "You wore it well."

Not that I had any idea what it did or how it worked.

"Let's just chalk up the whole episode to a win for the Guardians," Sir Edmund enthused.

"Let's not get carried away, dear," Lady Marie responded in a subdued voice. "We almost ruined everything."

We did, didn't we?

Underneath all of the excitement and magic, there was the very real possibility that we could have ended the world.

"The queen will have to be informed of our actions," Lady Marie concluded.

"I was afraid you were going to suggest that," Sir Edmund added.

"Sorry, Lady Marie, do you mean the queen of England?" I asked.

"Yes, Maggie. Guardians Rule #1: One must always take responsibility for one's own actions, no matter the cost," Lady Marie explained.

Guardians Rule #1!

But that means Lady Marie will confess to taking one of the Crown Jewels. She could still be arrested. I could be arrested. We all could be arrested.

"But…" I couldn't say any more words, my breath catching in my throat.

"Do not fear, Maggie." Lady Marie responded. "I didn't mislead you or the unit when I claimed that our queen would be receptive to our cause. She has served as a Guardian herself after all."

The queen of England was a Guardian!

"However, regardless of her reaction, I must confess to what we've done," Lady Marie added. "I will take full responsibility. I have to do this, or I cannot remain a Wayfinder leader. I almost lost my way, but I will get back on the right path, whatever it may cost me."

"Or us," Sir Edmund added. "I will stand by your side."

"Thank you, dear," Lady Marie responded, smiling slightly.

"I will too," Anahira announced, lifting her chin.

"Thank you, Anahira, but there is no need," Lady Marie

answered. "You were under my care and protection, under my guidance. Besides, the video footage from the glasses will provide all the evidence we need to present to the queen."

I shared a concerned look with Anahira.

"Girls, it is time for faith, not fear," Lady Marie added in a soothing voice. "We are Guardians. We have been sorely tested, and we must learn from this experience. Part of that learning is taking responsibility for what we have done. I will fully accept that responsibility, no matter the consequences. But I have faith that we did the right thing, even though the path we took was a perilous one. I have faith that our queen will understand the need for our actions, even though we should have consulted with her first."

I didn't know what to say in response, but I think I understood. Guardians Rule #1 said it all really, taking responsibility for our actions. So, as well as dealing with magical threats from other worlds, the Guardians had to own up to everything we did, even if we believed we were protecting the world. Although, I really could have done without any more surprises.

The Guardians.

"Girls united against random dimensional invasion and nasty surprises," I declared.

"What was that, Maggie?" Lady Marie asked.

"I've just realized what Guardians stands for," I replied.

"Girls united against..." Lady Marie paused.

"Random dimensional invasion..."

"And nasty surprises!" Anahira finished for me.

"I like it," Sir Edmund announced.

"So do I," Lady Studfall agreed. "Although we have had quite enough nasty surprises for one day, thank you very much."

We all laughed, and I noted we had turned onto my street.

The Rolls-Royce soon stopped outside my house, and I gave Anahira a massive hug.

"See you tomorrow," Anahira said as I got out of the car.

"Tomorrow?" I asked.

"Yeah, we've got to go to school."

Oh, yes, school. How could I forget?

Lady Marie walked me to the front door. "Rest now, Maggie. You have saved us all. Do not worry about my meeting with the queen. I've got this."

I smiled. Lady Marie was getting more comfortable using one of Anahira's sayings. I gave Lady Marie a hug and then watched as she walked back to the car. I waved at Anahira as the car pulled out and then turned to my front door. I took the key out of my meds bag, unlocked the door, and went inside. I found Mum walking toward me from the kitchen.

"Maggie! You're home. How was your evening?"

I hung up my meds bag and wondered if I should tell Mum that I needed a new epi-pen. I decided to use the spare one that is kept in the bathroom for now. The need for a new one could wait one more day.

I turned to the smiling face of my mum, who sat down on the sofa and urged me to join her and tell her all about my night.

I sat down.

"It was simply magical," I said with a smile.

EPILOGUE

Thaddeus Kraven stared at the large computer screen dominating his desk. Despite an unrelenting examination of the large amount of video footage, he could find very little evidence to support his knowledge of what had happened.

Just one camera angle in fact. One tiny piece of footage which, when slowed right down, briefly showed the Queen Mother's Crown without a center-piece diamond.

The authorities who would be investigating the remarkable events at the Tower of London would most likely miss it. Thaddeus's genius as a hacker had allowed him unrestricted access to the CCTV footage from the Jewel House, but he had only found the footage because he knew exactly what to look for.

It had been a crucial part of the plan after all.

Thaddeus had to admit the execution of that part of the plan had gone better than expected. He, for one, had never anticipated such a perfect diversion. The Warders and guards were helpless against the Trailfinder girls and completely unprepared for enchanted armor. The ravens were a nice touch too. Their presence in the Jewel House was not only impossible, but it was also highly distracting. The perfectly timed arrival of three enchanted suits of armor was equally distracting. It was hard to pay attention to anything else on the screen with the armor marching into the room.

A job well done, if a little overly flamboyant.

Thaddeus preferred the subtle approach. He had been sought out by the Master for his secretive methods. That and other reasons Thaddeus could only guess at.

Unfortunately, the Master wouldn't be entirely pleased with the eventual outcome of that evening. A group of Wayfinder Girls had somehow bested a prince of Faerie and returned the Mountain of Light to the Faerie Queen. Thaddeus hadn't thought it possible. Years of painstaking planning, of watching, and waiting for the perfect candidate, all ruined.

It was the Master who was the real power, cleverly manipulating the prince into believing the time was ripe for an attack on the queen. The Master who orchestrated the events, which saw Tylwyth and Teg leap at a chance to journey to the human world.

Thaddeus was not entirely sure who the Master was but believed him to be part of the world of Faerie. A being who, like Thaddeus, preferred to operate from the shadows.

The Master had recruited Thaddeus years earlier, promising wealth and power beyond belief. The initial gifts the Master showered upon Thaddeus proved his words were not empty. The assortment of small gems that the Master gifted Thaddeus had set him up for life. And there was still more to come.

The Master would have used the battle between the prince and the queen to strengthen his own hold on power, and Thaddeus was to have been richly rewarded for his part, especially in identifying a likely human contact for Tylwyth and Teg.

Maggie Thatcher had been perfect. A short and asthmatic girl suffering from food allergies. Thaddeus had even enjoyed playing with the whole Iron Lady connection. The Guardians even did the hard part in inviting Maggie to join their *secret* program. Thaddeus had a plan ready for getting Maggie involved if she hadn't been recruited, but it turned out his plan was unnecessary. The Guardians had made it all too easy.

Yet somehow the plan had been thwarted by the

Wayfinder Girls and their ridiculous Guardians program. As if they could keep the world safe from threats from other worlds.

It was a complete joke.

Although, to be fair. They had somehow managed to ruin the Master's plan.

Actually, ruin might have been the wrong word. Delay was more accurate. Yes, the Wayfinder Girls had only delayed the Master's plan.

Whilst the Faerie Queen had strengthened her position by reclaiming the Mountain of Light, the Earth had been weakened. The diamond's presence on Earth had kept many doorways firmly closed. But now, with its absence, those doors would begin to open.

The so-called Guardians were about to become awfully busy.

Thaddeus checked his screen one last time. If he blinked, he would have missed the moment the Mountain of Light had been removed from the Crown.

Thaddeus glanced at a locked wooden jewelry box sitting on the corner of his desk. He reached up to his neck and lifted a silver chain over his head. He used the small key hanging from the chain to unlock the box. He raised the lid and considered the glittering collection of jewelry items resting on the black velvet lining of the box.

Shards of the Mountain of Light.

Collecting the shards was the first mission the Master had tasked Thaddeus with, and despite his best efforts, he estimated he'd gathered less than half of the cuttings that existed in the world. Given that these cuttings took place in 1852, Thaddeus might have named it a job well done. But he was not satisfied. The Master had impressed upon Thaddeus the importance of gathering every last piece of the diamond.

Apparently, there was a way to reawaken the magic within the cuttings. Thaddeus would continue his search. He was a patient man, and the rewards would be substantial.

Thaddeus closed the lid, locked the box, and placed the chain back over his head. It was time to leave his den and return to his other, more acceptable life.

As he stood up, Thaddeus scratched his right arm. He was proud of the black dragon tattoos that covered both his arms. Maybe a bit eccentric, but easy to hide when needed.

For now, need dictated that he keep to the shadows.

The Master's plan would eventually succeed.

And Thaddeus would be ready.

COMING SOON

Maggie and the Cosmic Landfill

A Wayfinder Girls novel

PROLOGUE OF BOOK 2

Z lantarb Attikus, a blue-skinned number cruncher from the planet Vesca, had worked as a supervisor at the Bureau of Cosmic Waste Management for longer than he cared to admit. He'd performed his job with ruthless efficiency and should have secured a more senior position in any one of the last five circuits of Merit Advancements. Yet, here he was, still operating as a junior supervisor in one of the least-respected areas of responsibility; waste. But was it his fault the Union of Worlds had run out of room to store their rubbish? No!

Zlantarb had never really given much thought to the amount of waste the combined worlds produced, nor where all the waste went, but he was now up to his neck in it. The waste was starting to seriously irritate him. Nobody wanted waste dumped in their home world, nobody could afford to send their waste into deep space, not with the current exorbitant cost of energy, and nobody could burn the waste away, not with the toxic chemical mix that infected most of the waste. The problem had become so severe that a war had been fought over it. But war simply produced more waste.

Everyone expected Zlantarb to clean it all up. It was so infuriating.

He had worked hard to find a solution and had bet his name and reputation on the Portal Project, after consulting first with the Seers of Insight. The golden-haired Seers, with their piercing gray eyes, had assured him of unparalleled success. So he launched the project with great enthusiasm. It was a simple, yet elegant solution: find a non-Union world, establish a large portal in the air in that world, and then dump waste through the doorway from selected portals in the home worlds.

However, despite the raging success of the first established waste portal, the program had quickly suffered a serious setback.

Zlantarb had identified a second world, one which had seemed ideal, but as soon as he had started dumping waste, he received an urgent and angry communiqué from the Office of the President of the Union.

"Supervisor Attikus, cease your activity immediately!"

Zlantarb had stared at the message flashing on his screen. When he saw where the message originated from, his glands expanded so rapidly that his neck almost swallowed his face. He had never before received a message from the Office of the President.

Zlantarb was too shocked to respond, and the message that followed almost made him want to run and hide.

"Why are you dumping waste on the president's favorite place to go hunting?"

It turned out that what Zlantarb had identified as a non-Union world was actually the private and secret plaything of the current president. If Zlantarb hadn't stopped the waste-dumping operation immediately, and promised to remove every scrap of waste already dumped, he would have been reassigned to oversee the drainage of the vast Vescan peat bogs.

A bog-drainage supervisor didn't supervise progress from a position of comfort. Oh, no. A bog-drainage supervisor worked in the wet, smelly, and sticky bog. All day. They worked for as long as it took for the seemingly limitless bog to be drained.

It would have been an endless waste of Zlantarb's time and talent.

So Zlantarb had cleaned up the mess he'd made on the president's secret world, organizing the retrieval of all the waste that had been dumped. Then, at the demand of the Office of the President, Zlantarb had to create strict rules concerning any future portals.

The Waste Portal Protocols now governed all matters concerning the establishment of a portal into another world. Even though Zlantarb had written the protocols himself, he was not a fan. The inclusion of a notification clause had seemed logical, and the provision of adequate time to respond to any notification had seemed appropriate. But so far, the only effect of the notification period had been to give Zlantarb a long, painful headache.

Zlantarb had lost count of how many suitable worlds he'd identified, only to have those worlds rejected during the notification period. There was no end to the worlds the president claimed for his personal use. Likewise, the worlds claimed by the elite Houses that supported the president's rule. Worlds apparently needed for private hunts, family holidays, and the settling of certain individuals that the respected elites liked to visit, in secret. Which simply left Zlantarb with huge and steadily growing mountains of waste, with nowhere to put it.

The entire issue of waste was so terribly depressing.

"Excuse me, Supervisor Attikus, sir!"

Zlantarb lifted his head from his hands and glared at the worker who had invaded his personal pity party.

"What is it this time, Glelb?" Zlantarb responded, failing to keep the weariness out of his voice. Like Zlantarb, Glelb was from the planet Vesca. But unlike Zlantarb, Glelb was infuriatingly cheerful, seemingly content with his life as a lowly clerical worker in the Bureau of Cosmic Waste Management.

"Oh, I think you're going to like this, sir!" Glelb enthused.

"I've already told you that bring-a-pet-to-work day is not happening." Zlantarb replied angrily. Especially with the creatures Glelb regarded as pets. Like the ancient thing with tentacles that released a pool of slime whenever it got scared. Which was most of the time. Glelb had named it Colin for some unknown reason and had insisted it was far less messy than it was. But Zlantarb couldn't deal with any more mess.

"Oh, no, sir," Glelb replied. "I know how you feel about Colin."

"Then what is it?" Zlantarb asked impatiently.

"We have a new contact, sir!" Glelb exclaimed excitedly.

"A new contact? What do you mean?"

"It's a new portal, sir!"

A new portal?

What was the fool talking about? Zlantarb turned his head to his oversized screen and turned the setting to the Portal Monitoring Map. All of the portals were represented by tiny, glowing red lights, indicating they could not be used. Zlantarb turned his head to yell at Glelb when he noticed a tiny green light, right at the edge of his screen.

"What is it?" Zlantarb asked, more to himself than anyone else.

"It's a new portal, sir!" Glelb repeated with a wide grin. "It just appeared."

Zlantarb grimaced. "Where?"

Glelb checked a small notebook he had brought with him. "On a small planet in a distant system, sir! Our records show that the planet is called Earth."

Earth? Zlantarb had never heard of it before.

"Glelb, did you just say we have knowledge of this planet in our records?"

"Oh yes, sir!" Glelb responded ecstatically. "But our records also claimed that the portal was lost to us."

"Lost?" Zlantarb queried.

"Lost indeed, sir!" Glelb confirmed. "But now found. And open to us once more."

A lost portal?

That could be the answer to all of Zlantarb's problems.

"We must send a probe through the portal." Zlantarb declared.

"Already done, sir!" Glelb responded while clapping his hands.

Zlantarb hid his disapproval that Glelb had acted without proper authorization. Glelb would not have shared the existence of the new portal unless it was good news. And Zlantarb could use some good news right now.

"So, the world is uninhabited?" Zlantarb asked.

"Oh, no, sir!" Glelb replied. "Earth is fully inhabited. The most advanced inhabitants are called humans."

Zlantarb resisted the urge to reach out and throttle Glelb. There was no way the Waste Portal Protocols would allow Zlantarb to dump waste into a fully inhabited world. The new portal was yet another dead-end.

"Glelb, why are you wasting my time?"

"Sir! The human inhabitants do not care for their world."

Zlantarb actually perked up at this. The protocols allowed one exception to the ban on dumping waste on an inhabited world; if it could be proven that the inhabitants, these so-called humans, didn't care for their world.

"Do you have proof of this, Glelb? Tell me you have proof."

"Oh yes, sir!" Glelb responded, beaming like Vesca's twin suns. "Humans are causing extensive damage to the land, oceans, and atmosphere of their world. They are plundering Earth's resources to make products that don't last and then get thrown away. The amount of waste these humans create is absolutely staggering."

Zlantarb actually smiled. "That is good news, Glelb. Very good news. How soon can we initiate the transfer of our waste to Earth?"

"Well, sir, we must first give notice through the official channels of our intention to send our accumulated waste through the Earth portal."

"Oh, yes, Glelb. The notification period. How could I forget?" Although, given the fact that the portal had been lost, it was highly unlikely that there was any interest in Earth from the Union of Worlds. But the protocols dictated that notice must be given.

"I have already sent notice through the official channels, sir!" Glelb responded, as though reading one of Zlantarb's minds.

Zlantarb was too excited to have any sense of disapproval about Glelb's independent action. Earth could breathe new life into the Portal Project.

"How long do humans have to respond?" Zlantarb asked.

"They have one Earth day left, sir!" Glelb responded.

"And do you think humans monitor the official channels?"

"I very much doubt it, sir!"

Zlantarb smiled again. The protocols only required that notice be sent through the official channels. There was no stipulation on whether these channels were monitored or not. And the time given to respond depended on the distance between the Union of Worlds and the targeted world; the further away that world was, the shorter the time given to respond.

And the humans of Earth had just one of their days left.

Zlantarb could hardly wait.

MAGGIE AND THE MOUNTAIN OF LIGHT READER'S GUIDE

Are you ready for more of Maggie and the Mountain of Light? Check out the Monarch website for our free reader's guide. This educational resource is perfect for educators, librarians, book clubs, homeschoolers, small groups, and readers who want more of the Wayfinder Girls.

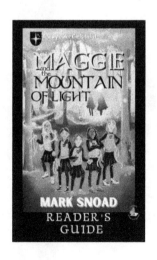

ACKNOWLEDGMENTS

First and foremost I would like to thank our Father in Heaven, the source and sustainer of life, and the creator of story. It is the meta-narrative of Jesus that continues to inspire, encourage and challenge.

My heartfelt thanks to Dr. Jen Lowry, founder of Monarch Press, and a cheerleader of Maggie since the beginning. Jen, thank you for your encouragement, optimism, and formidable dedication to the art of publishing. This book would not have been possible without your support.

Thank you to Kelly, Kara, Jessica, Sally, and Haley for being such a professional editorial team. I am very grateful for your craft and commitment, and for making the editing process such an enjoyable and rewarding experience.

Thank you to Korin for your artistic brilliance in bringing Maggie to life with your immersive and magical cover.

Thank you to my fellow Monarch authors. It is really nice to be in a team of supportive and caring writers, striving to be the best they can be.

Thank you to Ishrit Khangura for your astute feedback and reflections on the first draft of Maggie.

A massive thanks to Allergy New Zealand, and by extension, all those agencies working to support allergy sufferers throughout the world. Thank you for your advocacy work and for providing often life-saving information and care for people coping with allergies.

An equally massive thanks to GirlGuiding. Guiding allowed my daughter to participate fully in so many camps and activities, all in a safe and encouraging space. I will be forever grateful for the confidence and belief you helped nurture in my daughter.

Thank you to my family. I couldn't be prouder of my girls, Mikayla and Hannah, who make the world a better place to live in. And to my wife, Kimberley, thank you for journeying with me and smiling at all of my crazy ideas.

And finally, thank you to you, the reader. I hope you find something within these pages to make you smile and give you a sense of courage and hope.

ABOUT THE AUTHOR

Mark Snoad is an author and teacher living in Aotearoa New Zealand. As a professional make-believer, he strives to find the magic and joy in everyday life. It's definitely there, at the edges. You'll soon discover it, if you believe. Mark lives with his wife, two daughters and rascal dog, Wilbur.

ALSO BY MONARCH BOOKS

Our Monarch Collection

www.monarcheducationalservices.com

ALLERGY AWARENESS

If anyone needs support for dealing with food allergies, please check out any one of the following sites. All have helpful information and advice, and some will offer location specific support. There is definitely help out there and I know from experience how valuable expert insight can be. This is not an exhaustive list, check with your doctor for more resources.

https://www.allergy.org.nz/
https://kidswithfoodallergies.org/
https://www.allergy.org.au/
https://www.allergyuk.org/

CPSIA information can be obtained
at www.ICGtesting.com
Printed in the USA
LVHW090311110723
752023LV00003B/259